"Who are you?" Ian snarled.

He jerked his head to the side as Lily's hand traced streaks of fire down his left cheek. Grabbing her arms, he forced her back until her legs pressed against the bed frame. "Don't you know who I am? Have you not heard of Llywelyn's Dragon?"

Lily's gaze darted toward the bed, and her resistance increased. "Leave me be," she shouted, squirming against his hold.

Did she think he meant to bed her now? All he wanted were answers. Cursing, Ian wrapped his arms about her and pulled her flush to his body. Their eyes met, the heat of their breaths mingled between their lips.

Suddenly the fight seemed to leave her. She slumped against him, lowering her head until her hair veiled her face. "I cannot tell you who I am, milord…because I do not know."

Dear Reader,

Every year at this time, the editors at Harlequin Historicals have the unique opportunity of introducing our readers to four brand-new authors in our annual March Madness Promotion. These titles were chosen from among hundreds of manuscripts from unpublished authors, and we would like to take this time to thank all of the talented authors who made the effort to submit their projects to Harlequin Historicals for review.

Our choices for the month include *Heart of the Dragon* by Sharon Schulze, the medieval tale of a young woman in search of her identity, who must rely on the help of a fierce warrior willing to give up his freedom in order to protect her from harm, and *Emily's Captain* by Shari Anton, a story about a heroine whose desperate father sends a dashing Union spy to get her safely out of Georgia against her wishes.

The Phoenix of Love by Susan Schonberg, a Regency novel with a marriage of convenience between a reformed rake and a society ice princess who must overcome tortured pasts and present enemies before they are free to love, and *The Wicked Truth* by Lyn Stone, a second-place finisher in the 1995 Maggie Awards, about a woman with a ruined reputation and a straitlaced physician who join forces to discover a murderer in Victorian England, round out a terrific month.

Whatever your taste in reading, we hope you'll find a story written just for you between the covers of a Harlequin Historical.

Sincerely,

Tracy Farrell
Senior Editor

Please address questions and book requests to:
Harlequin Reader Service
U.S.: 3010 Walden Ave., P.O. Box 1325, Buffalo, NY 14269
Canadian: P.O. Box 609, Fort Erie, Ont. L2A 5X3

HEART
OF THE
DRAGON

Sharon Schulze

Harlequin Books

TORONTO • NEW YORK • LONDON
AMSTERDAM • PARIS • SYDNEY • HAMBURG
STOCKHOLM • ATHENS • TOKYO • MILAN
MADRID • WARSAW • BUDAPEST • AUCKLAND

ISBN 0-373-28956-1

HEART OF THE DRAGON

Copyright © 1997 by Sharon M. Schulze

SHARON SCHULZE

is a confirmed bookaholic who loves reading as much as writing. Although she has a degree in civil engineering, she's always been fascinated by history. Writing about the past gives her the chance to experience days gone by—without also encountering disease, vermin and archaic plumbing!

A New Hampshire native, she now makes her home in Connecticut with her husband, Cliff, teenagers Patrick and Christina, and their miniature dachshund, Samantha. She is current president of the Connecticut Chapter of RWA; in her spare time she enjoys movies, music and poking around in antique shops.

With love and thanks to my husband, Cliff,
and my children, Patrick and Christina.
I couldn't have done it without you.
To Julie Caille, Ellen Keefe and Nancy Block,
for encouragement, faith and steel-toed boots
when I needed them.
And with love to my parents,
Colleen Towle and Howard Cottrell.
You raised me to be stubborn—thank you!

Prologue

They called him Llywelyn's Dragon.

A warrior bold as the creatures of Welsh legend, his temper as fiery, Lord Ian ap Dafydd was the prince's right hand. Men of power quaked at word of his arrival, for he was the sword to carry out Llywelyn's judgment.

'Twas rumored he'd do any deed at the prince's bidding, avenge any slight to his master's name. Only Llywelyn had the might to direct the Dragon's fury, to shape the form of his vengeance.

Or so the prince believed.

But shrouded deep beneath that scaly hide, the Dragon's true nature slumbered.

Obscured by fire.

Hidden from harm.

Buried beyond the reach of pain.

Until he met her.

The woman with the power to free the heart of the Dragon.

Chapter One

Northern Wales, Spring 1215

Lily breathed deeply and stared up at the obstacle looming before her. Of rough stone, darkly menacing in the fitful moonlight, the curtain wall surrounding Dolwyddelan Keep rose above her like a vision from hell.

She loosened the strings of her cloak and slipped it off. Rolling it in a bundle, she hid it in the shadows at the base of the wall, next to the sack containing her meager belongings. The wind whipped about her, pressing her short tunic and loose braes snug against her quivering flesh.

The cold didn't make her shake, though she felt naked in the unfamiliar clothing. Nay, she'd borne worse. During the course of this ill-conceived trek, she'd encountered weather as unforgiving as the abbess herself.

She couldn't even call it fear. It was desperation that made her shiver—but it had also lent her the strength she needed in the weeks since her mother's death. Without that spur to goad her on, she'd never have escaped the confines of the cloister, let alone found Llywelyn.

For all the good it had done her.

Lily held her icy fingers to her lips in a vain attempt to blow some life into them. Exhaling deeply, she forced all her qualms to the back of her mind. It was no use thinking about it yet again. Some things had to be done, 'twas all. She focused upon the rough-cut stones and, hands and feet groping for purchase, began her ascent.

Ian leaned back against the wall, arms folded across his chest. If only he could shut out the noise as easily as the cool stone banished the heat of the overcrowded room! Tumultuous revelry filled Llywelyn's hall, spilling out into the anterooms and up the stairs to the gallery above. Wine, mead and ale flowed freely. He'd even caught a whiff of fiery Irish usquebaugh when the revelers reeled near in their drunken attempts at dancing.

But Ian stood apart, as alone among the raucous crowd as within the cool green depths of the forest. Ever silent, ever vigilant, he derived nothing more than a mild amusement from the scene unfolding before him. Once he might have joined the revelry, quaffed as deeply as the rest, but such foolishness no longer held appeal.

A woman stumbled toward him, skirts bunched in her hands and raised to the knees to expose her legs. "Care to dance, milord?" she asked coyly, leaning close until her abundant breasts pressed against his folded arms. She freed one hand to trail her fingers down the front of his tunic. "Come, I'll teach you," she said, her eyes promising more than a dance.

Something deep within him recoiled. Perhaps it was due to the smell rising from her tightly laced bliaut— old sweat and new ale—or mayhap it was simply her bold manner. Whatever the reason, he moved slightly away.

A burly soldier came up behind her and slipped his arm about her waist. "Here, Meg—are you mad? What d'ye want with him?"

The woman cast one last look at Ian, lips curled into a pout, before she allowed the man to lead her off. Breathing a sigh of relief, Ian shifted to a more comfortable position.

As he settled back again to observe the evening's entertainment, he noticed one of his men elbowing his way across the hall.

"Beg pardon, milord." Dai leaned close to speak near Ian's ear. "The guard on the south walk sent word someone's climbing the curtain wall." His lean face creased into a wry smile. "Appears they've lost their stomach for it partway up."

"By Christ, not another one." Ian pushed away from the wall and headed for the door, traversing the long room easily as a path opened before him. Not two weeks past, some half-wit from the hills had tried the climb at first light to prove his valor to Llywelyn. His scream of terror and the sight of his body lying broken at the rocky base of the wall should have been warning enough to any other fool tempted to follow his example.

Who could be so stupid as to attempt such a feat in the dark of night?

Ian ducked beneath the door frame and ran lightly up the stairs to the walk, tugging his cloak close about him against the icy wind blowing down from the mountains. The guard joined him as he peered over the crenel.

"Didn't hear him till he'd gotten near where he is now, milord." The guard's eyes shifted nervously beneath the brim of his helm as he made the admission, but he stood straight and his voice was strong. "At least 'tis just the one."

"Aye." This time, at any rate, Ian thought with disgust. He'd need to speak again to the captain of the guard, lest they wake some morn to find the keep taken.

"Bring me rope," he commanded, turning his attention to the dark shape huddled against the wall. "I'll deal with you later."

Ian scarcely noticed the guard's hasty retreat as he tossed aside his cloak and unbuckled his sword belt. His attention remained fixed on the motionless fool below him as he propped the weapon against the wall, then climbed onto the uneven embrasure. He lay on his stomach, booted feet hooked round the merlon, and hung as far over the edge as he could reach. "Are you hurt?" he shouted. "Or just afraid?"

The shadow shifted, the movement resolving the dark blob into the form of a man. "I fear nothing," he said. He slowly turned his head toward Ian in a surprisingly arrogant manner, revealing a face too youthful for a man full grown. "I'm simply resting."

"I should leave you here to 'rest' all night," Ian said. "Idiot halfling," he muttered to himself. Inching farther over the edge, he tried to judge whether his sword belt would reach, for he doubted the boy's strength would last much longer. Faint moonlight gleamed white off knuckles that held the wall in a death grip. Mayhap they'd have to lower someone to pry those rigid fingers free.

But another glimpse of that pale face convinced him the guard would return too late. Moving quickly, Ian pulled himself back, out of the embrasure, and slipped the scabbard from his belt. He untied the other belt he wore about his waist and joined the strips of leather with a firm knot.

Even with the two belts together, they didn't look quite long enough. He'd need to stretch as far as he could. "I'm going to lower a rope," he said, then whipped his tunic over his head and tossed it aside.

Ian wrapped the belt twice around his hand and, gripping the leather so tight that the metal studs bit into his palm, he levered himself over the lip of the wall and lowered himself and the makeshift rope.

The end stopped a bare foot short. "Look up." He kept his voice even, afraid the lad would loosen his hold. "See the rope?"

Face pressed tight against the rough stone, the boy tilted his head and opened his eyes. "Aye," he answered, then squeezed his eyes shut.

"You'll have to climb a bit more. Do you think you have the nerve for it, boy?" Ian asked, infusing the question with just enough mockery to raise the lad's ire. "Or do I need to come down after you?"

The boy immediately eased one hand from its death grip upon the stone. A quiet moan blended with the soughing wind as that hand inched closer to the dangling leather. The lad had courage, he'd give him that—despite this foolhardy climb.

The provocation had the desired effect. In no time at all, the lad had scrambled close enough to grab the belt. "Have a care," Ian warned, as the leather stretched taut beneath the youth's surprisingly meager weight. He wound the end tighter about his hand. Now, if the knot would hold...

Muscles bunching from the strain, Ian pulled the boy

toward him. Strong hands grabbed at his feet and held him, allowing him to haul the lad into his arms.

They flopped over the wall together and landed in a heap at the guard's feet.

Sweet Jesu save him, this was no lad! It had been some time since he'd held a woman, but he couldn't mistake the soft curves beneath the coarse male garments. Cursing, he shoved her aside and stood, tugging her upright to stand beside him.

The guard stepped forward to take her. Ian shook his head and jerked the woman's arms behind her. "You see to your duties," he told the other man. "I'll take care of this."

No need to have the guard carry this tale, at least not until he'd discovered why she'd attempted the wall. One hand a vise about her upper arm, Ian snatched up his sword and tunic and dragged the woman toward the stairs. They hadn't taken two steps before she dug in her heels and pulled to a halt.

"Come on," Ian growled. She remained rooted to the spot. His sword clattered against the walkway as he spun to face her. "Are you deaf, as well as stupid?"

"I wish to see Llywelyn."

The faint moonlight gilded her face, highlighting her mulish expression. But her stubbornness didn't matter. Two could play at this game—and he had no doubt that his strength of will could overpower any resistance. "Indeed?"

Her lips tightened into a grim line, and her chin rose another notch. "Aye. Take me to him, if you please." Her expression didn't change, making a mockery of her attempt at courtesy.

"Come." He tightened his grip on her elbow.

She pulled against his hold, mouth opening to speak.

Sweet Mary save him! Did she dare to defy him again? Tossing his belongings aside, Ian hoisted her over his shoulder, then scooped up his sword. She'd come with him whether she wanted to or not. Accompanied by a stream of insults from his captive, he ran lightly down the stairs, his lips curved into a smile.

Lily's breath ran short before her scant supply of curses did. His firm grip said as clearly as words that any attempt to free herself would be doomed from the start. She knew firsthand of his strength. How else could he have hauled someone as tall as she up and over the wall with such ease? She'd always felt huge and clumsy, towering as she did over the sisters—as well as the few men she'd met. But the top of her head came no higher than his shoulder. She'd do well to respect his size, and the power and confidence he wore like a mantle.

Besides, she was inside Llywelyn's keep, just where she wanted to be. In the company of a man of some authority, if the guard's reaction was any indication. Still, being carried thus certainly lacked dignity—as well as being painful. She tried to get more comfortable, but couldn't squirm into a position where his brawny shoulder didn't force the air from her lungs with every jolting step.

The heat on her face had more to do with the cursing she'd done than with hanging upside down. With blasphemy added to all the sins she'd committed of late, she'd be better off going back to the abbey and taking the veil in atonement. And likely doing penance the rest of her life.

Where was he taking her? The sounds of revelry soon

grew faint as he carried her toward a shadow-filled corner of the bailey.

She doubted she'd see Llywelyn this night.

Her ill-planned scheme didn't seem any more likely to bring her to the mighty prince's notice than anything else she'd tried. Although there didn't appear to be the strict social order in Llywelyn's court that she'd expected, she knew no one who could help her. Tonight's foolishness had been a desperate act, she'd known it from the start.

But then, she was a desperate woman.

However, clinging to the curtain wall had been less frightening than her present situation. A lifetime spent within the confines of the cloister hadn't prepared her for the darkness she'd seen in her captor's eyes.

As surefooted as a cat's, his step never faltered. The shadows grew deeper, closing about them until the moonlight was little more than a memory. They entered a building—she could feel the walls surrounding them, but she didn't realize it was a tower until they began to ascend the spiraling stairs.

They stopped, his sword clattering against stone. A faint, metallic jangle told her he held a ring of keys.

The door opened silently. Her captor kicked it wider, then crossed the chamber and dumped her from his shoulder.

She couldn't help grabbing for him, her only reality in this fearful sea of darkness. Her fingers grasped emptiness as she landed flat on her back on a soft pallet.

Did he think to bed her? Why else would he have carried her off to his lair? Sister Alyce maintained that men thought only of their pleasure whenever they were around a woman; 'twas the reason so many young girls sought the safety of the cloister. As unlikely as that seemed, she'd best take no chances. She scrambled to her knees, hands reaching for the edge of the mattress. Mayhap she could get away before he kindled a light, or at least—

The scent of burning tallow brought her head up, and the sight before her held her transfixed. The candles he held cast his features in harsh relief, lending a satanic aura to his face and giving credence to her fears. "Going somewhere?" he asked, raising an eyebrow in inquiry.

His voice was smooth, melodious. A shiver rose at her nape in response to its seductive timbre. Heart pounding wildly, Lily crawled off the bed and stood. He reminded her of a wild animal, beautiful, appealing and untamed. But she knew better than to show fear before him. Taking a deep breath, she stiffened her spine and met his gaze.

His eyes held her captive as he set aside the branch of candles and moved to stand before her. "If this is meant as a disguise," he said, slipping the cap off her hair, "it doesn't work. Not in the light." He took her chin in his hand, his fingers hard and warm against her skin, and tilted her head. "Only a fool would mistake you for anything but a woman."

Her pulse quickened at his touch, then spun out of control when he smoothed the tangled tresses from her face. She told herself 'twas fear made it so, and not the deep green of his eyes—dark as an emerald, and as cold. Yet despite their chill, she saw something there...

Loneliness? Yearning? Need?

A dark curl fell over his forehead. Her fingers itched to caress that silken bit of midnight.

She closed her eyes, but it mattered not. Something drew her to him still, made her want to move closer, even as he made her tremble. Had she gone so long without human touch that she longed for such from a stranger?

What sorcery was this?

The night's events had addled her brains. Speak, she told herself, do anything to break the spell. She opened her eyes, pulled together the tangled threads of thought and found her voice. "I wasn't trying to hide. 'Tis easier to climb in this than my usual clothes."

The sound of her own voice gave her the strength to move, to attempt to pull away. When she stirred in his grasp, he released her and crossed the small room to shut the door. Grateful for the reprieve, she drew a deep breath and let it out slowly, struggling to shake free of this enchantment.

"Why did you bring me here? I wish to see Llywelyn." 'Twas a pity she could think of nothing else to say; he'd surely believe her a simpleton.

Besides, her questions were for his master, she reminded herself. And she didn't know if even Llywelyn could provide the answers she sought.

What would she do if he couldn't? She had nowhere to go, no one to turn to. Llywelyn had to hold the key; beyond that, she refused to consider.

Ian leaned back against the rough wooden panels of the door, crossing his arms as he watched the woman, seeking some clue to her purpose here. He found her persistence astonishing. But then again, it took an immense amount of determination to do what she'd done this night. The idea of a woman attempting—and nearly succeeding—to scale the walls of Dolwyddelan was mind-boggling.

However, he hadn't brought her here to admire her tenacity. Or anything else about her, he reminded himself as he remembered the feel of her tall, slim body slung over his shoulder. He rubbed his back against the door, as if that would wipe away the lingering sensation. "Tell me who you are and why you wish to see him."

"My name is Lily." A trace of pain tinged her features, so fleeting he almost thought he'd imagined it. "Just Lily."

Her composure disturbed him. Didn't she realize the threat he posed? He couldn't recall the last time a woman had remained so calm while in his chamber. By Christ, even those he'd invited here generally quaked like frightened geese in his presence.

This woman presented a challenge, one he'd take on gladly. He'd never met anyone he could not break.

"What business could you possibly have with the mighty Llywelyn?" he asked, glancing at her threadbare garments with insulting deliberation. He noticed how they clung to her soft curves, and forced his gaze back to her dirt-smudged face. "He has no need of a filthy villein to warm his bed."

She gasped and took a few steps toward him. The candlelight hit her full in the face, giving him his first clear look at her and illuminating her tangled fall of hair.

'Twas her expression of outrage that caught his eye. He straightened and pushed away from the door. Perhaps all women looked thus, but he'd never noticed. By the rood, something about her face seemed so familiar, it caught his breath.

And her hair, pale copper, the color shining forth like a beacon...

What trickery was this?

He captured her chin in his hand once more, his fingers as harsh as his voice. "Where have you come from? And what do you here?'' He snatched the branch of candles off the table and brought them closer. "Who are you?''

For the first time since he'd pulled her from the curtain wall, she appeared frightened, and he could feel the fine tremor running through her. "I told you. Lily.''

Her voice shook, too. Good. Mayhap he could use her fear to get what he wanted. He set aside the candles and tightened his hold. "Lily who? You must have more name than that. Who are your people? Where do they live?'' He tugged at her until the heat of her body reached him through his linen shirt. "How could they permit a woman like you to wander the countryside alone?''

She shoved at his hand, to no avail. Her strength was no match for his. But she paid no heed to that fact—he began to doubt she was even aware of it. "Why should I tell you aught? My questions are for Llywelyn, not some lackey.'' Ignoring his tightening grip, she curled her fingers and raked at his face with her nails. "I demand you take me to him.''

"She-devil,'' he snarled as he jerked his head to the side—though not far enough. Twin streaks of fire trailed down his left cheek. "You demand?'' He grabbed her arms and forced her back until her legs pressed against the bed frame. "Don't you know who I am? Have you not heard of Llywelyn's Dragon?''

Her gaze darted toward the bed, and her resistance increased. "Answer me,'' he snarled, shaking her.

"Stop! Leave me be!'' she shouted. Renewing her struggles, she squirmed against his hold.

"Damn you.'' By Christ, did she think he meant to bed her now? All he wanted of her was answers. The heat rising in his blood meant naught. Any man would react thus, to feel a woman's softness pressed to his flesh.

But he would not let her go—not yet. In this battle of wills, he would yield nothing.

Cursing, Ian wrapped his arms about her and pulled her flush to his body. Their eyes met, the heat of their breath mingled between their lips. He fought the urge to lower his mouth to hers, to close the hairsbreadth separating him from sweet temptation.

Suddenly the fight seemed to leave her. She slumped against him, lowering her head until her hair veiled her face. "I cannot tell you who I am, milord...because I do not know."

Chapter Two

The feel of strong arms surrounding her, and the steady beat of his heart beneath her cheek, broke through Lily's sorrow. Horrified, she pushed herself away, swaying until she found her balance, her breath coming in sobbing gasps.

Her captor—the Dragon—stood staring down at her. She couldn't read his expression in the wavering light, but she doubted he planned to ease his lust upon her. He'd had ample chance just now, had that been his intention, but he'd let her move out of his hold. He'd sounded angry, almost puzzled, though why that should be his reaction, she did not know.

Chest still heaving, she stepped back. Her gaze never left him as she considered what to do.

Aye, she had heard of Llywelyn's Dragon. Who had not? He was legend among the village folk near the abbey. Even the sisters, their voices filled with a kind of fascinated horror, had been known to discuss the deeds he'd done in Llywelyn's name. In truth, she'd thought him to be older, although his size and strength proved no surprise.

And the aura of power she'd felt in his presence...

Yes, she could believe this man capable of every exploit attributed to him—and more. And yet she did not fear him.

When had she become such a fool?

His eyes measured her, examining her face with such intensity she feared he could see her very soul. Why should he stare at her thus? She tried not to squirm, but couldn't keep from swiping her sleeve over the hated tears filling her eyes.

"Why have you come here?" the Dragon asked, his voice calm now, the smooth sound an invitation to answer him.

Lily knew better than to fall into that trap; the abbess had used the same technique, usually as a prelude to some horrendous punishment. "I am sorry, milord. Where I've come from would mean nothing to you. 'Tis your master I must speak with. Only he can answer my questions."

He headed for a wooden chest beside the bed before she finished speaking and slammed the lid open with scant regard for the delicate carving adorning the piece. The tunic he chose was the same deep emerald shade as his eyes. She looked away when he tugged the garment over his head, unwilling to fall victim once again to the power of his gaze.

He snatched up the scabbarded sword leaning against the coffer and belted it about his trim hips. "You will not talk? So be it, then. Mayhap a night spent in the cellars will loosen your tongue." The expression on his face had her backing away, but he grabbed her by the arm. "Who knows? You might even get the chance to speak with my 'master'—if I'm of a mood to plead your case."

But the harshness in his eyes before he snuffed the

candles warned her there was little chance of that. Her heartbeat unsteady in the sudden darkness, Lily let the Dragon lead her from his lair.

Ian crossed the courtyard as the rising sun cast a rosy glow over the gray walls of Dolwyddelan. Icy puddles crackled beneath his boots, the perfect accompaniment to the wind whipping around the battlements.

He loved the brisk air, the cold serving to stoke the fire in his blood. It thrummed through his veins, lent energy to his steps as he descended the stairs into the vaults below the keep.

The promise of battle with a certain mysterious fiery-maned stranger had nothing to do with it.

The guard snapped to attention beside the cell door, then grinned his thanks when Ian dismissed him to break his fast abovestairs.

Ian shook his head at the young man's hasty retreat. No doubt he'd been bored to distraction standing here through the night, but perhaps 'twould teach the lad patience. That virtue was sadly lacking in most of the hot-tempered warriors who had gathered behind Llywelyn's banner.

He'd do well to control his own impatience before he unbarred the door and met with his captive once again. Last night, somewhere between the curtain wall and his chamber, he'd lost his usual impassive demeanor.

And try though he might, he hadn't regained it in the hours since he'd left the elusive Lily locked behind this door.

Taking a lantern from the hook beside the door, he removed the bar from its brackets and entered the cell.

Lily sat up, shielding her eyes from the light. She

leaned back against the damp stone wall and tried to ignore the way straw from the small heap she'd slept upon poked through her clothes. Although she knew she should stand—courtesy required it, not to mention the fact that she hated to have him tower over her—a night spent curled on the hard-packed dirt, after her midnight climb, had left her so stiff she could scarcely move. "Good morrow to you, Dragon," she said, infusing her voice with the strength her body refused to supply. "Have you word from your master?"

"I am Lord Ian ap Dafydd of Gwal Draig." He closed the door behind him and hung the lantern from a peg in the rafters. Three steps brought him across the narrow cell to stand at her feet. "No one calls me Dragon—to my face."

Did he give her his full name—and the name of his home—apurpose, to show her own lack? Rage and hurt overcame Lily's aches and brought her to her feet without pain. A glorious surge of power straightened her backbone and lifted her chin until she looked him in the eye. "I have never feared to be different, Lord Ian of Gwal Draig. I shall call you Dragon." She brushed straw from her clothes with apparent unconcern.

She expected him to do something…anything. For reasons she'd rather not examine too closely, she welcomed the chance to cross swords with him once again. Lily braced herself for the storm.

But he did nothing, nothing at all, if she discounted the slight gleam in his eyes. Did she see a challenge there?

'Twas a trick of the flickering light, more like. Lily bit her lip. She needed him to react, to lash back at her. Otherwise she'd never be able to sustain enough fire in her blood to do what she must. But his disregard of her meager show of defiance sapped her mettle. Fresh pain throbbed to life, making the simple act of standing torture. Shivers racked her, beyond her will to ignore.

Still silent, the Dragon left the chamber and returned with a three-legged stool. "Here, sit before you fall." He slammed the stool down and, grabbing her by the shoulders, pushed her onto the seat.

She closed her eyes and rubbed at her arms, certain she'd bear the imprint of his strong, callused fingers for days to come. But he'd spared her the indignity of collapsing at his feet.

Rough wool settled over her shoulders and startled her into opening her eyes. The warm folds of fabric enveloped her in her captor's scent. She tugged the cloak more tightly around her body and tried to ignore the sense of solace his unexpected gesture brought. It wouldn't be wise to feel grateful to him, to owe him anything. Who could tell what the Dragon might demand in return?

"Are you ready to talk today?" he demanded, his voice gruff. He leaned back against the wall with complete disregard for the cold, slimy stones and folded his arms across his chest. "I'm curious. Why must you see Llywelyn? What is so important that you'd risk your life to get to him?"

Lily fought the seductive slide into comfort as the cloak warmed her body. Within her mind raged a furious debate. Should she tell him? Sweet Mary, she knew little enough herself. But she'd heard it said that the Dragon had Llywelyn's favor—indeed, even his trust. He could help her, if he wished.

"Is Llywelyn even here?" The question had haunted her through the night. Until then, she hadn't allowed herself to consider that her efforts might be for naught.

The guard she'd spoken to—the one who'd refused her admittance to the keep even as he laughed at her request to see the mighty prince—had told her Llywelyn planned to stay at Dolwyddelan for a sennight more. But given his reaction to her, he might simply have been amusing himself further at her expense.

Lord Ian looked at her as if she were mad. "Do you mean to tell me you don't know? I thought your actions foolish before, but now—" He shook his head.

"Just tell me," she cried, rising from the stool and gathering the mantle about her. She wanted to pace, to move, but the chamber was too small and his cloak too long. She sighed her frustration. "Please."

"Aye, he's here. But I doubt he'll see you. His labors begin with the dawn, and continue without cease until the sun is set. In the evening he makes time for nothing but merriment." Did she detect scorn in his voice?

His face told her nothing, but what did his opinion of his master matter to her? She had run Llywelyn to ground at Dolwyddelan, climbed the curtain wall and survived. Relief weakened her already shaky knees. She plopped down on the stool. "Saints be praised," she said, smiling.

Ian stared. Her smile transformed her face, and her green eyes appeared lit from within. Although dirty streaks still covered her cheeks, she looked happy. And beautiful.

Christ on the cross, had he turned into a besotted fool? He shifted his gaze to the narrow beam of sunlight streaming through a slit high in the wall. Somehow, this woman had addled his brain.

But he refused to give in to the temptation she presented. The image of a strong, unified Wales rose in his mind, the shrine he worshiped above all others. He'd likely given up all hope of heaven, of family and a life of his own, to attain that goal. A mere slip of a woman would not keep him from it.

He'd ignored far more compelling distractions, he reminded himself as he forced himself to look at her again.

Her smile had disappeared. Perhaps God's light still shone upon him, after all.

"Would you plead my case, milord?" she asked. "It truly is important. I'd never have tried so hard to see him, otherwise."

What harm could there be in it? Christ knew, she'd shown more valor than many a noble warrior. She'd earned her chance to speak—to him, at least. "I'll hear what you have to say."

"Thank you, sir." Lily settled herself on the stool, her spine straight as an arrow, despite the fact that she had to ache like the devil. "I searched for the prince for more than a fortnight, though it seems as though my quest had gone on forever."

"Where have you come from?"

"I've lived in the abbey of Saint Winifred all my life. My mother and I were boarders there."

"What is your mother about, to permit you to wander the countryside alone?" He began to revise his initial opinion of her. No one of low degree boarded at an abbey, especially an abbey as wealthy as Saint Winifred's. And her speech carried the refined tones of the nobility. His wits had gone begging. He should have noticed that immediately.

"My mother is dead, milord, this month past." She made the sign of the cross. "May God grant her peace." She closed her eyes, sadness etched upon her face.

Perhaps grief at her mother's death had confused her,

sent her upon this senseless journey. "Surely you must have family," he said, ignoring the way her eyes had filled with tears—just as they had last night. "Someone must have paid the abbey to keep you. The Church's charity doesn't stretch that far."

Lily shook her head and met his gaze. She believed what she told him, he could see it. And no cloud of madness or confusion tainted the clear emerald of her eyes. "The abbess, Sister Maud, swore my mother was the only family I had. And that our board had been paid, and would continue to be paid, by a benefactor unknown to her."

"Surely the bishop—"

"I sought him out first of all, once I'd escaped the confines of the abbey."

"Escaped? They had no right to hold you," Ian said. The more she told him, the less he understood. Nothing she'd said made sense.

She stood up, slipped his cloak from her shoulders and placed it carefully on the stool. "There are many ways to hold someone close by without making them a prisoner, Dragon. The sisters never locked me up. They simply made certain I had no opportunity to leave." A winsome smile lit her face. "But I used their own ways against them. All my life they sought to school me to patience. So I bided my time and lulled their suspicions. Eventually a chance arose and I took it." She laughed. "I truly doubt they care that I am gone—I've been a trial to them since I first learned to speak."

He could imagine it. "What did the bishop say?"

She paced the narrow confines of the cell before she replied. "I never saw the bishop himself. But his clerk assured me the bishop knew nothing about my situation.

And I could scarce return to Saint Winifred's to question the abbess. I'd never get away again.''

When would she come to the point? He could have growled with frustration, but he pushed the feeling deep. If only he had patience, he'd learn what he wanted to know—sooner or later.

But he had more important things to do than listen to a mysterious young woman recount her meandering tale. "How does Llywelyn fit into this? He isn't a patron of Saint Winifred's, I know that for a fact. And I doubt even he has the power to force the bishop to tell you anything." Straightening, he crossed the room and stood before her. "What is it you want from Llywelyn?"

"I think he knows who I am."

Ian shook his head in disbelief and bit back a laugh. "Do you think the prince so powerful he knows all— and everyone—within his domain? I cannot believe God himself has such dominion."

Lily looked at him as if he, and not she, were the fool. "While my mother lay close to death, I could swear I heard one of the sisters ask another if they should send word to Llywelyn. When I mentioned it to the abbess, she turned my question around and never gave me an answer. That way she did not have to lie, if it were true. Sister Maud prides herself on her honesty," she added, her voice scornful.

She held her hand out to him in supplication. "My mother was all I had, though she rarely knew me. I have nowhere else to turn, milord, and nothing left to lose. I am tired of being alone. All I want is to find some place where I belong."

That, he could understand. It did not bother him to be on his own, but he also had his sister, Catrin, and his cousin Gillian, to turn to when he tired of his own company. And Llywelyn was his kinsman, as well as his overlord.

He chose to live a solitary life. Lily didn't have that choice.

"Is there anything else I should know? Your mother's name, at least—you must know that."

"Nay. Everyone called her 'milady.' I never heard her name." She sighed. "You must understand—she lived in a world all her own, a world filled with people who didn't exist. I believe 'twas why she'd been sent to the abbey. No one wanted to care for her, most like. But she wasn't mad, just filled with sadness. No one could lift her from it."

Something inside Ian recoiled at the lonely life Lily had led and the matter-of-fact way she spoke of it. He couldn't imagine a childhood spent without a mother's love. And it didn't sound as though the sisters of Saint Winifred's Abbey had spared any affection for Lily. His parents had been everything to him; he would have done anything to save them, if he could. Their loss was a pain he buried deep and refused to expose.

Perhaps he could help her. "I will do what I can for you."

She reached out and took his arm in a firm clasp. "Thank you. You have no idea how grateful I am, milord."

He looked down at her hand. He liked the way it felt, far too much. So he did what he had to to make the feeling go away. "I make you no promises. Llywelyn may not wish to hear what I have to say. He has little time to waste on one person's petty concerns."

She released him immediately. But the wounded expression in her eyes lingered, long after the warmth of her touch faded from his arm. "I understand. And I appreciate whatever you can do, sir." She turned and picked up his cloak. "I'll bother you no further," she said, holding the bundle out to him.

"Keep it." He crossed the room swiftly, feeling as if he'd kicked a helpless animal. "You need it more than I." Cursing under his breath, he jerked the door open and made good his escape before he did something even more gallant.

And more stupid.

Lily huddled within the welcoming folds of the Dragon's cloak and struggled yet again to recall any snippet of information useful to her quest. She'd racked her brain on numerous occasions over the course of her journey, but so far, she could remember very little.

Her life at the abbey had consisted mainly of endless days of stultifying boredom. The only child among the few boarders, she'd counted herself fortunate when an elderly noblewoman enlisted her help to spin or sew. Rarer still had been the chance to venture beyond the cloister walls into town. The games the village children played in the meadows, running and shrieking with joyous abandon, were as foreign to her as the sight of a man of fewer than fifty years. Other than their elderly priest, she'd seen men only from a distance. The sisters had been careful to keep her close by on their infrequent forays into the village.

She'd been astounded by the size and strength of men when her travels took her into a town, alone. And their crude suggestions had shocked her, though not for long. But she didn't fear them, a fact that surprised her. Indeed, she found nearly everyone she encountered a refreshing change from the occupants of the abbey, with their regimented lives and devotion to duty.

In a way, this journey was the embodiment of a childhood dream. How many times had she lain in the grass, staring at the birds flying overhead and envying them their freedom? She'd always known a whole new world existed beyond the abbey walls. Now she had the opportunity to explore it.

There had been a gatekeeper at the abbey years ago, a very old man who'd traveled far and wide. He told her of lands and people different from any she'd ever known. His brief stay at the abbey shone as a rare bright spot in her memory. She'd never forgotten the tales he'd shared with her.

If the Dragon couldn't help her, perhaps she'd make her way south, to Pembroke or Manorbier. Each castle had its own town, of a size she could scarcely imagine. Strangers from foreign lands came there to trade, bringing with them news of places far beyond her ken.

Though she knew that for many the cloister provided a safe haven, to her it had been a prison. She'd never return, no matter what she had to do to survive.

The sound of the bar thumping against the door startled her. Her heart pounding wildly, she stood and tossed aside the cloak. Had the Dragon returned so soon?

The door flew open beneath the force of two brawny men. Before she could do more than gasp, one entered the cell and grabbed her roughly by the arm, while the other stood guard in the doorway.

He pulled her arms behind her and bound them with a coarse rope. "What are you doing?" she asked. Already her shoulders throbbed with pain, so tight were the bonds. "Did Lord Ian order this?"

"Ye're to come with us," the guard said. "Don't give us trouble, missy, else ye might get hurt." He wrapped a musty rag around her mouth and tied it behind her head.

He gave her a shove to start her moving. Her feet slipped in the loose straw, and she scrambled for purchase, stumbled and almost fell on her face. Her burly escort saved her from that fate, but her arms felt wrenched from their sockets.

For the first time since the Dragon hauled her up the wall, she felt afraid. Her guards set a hellish pace. She tried to keep up, but they made no accommodation for her shorter legs as they hauled her through a maze of dark, winding corridors. The filthy gag made her cough; the fear in her throat made it almost impossible to breathe.

The ground sloped downward, the hard-packed dirt grew uneven. The distance between torches grew so great that she could scarce make out the walls. For all she knew, this might be the passageway to hell itself.

Her arms numb, Lily struggled to find her way, a task made more difficult when the hallway narrowed. One of the men continued to shove her ahead of him, pushing her into the rough-hewn stones whenever the walls curved.

Suddenly he jerked back on her bonds. Lily bit back a groan; her arms still had feeling, after all. Cruel hands dug at the knot holding her arms, then jerked the gag from her mouth before spinning her about and thrusting her into the shadows.

She landed on her hands and knees. The impact sent unbearable pain through her already aching body. But she found her footing and crawled to her feet. "Wait!" she cried. "Where have you brought me?"

Silence was her only reply.

Then metal clanged against metal, and the darkness became complete.

Chapter Three

Lily bit back a whimper. The shadows pressed in on her from all sides as she wavered on her feet, then sank to her knees beneath their weight.

Her arms hung, useless, from her shoulders, yet already they tingled with the return of sensation. She forced her fingers to move despite the fiery pain, hoping to speed up the process. For now, any further motion was impossible.

Only darkness met her frantic gaze. Darkness meant the unknown. Her mind envisioned a thousand formless terrors lurking all around her. She drew a deep breath. Perhaps if she learned the bounds of her new prison, it would cease to frighten her. Since she could not see in the impenetrable gloom, she closed her eyes and concentrated on her other senses. The air tasted dank and moist upon her tongue. A foul stench emanated from somewhere to her left; she'd be careful not to move in that direction.

She had no intention of standing up, lest there be spiders or some other horrid creatures above her.

The faint sound of scurrying she recognized. Rats, loathsome but familiar. So long as they kept their dis-

tance, she had no objection to sharing her cell with
them. She found their company preferable to that of the
men who'd dragged her here.

Why had they brought her here?

She hadn't been surprised when the Dragon had
locked her up. Though she posed no threat to anyone,
she could see the need for caution, especially in the
prince's keep. If the guards had been willing to allow
a stranger in to see Llywelyn, she wouldn't have ended
up on the wall—or in the Dragon's custody.

The sudden chill in her heart rivaled the cold air surrounding her. The Dragon had to be responsible for her
new accommodations. She thought he understood her
dilemma, the need that had driven her to Dolwyddelan.

How could he do this to her? And why?

Lily huddled in a ball on the floor, her arms wrapped
tight about her knees for warmth and comfort. His betrayal cut deep. Although she'd confided in him, trusted
him with her story, he owed her nothing. And the pull
of attraction she felt in his presence simply meant she
was ignorant of men, a fool.

Shame and anger jolted her. Self-pity solved nothing.
Her journey thus far hadn't been easy, but she knew her
situation could be worse. Battered and bruised, cold and
hungry—she'd been all those things before. But she was
still whole and healthy, with a spirit to match.

She would survive. And triumph.

A lifetime spent within the imprisoning walls of Saint
Winifred's Abbey had taught her the value of patience.
She'd use that patience again. What else could she do
but familiarize herself with her surroundings and make
her plans? In time she would discover what the Dragon
wanted of her, why he'd sent her here.

And he would learn her spirit would not break so easily.

Ian's interview with Llywelyn haunted him long after he left his overlord's presence. Something about the meeting disturbed him, though he had yet to figure out why. Llywelyn had listened to his words and agreed to consider permitting Lily to meet with him soon. There was nothing unusual about that, contrary to what he'd led Lily to believe. Llywelyn possessed a deep sense of curiosity and a well-developed mind. Ian admired his ability to look ahead and plan for the future.

It was their shared vision of a united Welsh people that had led Ian to join forces with Llywelyn. Llywelyn could bring that dream to fruition, draw together the independent nobles into a power to be reckoned with, whether dealing with Norman tyrants—or Welsh ones.

In this quest, he'd committed deeds he could never have imagined in his youth, before the destruction of his family. The bastards responsible for his parents' deaths had paid with their worthless lives long ago, but his desire for justice remained. He knew his sister wondered at the change in him, perhaps even mourned the loss of the man he had once been. When he looked back at that innocent, he did not recognize himself. But what did that matter, in the greater scheme of things?

He would do anything necessary to achieve his goal.

At times, that task seemed nigh impossible. His latest chore promised to tax his patience—and that of his small company from Gwal Draig—to the limit. Dai and several others had joined him in the bailey to watch as ten young men from the hills—future warriors all, he reminded himself with a snort of disbelief—played at mock combat.

"D'ye think any of them has ever seen a weapon close up, milord?" Dai asked, his voice choked with pent-up laughter. "Look at how they're holding their swords. Were we ever so daft?"

"I hope 'tis just ignorance, not stupidity. We'll find out soon enough." He saw nothing to laugh about in the chaotic scene. Rarely did they find men like these, freemen without an overlord to command their loyalty. With luck, they'd gain some decent fighters, always in short supply. If not, he didn't doubt he could find some task for them. He'd suggested this exercise to determine what he had to work with.

But he could tell right off. Shepherds and farmers, the lot of them. When he could no longer stand to watch their clumsy attempts, he stripped off his shirt and tunic and, snatching a practice sword off the ground, leaped into the fray.

His first battle roar sent half the company to the curtain wall, backs pressed against the stone. They blanched and shook with terror, much to the onlookers' amusement. Once he began to lay about him with the dull blade, only two men held their ground to parry his attack.

Their movements were awkward, but he saw their confidence increase with every swing of his sword. He didn't try to overpower them—he wanted to test their mettle, if they had any, not scare them off. But, unlike the others, they rose to the challenge and worked harder still.

After a time, one stepped away, sweat streaming down his face as he gasped for breath. But the other pressed on, grinning, his eyes alight with the joy of battle.

Ian pushed harder and brought him to his knees, the blade at his throat. "Do you yield?"

"Aye, m-milord," the youth stammered. He looked Ian straight in the eyes. "But only 'cause I got no choice."

"Get up." Ian handed the sword to one of his men and picked up his shirt. "You and you—" he nodded to his other opponent "—come with me. The rest of you," he said, raising his voice to reach the men along the wall, "stay here with Dai. See if you can learn something from him."

Dai rolled his eyes and offered a mocking salute. "Whatever I did to offend you, milord, I apologize—a thousand times over. By Christ, you don't really expect me to make fighters out a them, do you?"

"We need every man we can get. If you can't teach them to use a sword or a bow, at the least they should be able to handle a spear. It's not too different from a shepherd's crook," he added dryly. He tugged his shirt over his head. "When you've finished here for the afternoon, come to me in my chamber. I've another task for you, one I'm sure you'll find more to your liking."

Laughing at Dai's grumbled curses, Ian led his two apprentices away.

He practiced with them until they looked ready to drop and he'd worked up a sweat, as well. But the labor brought satisfaction, as hard work always did; he couldn't help smiling as he returned to his room to wash and change his filthy clothing before the evening meal.

He found Dai leaning against the wall outside his room. His lieutenant's sparse, grizzled locks stood out from his head as though he'd dragged his hands though them more than once. "Seems you had a good afternoon," he snarled as Ian unlocked the door and motioned him into the room. He flopped onto a stool with the ease of long acquaintance. "Wish I could say the same."

Ian grinned. "I think we'll make fighters out of those two." He filled a pair of mugs with mead and handed one to Dai. "Here. Your favorite, made by my sister's own hands. I can see you need it. Getting too old for this work? You know there's a place for you at Gwal Draig." He tried not to laugh at Dai's expression of disgust at the familiar taunt—and his typical reply.

"Aye, beneath six feet of dirt." Dai drained the brew, then stood up and helped himself to more. "They worked you over good, eh, lad?" he asked, tugging on the trailing cuff of Ian's sleeve.

"Not a scratch on me. They look worse than I do. I doubt they'll be jumping too lively with the ladies tonight." He finished his mead in one swallow, then poured water to wash. "Did you have any luck with the others?" he asked, without much hope. Yawning, he stripped off his shirt and tossed it onto the chest, then stretched the kinks out of his shoulders.

"Are you daft? You know as well as I, that lot'll never be ready. Even after all I put them through," he said, his voice tinged with exasperation, "or mayhap because of it, most of them will still turn tail at the first sign of battle." He sipped at his mead, then asked, "What of the lad you pulled from the wall last night? Anyone willing to try that must have a measure of courage."

In the process of scooping cold water over his head, Ian chuckled, and he came up sputtering. He groped for the drying cloth. "That she does."

"Something wrong with my ears, lad? I could swear ye said 'she.'"

"I did."

He took his time drying off, savoring the other man's glare. Dai hated to wait more than almost anything. 'Twould do him good to learn patience. By the time Ian had tugged a clean shirt over his head and picked up his comb, Dai looked ready to explode. "She's the reason I asked you here."

"Who is she?"

"She says she doesn't know."

Dai leaped to his feet. "Did she hit her head on the way up the wall?" He slammed his empty cup onto the table. "Or did you hit yours? Enough of your foolery, milord. 'Tis a jest, am I right?"

"'Tis no jest. 'Tis more a puzzle." He walked over to the bed and stared down at the place where Lily had sprawled. He could see her there still, her hair shining against the dull gray coverlet. That image had haunted his dreams, just as the look on her face when he agreed to help her had dominated his thoughts throughout the day. Mayhap he'd have time to see her before the evening meal. He'd take Dai to meet her, he decided, instead of simply sending him—

"Come on then, milord," Dai said, cutting into his thoughts. "Can't say something like that, then leave me hanging. Tell me more."

"In good time. Will you allow me to finish dressing, or must I parade through the bailey bare-assed?" Ian asked as he settled a clean tunic over his shirt and leggings.

Dai snorted. "Aye, the ladies'd like that, I make no doubt. Not that you'd notice. Never saw a man turn away so many invitations as you, milord."

"It's not me they want, but the chance to bed the Dragon. Besides, 'tis damned difficult to lay a wench

who's staring at you with fear in her eyes," Ian said
with disgust.

"So don't look at their eyes. Christ, how'd you get
so choosy? If the lass is a toothsome armful and willing,
what does the rest matter?"

"It matters to me." Ian scanned the room for his
cloak before he remembered he'd left it with Lily. He
didn't need it, anyway. His blood had flowed hot from
the moment he first tussled with her. The feel of her in
his arms remained imprinted upon his body.

And his mind.

Dai's words made him think of her vivid green eyes.
He had recognized many things in her gaze when it
rested so steadily upon him. But he hadn't seen fear
among them.

Jesu, he grew maudlin! Next thing he knew, he'd start
composing a song about the way her hair glowed in the
candlelight. Perhaps he'd spent too much time in his
Norman brother-in-law's company and his courtly manners had rubbed off on him.

A quick glance at the sky through the window slit
showed the sun hovering just above the horizon. If he
wanted to take Dai to meet Lily before supper, they had
best go now.

"Come along, old man," he said, urging Dai away
from the mead and out the door. "I'll show you a
woman who doesn't know how to fear."

"Indeed, milord." Dai squinted at his face in the dim
light of the corridor; Ian felt the measuring weight of
his scrutiny. "And how would you know that?"

"She calls me Dragon."

Ian fought back a smile as they left the tower and
crossed the bailey. Seldom did he move Dai to silence,

but the other man hadn't said a word since his last comment. Although he valued Dai's counsel, and trusted him implicitly, he often found himself only half listening as he prattled on.

He picked up his pace as he led the way down the stairs into the cellars, but then stopped dead in the corridor. No guard stood outside the cell.

And the bar to the door lay on the floor, as though tossed aside in haste.

Motioning to Dai to keep silent, Ian drew his sword and crept forward, then pushed on the door. It swung inward in a slow, creaking arc, revealing the darkness within.

Dai snatched a torch from the wall and handed it to him. Sword at the ready, Ian entered the cell.

He paced the narrow boundaries, but of Lily he found no sign. The three-legged stool sat where he'd placed it, his cloak draped over the seat, the only clues that his visit hadn't been a dream.

"Lord Ian."

He whirled at the sound of Dai's voice, then kicked the stool aside and snatched his cloak off the floor. "Where is she?"

The formless suspicions he'd harbored after meeting with Llywelyn crowded into his head, a jumble of curiosity and accusation, barely noticed hints that something wasn't right. He should have followed his instincts, sent Dai off to investigate sooner, instead of—

"Mayhap Llywelyn let her go," Dai commented.

"He hadn't agreed to see her. Even if he decided to meet with her, he would have sent for me to be there, as well. I'm the one who questioned her."

"What does it matter, lad? She was here, now she's gone. You said yourself she didn't know who she was."

Dai shook his head. "I know for a fact you've got more important work to do than this."

But it did matter. "There's something strange about this. The situation Lily described seemed odd." He righted the stool and sat down, his mind working furiously. "I want you to go to Saint Winifred's Abbey once we discover what has happened here. I'm certain you'll have better luck finding answers than a lone young woman would," he said pointedly.

"Aye, milord."

"But first we need to find her." Ian rose to his feet. "Come. Let's see what Llywelyn has to say about this."

The prince had yet to leave his chamber for supper, which suited Ian's purpose. He'd rather not discuss the mysterious Lily before all and sundry in the hall.

Once the meal ended, the revelry would begin. And when the wine began to flow, any kind of conversation would be impossible.

"May we speak with you privately, milord?" Ian asked. At Llywelyn's nod, he ushered Dai into the chamber. "I've matters of importance to discuss."

Llywelyn returned his attention to a basin of water as Ian pulled the door closed with a sharp snap. His expression revealed nothing but impatience as he took his time drying his hands on a strip of fine linen.

Tossing the towel aside, he crossed the room to a table in the center and picked up a jeweled chalice. "Would you care for wine?" He poured the deep red liquid from a pitcher, sending the scent of spices wafting through the air.

Ian declined the wine and the offer of a chair, then waited impatiently as Dai accepted a goblet and joined the prince at the table. Finally the niceties were satisfied, and Ian got down to business.

"I went back to see the girl, to tell her you would deal with her once you had more time." He watched his kinsman's face with interest, although he kept his own expression casual, disinterested. "I planned to release her from the cell, since she poses no threat to anyone." He toyed with a thread on the sleeve of his tunic, continuing to observe Llywelyn from beneath lowered brows. "I was surprised to find she wasn't there."

All Llywelyn's attention seemed focused upon his wine. Then he glanced up and met Ian's gaze. Ian could see nothing in the other man's face but a mild annoyance, gone so swiftly he might have imagined it.

"You needn't have bothered," Llywelyn said. "Any more than you should have bothered me with her tale in the first place. I know nothing of her or her mother, and so I told her."

"Then where is she?" Ian demanded.

"She had no wish to stay, once she saw I could not help her. A guard escorted her from the castle." Llywelyn raised the goblet to his lips and avoided Ian's scrutiny. "She's here no longer. Beyond that, I cannot say."

Chapter Four

A light glowed before her, shining through a small slit set high in the door. She had to be dreaming. Lily raised her head from her updrawn knees and rubbed the sleep from her eyes. She looked again, but the light didn't disappear. Instead, it shone brighter.

"Who's there?" she called, slowly rising to her feet. A strange shuffling noise, accompanied by the rustle of fabric, came from the corridor. No one answered.

She had no way to mark the passage of time, but her rumbling stomach told her that many hours had passed since she'd broken her fast. Perhaps one of the guards had returned with food. They had to feed her some-time—didn't they?

Though her body protested with every step, she made her way toward the door. The wide, metal-banded planks felt solid and impenetrable when she leaned her weight against them. She ran her hand along the edge, where the door met rough plaster and stone, but she couldn't find a handle. Anyone lodged here was meant to stay.

She had to crane her neck to see out the window. The glare from a torch blinded her, but her nose worked all too well. Coughing, she moved down from the opening and slumped back against the wall.

She couldn't imagine anything that could cause such an indescribable stench. Whatever it was had to be on the other side of the door. Even the dank, fetid air of her cell smelled better.

She filled her lungs before rising on tiptoe to peer out once more. She blinked several times, until her vision adjusted to the brightness.

The sight that met her eyes had to be a fiend of Satan. She couldn't imagine how anyone could suffer such injuries and live. She'd seen cripples before—many had come to the abbey for help—but never had she encountered such a horrifying combination of infirmities.

Bent almost double, he leaned on a rough stick, one misshapen foot twisted at an unnatural angle. A scraggly beard covered most of his face, but through the silver-shot hair she could see that his nose and one cheek had been smashed nearly flat. His left eyelid drooped closed. His forehead, and the hand that held the torch in an unsteady grip, were covered with scars.

"Might not want to look," he rasped. "I'm not a pretty sight." His laugh had a maniacal quality to it, sending a shiver down Lily's spine. She crossed herself, thanking God this unfortunate creature couldn't see her—or the loathing and pity she couldn't hide.

"Who are you? Why have you come here?" she asked when she found her voice. She backed away from the door to catch a breath. "Are you here to let me out?"

"Nay. I saw the guards bring you here. 'Tis the first chance I've had to follow. I wanted to see for myself." He shuffled away from the door and placed the torch in a bracket on the wall. "A shame I can't reach the window—I didn't get a good look when they dragged you from the other cell. But I heard about you.''

He'd heard about her? Was his mind as twisted as his body? Even if she had the Dragon to thank for her new accommodations, she couldn't believe he'd discussed her with that…creature out there.

''Who are you?'' she demanded.

He laughed again, a humorless sound. ''I had a noble name, and power, once, not so long ago. But that man is dead—or so I hear.'' He coughed, sounding as if he were choking. ''Until I can prove them wrong. You can call me Toad. 'Tis as good a name as any, for now.''

She stared at him again, forcing herself to take in every wretched detail. *He must be a madman.* He could no more be noble than she.

But even a madman deserved pity, as long as he did no harm. And from the sound of him, he wasn't long for this world—a blessing, she had no doubt. She'd listen to him ramble, just to hear another human voice. But she didn't have to look at him.

She stepped away from the door. Sweet Mary, his image was already etched upon her mind's eye. And he wouldn't know whether she could see him or not.

She moved to the middle of the floor and sank down upon the cold stones, drawing her knees to her chest and gulping great breaths of fresher air. ''So tell me, Toad, what have you heard of me? I've been here but a day—hardly anyone knows I'm here.''

''My honored kinsman knows. Though he isn't quite certain what to do with you. Have a care, girl—you've upset his schemes. He doesn't like it when that happens.''

Did all madmen speak in riddles? Just so had her mother rambled on. Their words made no sense to any but themselves, and woe betide those who tried to understand them. She'd found 'twas best to let them wander. It harmed no one—although it frustrated Lily no end not to understand.

"Should I fear for my life, then?" God knew, she'd thought of little else since the cell door had slammed shut behind her.

He chuckled again, an evil sound over the restless shuffling as he moved about. "Perhaps."

She'd kept her gaze on the window while they spoke, grateful for even the dim glow from the corridor. But suddenly the light faded. "Wait!" She sprang to her feet and rushed to the door. "You cannot leave!"

Especially not after his last remark. She needed to know more—

Lily stretched, catching a glimpse of him, but he'd almost disappeared from view. "Toad! Come back!"

"Sleep well, milady," he called as he rounded a bend in the corridor.

Leaving her in total darkness once more.

Frustration left Ian feeling like a caged beast. He prowled the confines of his chamber, his body as restless as his mind. He knew Llywelyn had lied to him, could feel it deep within his bones. He'd witnessed that act of innocence too often not to recognize it now. He simply didn't understand why Llywelyn would treat him thus.

"Quit your pacing and sit down, milord," Dai snapped. He shoved a stool in Ian's direction. "All this stomping about is making me daft. You're acting like a spoiled little lordling. Christ, man, use the brain God gave ye."

He forced himself to stop, and faced Dai, letting the

words sink in. When would he learn to listen with his head, instead of his emotions? Most of the time, he could keep his temper contained. But Dai had witnessed it often enough in private that it had no effect on him— except to exasperate him.

Nodding, Ian righted the stool and sat down. "He's lying. We both know it."

"Aye. And why would he do that, milord? I think you'd better tell me more about this girl."

"Woman," he corrected absently. "She's a woman full grown."

"Is she? Is that what's got your head in a spin, lad? I'd never have believed it of ye, but there's a first time for everything. Even a dragon needs a mate."

Dai knew him too well.

"Something about her haunts me," he admitted. "Although she's dirty, and wears men's clothes, there's a...beauty about her. She won't leave me alone."

"Tell me about her, and what you want me to do."

It didn't take long, he knew so little.

"I want you to go to Saint Winifred's Abbey and find out all you can. Something about this bothers me— all the more because of Llywelyn's reaction. I'll nose around tonight. She could still be here."

"Should I wait till the morn to leave?" Dai asked.

"Aye. No need to arouse suspicions. Take two men with you. If anyone asks, I'll say you have business for me at Gwal Draig. But get back to Gwal Draig as swiftly as you can. If I cannot meet you there, I'll send word. I mislike this entire situation."

He ushered Dai out, then went to stand by the window. Darkness had fallen. He stared out into the welcoming shadows and sought counsel from the night.

The wisest course would be to return to the hall, as

he did most evenings, but the chances he'd learn any-thing of value there were virtually nonexistent. Perhaps he ought to share a few ales with the castle guard in their quarters. No one would think anything of it. He'd done so before.

Whether Lily had left Dolwyddelan of her own vo-lition, as Llywelyn maintained, or had simply been moved, someone had to have seen her.

He would find her.

And when he did, somebody would pay.

By midnight, Ian felt awash in ale but no closer to finding Lily. His feet heavy on the tower stairs, he sought the cool night air. He needed to clear his head before deciding what to do next. After half a night spent dicing and drinking, the only information he had was that no one had seen her leave.

So either Llywelyn had lied to him, or the guards at the castle gates had all gone blind. In his present mood, 'twas all he could do to prevent himself confronting his princely kinsman and demanding the truth.

That would gain him nothing.

No one had seen Lily outside, but there were bound to be passageways throughout the keep that he didn't know about. A smart man always left himself an escape route. He would return to Lily's cell and investigate further.

There wouldn't be a better time. No one had any business in the cellars at this time of night.

He moved quickly through the shadows and retrieved a shuttered lantern and his cloak from his chamber. He saw no one as he slipped into the cellars and closed the door behind him.

As far as he knew, none of the cells held prisoners.

He should be able to search to his heart's content. A rabbit warren of corridors lay deep beneath the keep. He'd never had reason to explore them before, so he set about it in a methodical fashion.

From the number of undisturbed spiderwebs he found, he knew that some areas hadn't been occupied in quite a while. But several passages could have been used recently. He chose the widest and set off.

He hadn't gone more than fifteen paces before the corridor ended in a wall.

Ian smiled.

Only a fool built a passageway leading nowhere. He set the lantern on the floor, then felt around the edges of the wall, pushing and prodding at the stones until his patience was rewarded. Just as he had suspected, the wall was actually a door. Surprisingly silent, it opened inward. Picking up the lamp, he pushed on.

The air had a sweetish scent overlaying a dank, earthy odor, as if something had died. The stench, combined with the ale he'd consumed, made his stomach roil in protest. But he kept walking. The ceiling dropped so low his hair brushed against the splintery planks above him. Crouched low over the lantern, he almost missed the two doors to his left.

"Lily?" he called, banging on the first door with his fist. "Are you here?"

He heard the sound of footsteps, then pounding on the other door. "Dragon?"

He couldn't mistake that voice.

And no one else called him Dragon.

Holding the lantern high, he turned toward the door. "Aye, Lily, it's me."

He tugged on the door, but the lock held firm.

"There's no key," he said after scanning the area. "I'll have to try my dirk."

When he lowered the lamp to the floor, Lily called out, "Don't take away the light." He could understand her plea; it must be black as pitch inside the cell. He hooked the lantern over the wall pricket and drew out his dirk.

The blade scarcely fit in the lock, but Ian took his time. If he snapped the knife off, he'd never get her out on his own.

And he had no intention of seeking help, now that he saw where they'd put her. Locking her away down here could only be a deliberate attempt to keep her hidden.

Most likely from him.

Slowly, gently, he wiggled the knife, until he felt the lock give. He pulled the dirk free, shoved it back in its scabbard and yanked the door open.

Lily leaped into his arms with an inarticulate cry.

He gathered her quivering body close and held her tight, smoothing his hand over her tangled hair. "Hush," he whispered. She tried to speak, but the words came out jumbled and indistinct. "Slowly, sweeting. Hush. It's all right."

He held her as he would an injured child, trying not to notice the way her body fit so well to his, nor the softness of her hair beneath his cheek.

But his body would not listen. Heat rose in his blood, intensifying her scent, magnifying the feel of her pliant curves pressed against his hardness.

Carrying her with him, he stepped back into the corridor, into the light. He framed her face with his hands and stared into the eyes that had haunted him, asleep and awake, for the past day. She met his gaze, stare for stare, until, with a muttered curse, he crushed his lips to hers.

Her mouth didn't move, but neither did she try to push him away. She kissed like a child, lips pressed to lips. He gentled his hold and showed her another way.

He outlined her mouth with his tongue, then nibbled at her lips until they opened enough to allow him entrance. Pressing on the corners of her mouth with his thumbs, he urged her to give him more.

She sighed and took a step back, her eyes wide. Then, grabbing the front of his tunic in her fists, she pulled him close again.

But this time she burrowed her face against his chest and clung to him. "Why did you send me here?"

"How could you think that?" He drew back enough to see her face. That she believed what she said, he could not doubt, not after searching her eyes.

"No one else knew about me." She eased her hands from his mantle and smoothed the wrinkled fabric. "And you'd locked me away already."

"Only because I didn't know what else to do with you. I've never found a woman scaling the castle walls to see Llywelyn before," he said, his heart pounding harder in remembrance. "I did not send you here." He held her gaze until he thought she believed him.

A shiver coursed through her; her skin felt icy beneath his hands. He drew his cloak off and wrapped her securely within its warm folds. "They didn't give me a chance to take this," she said, her voice faint.

He pulled her into his arms again, just to warm her, he told himself. Never mind that holding her brought him a measure of comfort, as well.

"Who brought you here? And when?"

Lily closed her eyes, as if trying to remember—or to

forget. "Two men burst into my cell, before midday, I think. They bound my arms and gagged me, then dragged me here. 'Twas too dark—I could not see. Before I realized what they were about, they untied me and shoved me in here."

He could feel the effort it took for her to recount the tale so calmly. But her voice stayed even, almost emotionless. He knew she was frightened, but she hid it well. Few men had her courage. He brushed a kiss across her brow and held her close a moment longer.

"We must leave," he told her. "You'll be safer away from this place, while we decide what to do." He released her slowly, reluctant to let go.

Lily grabbed his sleeve. "If you didn't send me here, who did?"

"I'll tell you later, once we're away from here. Come, don't you want to leave?" He'd rather wait until she'd had a chance to eat and get warm before he told her his suspicions.

Besides, he wanted to learn more before he leveled his accusations against the man she'd come to for help.

Llywelyn.

He drew his knife again, weapon enough in such close quarters, should he need it. She stared at the dirk, then his face, for what seemed forever, thinking he knew not what. But she must have found what she sought, for she nodded once. "Lead the way, Dragon," she said. She unhooked the lantern from the wall, then tucked her hand in the crook of his arm. "I trust you."

He might well be the only person here she could trust, he thought as he closed the cell door.

He'd do whatever he must to prove himself worthy of it.

* * *

Lily clung to the Dragon's arm, her grip barely short of desperation, as he led her through the labyrinth of passageways. She expected Toad—or some other creature like him—to slither into their path at any moment. Even with enough light to see, 'twas a frightening place.

The relief she felt at the knowledge that Lord Ian hadn't sent her into the cryptlike cell was near overwhelming.

But if not the Dragon, then who?

Toad said he knew who had sent her there, and much else, besides. But how could she believe such an obviously deranged person? Nothing he'd told her made any sense.

And he certainly didn't appear to be someone a prince would confide in.

No, she'd simply have to be patient. The Dragon would tell her what he knew, when the time was right. She knew he'd keep her safe.

She knew he was worthy of her trust.

When the corridor seemed to end, he gently eased her hand from his arm and took the lantern. "In case anyone's watching," he said, extinguishing the light and plunging them into complete darkness once more. Before she could ask him what he was about, the Dragon pushed on the edge of the wall and a door pivoted toward them. He stood silently for a moment— listening, she concluded—then handed her the lantern. "Come—no one will see us now," he whispered. Grasping her by the elbow, he led her through the corridor.

"Where are you taking me?" she asked. Not back to the other cell, surely?

"To my chamber, for now. We'll decide what else to do in the morning."

They skulked around the dimly lit boundary of the bailey with far more stealth than on the previous night. But except for the fact that this time she was able to walk, instead of riding slung over the Dragon's shoulder, it felt much the same.

Lord Ian ap Dafydd seemed most comfortable lurking in the shadows, from what she'd seen of him thus far. She could feel a darkness within him; perhaps 'twas why he sought the shadows instinctively.

But although she should probably fear that side of him, it intrigued her.

Especially since he'd kissed her.

She sensed he'd held himself in check—his touch had been quite gentle—but she'd felt a wildness simmering on the edge of her awareness.

That might have been nothing more than a reflection of the heat that bubbled through her veins at the mere thought of his lips touching hers. He drew her to him by means of some invisible thread—a look, a touch, all it took to make her want to return to his arms.

No doubt he'd be horrified if he knew. She was naught but a stranger to him, ignorant of men and women, no one of importance.

And he was Llywelyn's Dragon.

She'd know better the next time her emotions threatened to overwhelm her. The first time, she could pass off as an accident; if she did it again, he'd know her for a fool.

With luck, she'd find out what she needed to know soon, perhaps on the morrow. Then she'd be on her way.

And the Dragon need never know how he'd singed her heart.

Chapter Five

Once again Lily waited outside the Dragon's chamber while he found his key, then turned it in the lock. But this time he kept her behind him when he slipped through the door into the dark room, his dagger in one hand, the other wrapped about the hilt of his sword.

She wondered at his caution, until he shoved her backward as the room filled with light. She fell sideways into the corridor, landing on the floor and bumping her head against the stone wall. Though her head reeled, she sat up and groped for the lantern to use as a weapon. Before she got a good grip on the handle, someone wrenched it from her hand. She glared up at the soldier, then slumped back against the doorway.

The Dragon slashed wildly at two armed men and laid open the face of one with his knife. As the fighter spun away, a voice cried, "Hold, Ian! Would you murder our own people?"

Lily blinked to clear her foggy vision. Lord Ian slowly lowered his sword and stepped closer to her. "Nay, milord," he said. Without turning to face her, he reached down to help her to her feet. She took his hand and pulled herself up beside him. He gestured to the four guards in the room, meeting the wounded man's glare with a mirthless smile. "Do you threaten us?"

The speaker came toward them from the shadowy end of the room. Though dressed no differently than the others, he wore authority as if it were a mantle. He could only be Llywelyn, prince of Wales.

She couldn't interpret the look he sent the Dragon, but she knew it didn't bode well for him. "I see she didn't leave after all," Llywelyn said with a wry smile. "Clearly someone made a mistake—a costly one for him, I'm sure."

The Dragon sheathed his sword, but kept his dirk in his hand. "No doubt," he agreed. "Mistakes happen."

Llywelyn moved closer. His gaze swept over her, taking her measure, then staring into her eyes. She couldn't tell if she passed muster, or if he found her lacking. But she refused to back down or look away first. It was a relief when he ceased his scrutiny and returned his attention to the Dragon.

"Trust you to find her before any knew she was missing, Ian. I've always known I could count on you for anything," Llywelyn said. He motioned to one of his men. "Take this woman to her quarters. 'Tis too late to discuss anything of importance now." When the Dragon stepped forward, he added, "She'll be perfectly safe, Ian. You've done your duty. 'Tis no longer your concern. I've other work for you."

Lily placed her hand on the Dragon's arm and looked earnestly at Llywelyn. She couldn't understand why he refused to meet her gaze. "Milord, I don't wish—"

At Llywelyn's nod, the guard took her by the elbow, tugging her away from her protector and out of the room. Ian turned to watch as they led her away, his expression unreadable.

Outwardly calm, Ian watched the two men lead Lily away. But inside he seethed with fury, a fury he did not intend to show Llywelyn.

He needed to tread warily. By looking for Lily after Llywelyn told him she'd left, he'd already committed a grave error. He didn't wish to compound his mistake now.

The results were too important.

Llywelyn had made a mistake, as well, and Ian had caught him out.

Llywelyn knew something about her, something he wanted to keep hidden.

The trick would be to discover that secret—and soon.

With a nod toward the door, the prince ordered the other men from the room. Ian closed the door and leaned against it, waiting for the ax to fall.

He didn't have long to wait.

Llywelyn stood tall, an imposing figure, though he didn't intimidate Ian. He'd committed too many sins in Llywelyn's name—the other man owed him too much. But Ian wasn't a fool. He knew how easily a powerful man's favor could turn to vengeance.

"What were you about, Ian? Do you doubt my word now, that you must go behind my back and foul my plans? If I thought you needed to know where the girl was, I would have told you."

Thus he gave himself away. Ian hid his satisfaction, and sought the words to free himself from this coil. "I understand that, milord. And I didn't doubt you. But I hear things from many sources. Word reached me that led me to believe you'd been given false information. I merely wished to verify what I'd heard. There's no harm done. She's back in your possession, to do with as you will."

For the moment, Ian added to himself.

Llywelyn eyed him assessingly. He evidently passed muster. Ian saw nothing but approval in the other man's expression. "Very well. 'Tis forgotten. Besides, I have need of your expertise in the trouble with my nephew Rhys. He's begun making noise about reclaiming his lands. I want you to find him, make him understand my position before he goes too far. I'd rather not be forced to harm my own kin," he added, his gaze steady. "Leave as soon as you can, and take as long as you need to make him see reason. We'll manage fine until you return." He nodded and headed for the door.

"As you wish, milord," Ian said, opening the door and bowing as Llywelyn walked past.

His movements slow, he pushed the door closed, then turned the key in the lock. He stared at the worthless piece of metal, then heaved it across the room.

Damnation! It didn't do much good to lock the door when someone else had a key.

He couldn't have done worse tonight if he tried. Now Llywelyn had taken Lily away. If Llywelyn tried to hide her again, Ian could be certain he wouldn't find her this time, unless Llywelyn allowed him to. And that wasn't likely to happen.

By the time he returned from placating Rhys, she'd be so well hidden, he'd never find her. Assuming, of course, that they let her live. Considering where he'd found her, that was not a certainty.

Weary beyond belief, he removed his sword and dagger and placed them within easy reach before he stripped off his clothes and fell into bed. He didn't even bother to douse the light, hoping the brightness burning through his eyelids would show him whatever clue he kept missing.

Letting his mind drift, it filled immediately with images of Lily. He would never forget the expression of joy on her face when he'd opened the door to her cell. Again that jolt of familiarity assailed him, the sense that the knowledge he sought hovered just beyond his reach.

Her smile lingered, and he focused on it, the way her green eyes glowed, the slight tilt of her lips at one corner...

He sat bolt upright. He knew that smile, had seen it a thousand times before. When he added the green eyes and coppery hair—similar, but not quite the same—he truly thought he'd gone mad.

What he had in mind was impossible. There was no way that Lily could be related to Gillian de l'Eau Clair FitzClifford, marcher baroness.

His cousin.

The soldiers hustled Lily across the bailey and into the keep itself. She followed where they led; 'twas the least she could do, since this time they hadn't bound or gagged her. She scarcely had the energy to walk, let alone try to escape. Besides, running would avail her nothing, for she had nowhere left to go.

She returned the stares of the revelers they met on the stairway. Never had she seen such fine clothes, nor so many people the worse for drink. Several women, their bliauts laced so tight she could have seen a flea bound beneath them, smiled invitingly at the guards and frowned at her.

It was a relief when they stopped outside a chamber at the top of the stairs. She almost didn't care where they put her, so long as it was bright and warm. And if they brought her food, as well, she'd think she'd gone to heaven.

They unlocked the door and motioned for her to enter. A maid followed her in and placed a tray on a stool next to the straw pallet. A chamber pot in the corner completed the furnishings.

The maid and one of the guards left. The other guard kindled a lamp hanging next to the door. "Stay quiet and give us no trouble," he said gruffly before pulling the door closed.

She heard the key turn in the lock with a curious sense of pleasure. This, her third prison of the day, was certainly the best appointed. It met her simple requirements amply.

She'd already noticed that there was no window in this door, so she availed herself of the facilities with a sigh of relief. There was even a ewer of water; she scrubbed off as much of the past few days' filth as she could before investigating the contents of the tray.

'Twas simple fare, coarse bread and hard cheese, with a mug of warm ale. To Lily it seemed manna from heaven. She savored every bite, setting aside half, lest they bring her nothing on the morrow. Besides, after the scanty meals she'd had the past few weeks, her stomach could bear no more.

More comfortable than she'd been since her mother's death, she settled on the pallet to mull over everything that had happened. She'd believed that coming to Dolwyddelan would give her answers; instead, she had more questions than before. But she couldn't regret that she'd come here, despite her sojourn in the bowels of the castle.

She couldn't regret meeting the Dragon.

Absently working her fingers through her tangled hair, she tried to think, but her brain reeled with exhaustion and confusion, not to mention the lump still swelling on the side of her head.

She needed sleep to clear her mind. Only then could she make sense of everything.

But she'd no sooner closed her eyes than she heard the rattle of a key in the door.

Sweet Mary, what did they want now? Had they permitted her the luxury of refreshing herself, of food and drink, only to drag her back to the pit? If that was their plan, she would not go.

She'd been too compliant, not wishing to anger Llywelyn. By God, what more could he ask? She refused to go against her nature any longer.

When the door swung open, she stood ready with the tray, prepared to knock her jailer over the head, if need be. She hit the man in the head three times before he managed to wrest it from her, although she inflicted little damage.

"Leave me be!" she shrieked. "All I want is a decent night's rest! I'll go wherever you wish tomorrow!"

He held her wrists in one meaty hand, making a mockery of her struggles. "You'll do as I wish, girl, else you'll pay for it." He chuckled, the sound resonating from deep within his massive chest. "They told me you were a quiet thing, and meek. Ha! What do those Welsh bastards know? Puny little runts, most of them, with brains to match."

Lily stared up into his face, intrigued by his strange looks and accent—and intimidated by his sheer size. He towered over her. Hair so fair it looked almost white hung past his shoulders, and his eyes gleamed an icy blue in his deeply tanned face. Even his clothing was odd, the fur-and-skin tunic leaving his arms and part of his chest bare. Despite his forbidding mien, laugh lines crinkled the corners of his eyes; indeed, he was smiling down at her now, clearly amused by her meager show of rebellion.

"Who are you?" she asked. And, more important to her—why was he here? He couldn't be Welsh. What business could he have with her?

"I am called Swen Siwardson. Your prince sent me to take you to your new home. Here," he said, releasing her and tossing a bundle on the bed, "I have brought you proper clothes." His gaze swept her from head to toe. "Though I like what you wear now well enough."

He made her feel awkward—naked—in her tunic and leggings. Turning away, she wrapped her arms about herself for a moment, then unfolded the packet.

It contained an underdress of linen, softened by many washings, and a faded wool bliaut. Though well-worn, they smelled clean. Lily held them up—they should fit, with room to spare.

But she still didn't intend to go anywhere.

"You put them on, then we will leave," Swen told her. He stood in front of the door and, drawing his dagger, flipped it through the air. It landed, quivering, in the opposite wall.

"Would you go out into the hallway to wait?" she asked when she found her voice. If he'd done that trick to intimidate her, it had worked.

"Nay. You get dressed now." He crossed the room in three strides and retrieved his knife. "We must be far from here before dawn." Another flick of the wrist, and he sent the blade into the wall just past her head.

He'd made his point. Hands shaking, Lily picked up the undertunic and pulled it over her head, then, using the roomy garment as if it were a tent, slipped out of her old clothes.

She had trouble lacing up the bliaut, but what did it matter, so long as she didn't trip over the excess fabric? At least Swen didn't watch her dress—not so she could tell, anyway. The thought of traveling to some unknown destination with him frightened her, but she didn't seem to have a choice. She might as well go with him willingly; he looked capable of killing her with his bare hands. He'd probably enjoy it, too.

After she gathered the Dragon's cloak about her, she ripped a square of material from her shirt and wrapped the extra food to take with her, then joined Swen by the door.

Reaching into a pouch at his waist, Swen pulled out a slender piece of rope. Sweet Mary save her, but she was growing tired of this! She remained silent while he took her bundle of food, then bound her wrists. He picked up her torn shirt from the floor and eyed her consideringly. "You going to be quiet, or do I need to tie your mouth, too?"

"I won't say a word, I swear," she assured him.

He nodded, a grin on his face. "Good. But it won't matter if you do. No one will hear you where we're going." Swen moved to the wall and shoved at one of the wooden panels. It slid open to reveal a dark, gaping passage. "Come on, then, girl."

Grabbing her by the rope wound about her wrists, he drew her into the wall with him, and they plunged into darkness.

She would never forget her journey with Swen so long as she lived. The man didn't understand how it felt to be tired, he just plodded along and carried her with him, alternately bullying her and encouraging her to keep her moving. They traveled through the passageway seemingly for hours before they emerged from a rocky outcropping well outside the castle walls. No one would even know she'd left, unless they came looking for her.

Since no one had seen them leave, how long might it be before that happened?

A horse stood tethered in a copse of trees, loaded with several small packs, awaiting their arrival. After checking the area to be sure they were alone, Swen tossed her into the saddle, then climbed up behind her.

He held her steady before him, but she didn't like his arm wrapped around her waist, nor his body pressed against her back. He was larger and more muscular than the Dragon, but she'd far rather have had that enigmatic Welsh lord holding her close than this blond giant.

However, she didn't have a choice.

Looking back over his shoulder, Lily caught her last glimpse of Dolwyddelan Castle as the moon set behind the towers. Would she ever see it—or the Dragon— again?

That question haunted her as they jogged along, both man and horse apparently tireless. Lily fought sleep as long as she could; once the sun rose, she concentrated on taking note of anything unusual along the way. If she managed to escape Swen, she needed to know the route back to Dolwyddelan.

Not if, she reminded herself firmly as she stifled another yawn. When. When an opportunity to escape presented itself, she must take it. Her chances of getting away—and staying out of his reach—were much better here in the hills and forest than they'd be once he locked her up again.

If Swen hadn't been her captor, she'd likely have found him an amusing companion. He loved to talk, and it didn't seem to matter whether she answered him or not. He just kept up a steady stream of comment, his deep voice droning on in her ear until she could ignore him no longer.

"I don't know where you're from, but do all people in your homeland talk as much as you?" she asked in exasperation.

He chuckled. "Not all, but most. My home is far north of the Frankish lands. 'Tis cold there much of the year, not like this place. In winter the nights are very long. We like to gather round the fire, drink ale and tell stories. Much like your Welsh bards, only merrier."

Here was a chance to quench her insatiable thirst for news of foreign places. "You miss it." She heard it in his voice.

"Aye."

"Then why have you come here?" She looked back at his face. "Why are you doing this?"

His expression told her nothing. What made men so inscrutable? She found it far easier to read women's faces, though perhaps 'twas only that she'd had more practice.

She poked him in the gut with her elbow. He grunted, but appeared unharmed. "You cannot go silent on me now," she chided. "Do you owe Llywelyn a debt? Or has he offered you riches? I don't understand why he wants me locked away. It makes no sense, since I cannot possibly be of any value to him, but nothing that's happened since I scaled the castle wall has—"

"You climbed the wall?" He gave a muffled grunt of laughter. "I would like to have seen that. Did you make it all the way up?"

"Almost. The Dragon pulled me over the top of the wall."

Grabbing her chin in his callused palm, he turned her

head and stared down at her face. Finally he shook his head. "Quiet and meek! Llywelyn's men are fools. And I worried that this would be an easy task, boring, a waste of my talents. I will need to watch you carefully," he said. A wide smile split his face. "Good."

Lily jerked free of his hand and turned her back to him. That slip of the tongue would cost her dearly. The last thing she wanted was Swen watching her more closely; those pale eyes already saw too much. Beneath his affable mien a sharp mind—and a dangerous man. She'd been a fool to underestimate him.

Exhaustion made her mind too dull to focus on anything important now. Instead, she badgered Swen for more information about his home. Finally, his deep voice rumbling in her ear, she drifted off to sleep.

Swen looked down at the girl, her face resting back against his shoulder, her body slumped against him with the bonelessness of utter exhaustion. She surprised him. As he'd told her, she was nothing like those idiots had led him to believe. Perhaps everything else they'd told him was a lie, too.

They expected him to accept her as a convent-bred lady, escaped from the abbey to run off with a Norman churl? It hadn't rung true even before he met her. And now that he had...

He didn't believe a word of it.

Llywelyn wanted her out of Dolwyddelan, Swen knew that much. She hadn't wanted to leave. And the look in her eyes—and something in her voice when she said his name—pointed toward the Dragon as the man Llywelyn wanted to separate her from.

For her protection, or the Dragon's?

This grew more interesting by the moment.

Swen shifted the girl in his arms, savoring the way

she nestled against him. If she belonged to the Dragon, he had no intention of enjoying more than this. A pity, but he didn't poach on another man's territory.

Especially the Dragon's.

Lord Ian could be on their trail even now. Swen's blood heated in anticipation. This situation might prove to be far more enjoyable than he'd imagined.

He gazed at Lily's face once more. Soft skin, vivid eyes, hair of flame.

And courage.

The Dragon would find them.

Swen smiled. He loved a good fight.

Chapter Six

Before dawn, Ian stood outside Lily's chamber, key in hand. Fortunately for him, the man on guard at the foot of the stairs owed him a favor, one he'd never imagined he'd bother to collect. But he needed to see Lily, without Llywelyn's learning of it. This was the only way.

He unlocked the door and slipped in quietly. Flickering lamplight cast an eerie glow over the small room, but nowhere did he see Lily.

Hell and damnation. He swiftly drew the door closed and leaned his forehead against the planks. Llywelyn had done it again.

Heart pounding hard with frustration and concern for Lily's safety, he stalked over to the pallet and picked up the clothes tossed carelessly aside. At least she'd gotten a chance to change, hopefully into something better. He forced himself to calm, and looked about the room with more care.

A wooden tray lay near the door, bread crumbs scattered around it on the floor. Her shirt had been torn, but it didn't appear to have been ripped from her body, thank God. A square of the fabric was missing. A bandage? He searched the area around the pallet, but he didn't find any blood.

However, he did notice several blade marks in the walls. The wood appeared fresh-cut. Lily didn't have a knife, not even an eating knife, though these cuts had been made by something larger, thrown with force, to judge by the depth.

Ian clenched his fist around the remains of Lily's shirt. He knew of only one man with the habit of tossing his knife.

Swen Siwardson.

Had that arrogant Viking bastard been in this room—with Lily?

Siwardson had arrived at Llywelyn's court scarce three months ago, sent by his father to handle trade negotiations. Almost immediately he'd wormed his way into the prince's favor.

Ian felt no jealousy over that fact, but he didn't trust the Viking's constant jovial manner. Unless the man was daft, how could he be so happy all the time? His size and strength, combined with his unusual looks and good humor, made him near as popular with the ladies as the Dragon, though he took more advantage of that popularity than Ian ever would. He couldn't fault the man for that.

But what business did he have in this chamber with Lily? He couldn't have gotten in without a key. Ian could see Llywelyn's hand in this. Clearly, his overlord intended to take no chances with the Dragon's obedience. If Lily wasn't there, she couldn't tempt him away from his duty.

Or so Llywelyn thought.

Since he'd come to realize that Lily reminded him of Gillian, his mind hadn't stopped conjuring up reasons

to explain the resemblance. Every explanation that came
to mind was far too bizarre to contemplate. He hoped
Dai would discover something useful. Llywelyn's actions only served to reinforce the feeling that there was
more to Lily's tale than he'd first thought.

He had to find her.

By the time the sun crept up over the horizon, Ian
had left Dolwyddelan. He took a company of six men
with him, including the two he'd chosen to train the
previous afternoon. They knew next to nothing about
fighting, but that wouldn't matter. They had good
hearts, and already their loyalties lay with him.

As soon as they traveled out of sight of the castle, he
parted company with his men. They would go on to
l'Eau Clair, his cousin's keep in the marches, while he
searched for Lily. Instinct told him that the answers to
Lily's questions could be found there.

Cautious investigation before he left revealed that no
mounted men had left Dolwyddelan in the night, and
that Siwardson was nowhere to be found. Apparently
the Viking had spent the night away from the castle. A
convenient excuse. But Ian felt certain Siwardson had
taken Lily.

Now he needed to discover where they'd gone.

He backtracked to the outskirts of Dolwyddelan. Siwardson must have had horses waiting somewhere outside. Hopefully they'd left some sign or trail he could
follow.

He searched for a while before he found the faint
hoofprints of one horse, leading toward the forest from
a remote area beyond the craggy outcropping that
formed Dolwyddelan's foundation. Lacking any other
trail, he headed into the woods.

Unfortunately, there was no snow on the ground, although there were enough soil-covered areas to show an occasional hoof mark. As the day wore on, Ian couldn't help but be impressed with the other man's ability to travel without leaving a well-marked trail. But he still managed to follow along.

He made good time, considering the terrain and the lack of clues, but he didn't feel he'd gained much ground when he paused in midafternoon. They must have left the castle in the middle of the night to have so large a lead. He had an advantage, however; Siwardson's mount carried a double load. Soon, he hoped, he'd begin to catch up to them.

Ian's lack of sleep the past two nights began to catch up with him as the day faded into twilight. He paused to eat, and to rest his mount. As soon as the moon rose high enough to light his way, he continued on. Siwardson would have to stop eventually, if only to give his overburdened horse a rest. That might allow him to catch up with them.

He wondered how Lily fared. He'd tried not to think of her too often as the day passed. Only by detaching himself from this venture could he hold the frantic feeling pushing at his heart and mind at bay. As he'd done with so many of the tasks Llywelyn set him to, he treated it as a necessary duty, distancing himself from the reality of it. It was the only way he would succeed.

But as he rode through the shadowy trees, pausing every so often to look for signs they'd passed this way, Ian found himself thinking of Lily more and more, until she filled his thoughts. How would she look in ladies' garb, her hair brushed smooth? He could not forget the way she'd clung to him in the cell, her lips so soft beneath his. Their bodies had fit together perfectly, her height a match for his. When he held her in his arms, her head had just reached his shoulder.

She'd felt as if she belonged there.

Would the Viking try to kiss her, or make too free with his hands? He didn't fear that Siwardson would harm her. By all accounts, he loved women. That was the problem. Ian didn't want him to so much as look at Lily.

The thought made his blood rage with a fire completely foreign to him. But even though he had never felt it before, he knew what it was.

Jealousy.

He urged his mount to move faster.

The trees grew thick in this part of the forest, making the going rough. He dismounted and led his horse. When he heard a noise different from the usual night sounds, he stopped. He stood listening, and heard it again. Voices, to his left. He tied the reins to a sturdy tree and, drawing his sword, continued on foot.

He walked with care through the sparse underbrush, scarcely able to see in the faint moonlight that filtered through the towering firs. Firelight flickered from behind a granite outcropping. He crept around the rocks and stood on the edge of a small clearing.

Lily sat leaning against a saddle, wrapped in his cloak, her bound hands resting in her lap. She appeared to be unharmed, though even in this light she looked exhausted.

Siwardson sat several feet away from her, his knife, as always, in his hand. "I wondered how long before you'd find us," he said, staring across the fire. He didn't seem surprised—or concerned—that the Dragon had located his prey.

Ian stepped into the clearing. "You did well at hiding

your trail. I compliment your skill. And you traveled far, considering your burden.''

Siwardson laughed, the sound grating on Ian's nerves. "She is no burden, as I'm sure you know, milord. I find her...delightful.''

Lily struggled to her feet, heart pounding wildly. The Dragon looked like an avenging angel, the firelight shining off his dark hair, and his sword held ready at his side. She had prayed Lord Ian would find her, though she'd had no reason to believe he would come after her.

But why didn't he do something? "Do you two intend to stand here all night exchanging pleasantries? If you've come for me, Dragon, I'm quite ready to leave.'' She took a step toward him.

Swen stood and moved to her side in one swift motion, his knife discarded for a sword. Gone was the jovial giant, in his place a steely-eyed warrior. He grabbed her elbow and pulled her close. "I think not. Your prince has charged me to deliver you to your new home, milady. I am sorry. I have no quarrel with Lord Ian, but I cannot allow you to go with him.''

"I don't understand why Llywelyn wishes me locked away, but I've done nothing to warrant such treatment. You've been kind to me, sir." She looked Swen straight in the eyes, hoping he'd see the truth in her claim—and how important this was to her. "Please, let me go.''

She could have sworn he wanted to do as she asked, but it was also clear to her that he would not. Instead, he released her arm, then pushed her behind him, out of the light.

Lily tumbled to the ground, then scrambled to her knees in time to see the two men move to face each other near the fire. "What say you, Dragon?'' Swen asked, a grin splitting his tanned face. The flames lent a devilish glow to his eyes, washing away any hint of levity. "Will you permit me to carry out your master's bidding? No harm shall come to her within my care—you have my word."

The Dragon raised his sword and held it ready. "I believe you, Viking. But she will not be in your charge forever. And who can say what will happen then?" He kicked aside the small pile of firewood. Sticks landed in the fire and sent a plume of sparks flying. "I'll take her with me now. Will you allow it?"

"Nay!" Swen cried as he swung his sword in a wide arc.

The Dragon met him blow for blow. The blades sang with a metallic ring, accompanying both men's grunts of exertion.

Lily tried again to stand, but her cloak and skirts had tangled round her legs. She crawled backward to the edge of the clearing, unwilling to miss a moment of the battle raging before her. She doubted they even knew she was there, for she could see that all their attention was focused on the task at hand.

She quickly learned that swordplay was hard, dirty, graceless work. They used their feet as often as their blades, shoving at each other, kicking and pushing—anything to force the opponent to the ground. Swen still grinned widely, as though the entire proceeding were a huge joke, but the Dragon's features showed nothing but determination.

He would win, or die trying.

The Dragon kicked at Swen's feet and knocked him to the ground, but Swen managed to grab his leg and pull him down, as well. The two men rolled across the clearing, hands at each other's throats. They landed in the edge of the fire, sending off the stink of scorched wool, then fell, writhing together, on the other side of the clearing.

Lily couldn't tell which man had the upper hand, and since her wrists were still bound, there was little she could do to help the Dragon. Then she remembered Swen's knife.

When he unsheathed his sword and stepped close to her, he'd flipped the dagger aside. He hadn't had a chance to pick it up; it must still be on the ground. Keeping an eye on the struggling men, she scuttled around the fire on her knees until she found the knife.

She grabbed it, then somehow propped it between her feet and held it tight while she rubbed the bindings against the blade. Thank God 'twas sharp, she thought as she felt the rope give. Though her hands felt numb, she shoved her skirts out of the way, snatched up the knife and headed for the men.

Both were bloodied and dirt-smeared. She reached them just as the Dragon punched Swen in the face twice, in rapid succession. The Viking's eyes rolled back and he slumped to the ground.

Ian flopped to the dirt beside him, breathing heavily through his mouth. Blood trickled from a cut above his left eye, and his lower lip looked bruised and swollen.

His movements clumsy, he untied a pouch from his belt and tried to open it. "Let me," Lily offered, dropping to her knees beside him.

"There's rope in it." His voice sounded odd, no doubt muffled by his split lip.

She held the bag up to the light and peered inside until she located the cord. He took it and flipped Swen onto his stomach.

"Don't want to leave him to die," he said as he wrapped the rope around Swen's wrists, then secured it.

"But we cannot bring him with us, either." He hoisted Swen up onto his shoulder—an amazing feat—and carted him over to a clump of bushes. She followed, wondering what he intended to do with the Viking.

He looped Swen's arms about the branches, then took the pouch from her, pulled out a thick leather strap and used it to bind Swen's legs loosely around the base of the bushes. "He'll be able to free himself, but not for a while. It will give us time to get away."

Moving without his usual grace, the Dragon took her by the arm and led her back to her seat near the fire. He searched through one of Swen's packs and pulled out a small flask, uncorked it, and sniffed the contents. His face relaxed into a smile, surprising her.

As fleeting as the smile was, it transformed his face. He looked almost carefree—and even more handsome, if that was possible—despite the blood smeared on his chin and forehead. Lily reached out and dabbed at his face with the trailing cuff of her sleeve.

He remained motionless until she'd finished, then nodded his thanks. "Have you eaten?" he asked.

Content to watch him, she settled back against the saddle and sighed. "Aye. I had saved half the meal they brought me last night. It was plenty. Swen has food in the other pack, if you're hungry."

He shook his head. "No, I've eaten." He brought the flask. "But this is an unexpected boon." He brought the bottle to his lips and drank deeply of the contents. "Usquebaugh." She sent him a questioning look. "The Irish make it. I'm not certain exactly what it is, but it's powerful. Makes ale and wine seem like water." He took another swallow before replacing the stopper. "Too much will make a man feel sick unto death, but a little warms the blood and takes the pain away."

He started to put it back into the pack, then hesitated. "Do you want some?"

"Why not?" What harm could it do? It certainly seemed to please him.

He knelt beside her and handed her the flask, his fingers brushing against hers and lingering, so it seemed. Although she hadn't drunk yet, heat streaked up her arm and through her blood. Her fingers shaking, she uncorked the bottle and, raising it to her lips, took a sip. "Jesu," she gasped, as liquid fire burned all the way to her stomach.

Ian chuckled. "Had enough?"

Not certain her voice would work, she nodded and handed it back. This time she knew the touch of his hand on hers was no accident, for his fingers intertwined with hers for a fleeting, heart-stopping moment.

Before she could react, he rose to his feet and started gathering up Swen's supplies. "I don't want to make this too easy for him," he said. Using his sword, he lifted the packs high and hung them from the branches above Swen's head. "I imagine he'll see them—probably long before he can reach them." Again she saw that fleeting smile, and again her heart raced. She looked away. Did she react so strongly to his smile because she never knew when to expect it?

She stood so that he could take the saddle. "Where are your horses?" she asked. He must have left them far away, for she'd not heard his approach, nor the whickering of any horse but Swen's.

He hefted the saddle up into a tree, then picked his sword up off the ground. "I only brought one mount." He kicked dirt into the fire and stomped out the embers. "You'll have to ride with me."

She felt blind in the sudden absence of light. However, she was glad he wouldn't be able to see her response to his comment. She knew that riding in the Dragon's embrace would be nothing like riding with Swen. Frowning, she let Ian lead her by the arm through the thick trees. Now she would learn what purgatory was.

Her other senses seemed more finely attuned than normal. His strong fingers held her arm in a firm yet gentle grip, sending that insidious heat winding through her veins again. Despite the piny odor of the forest, she could smell his clean, masculine scent. She'd have recognized it—and him—anywhere. The thought was strangely comforting.

His horse stood patiently waiting, not even shifting or stomping when they approached. Perhaps warriors trained their mounts thus, for Swen's had been the same. Whatever the reason, Lily couldn't help but be glad of it. She'd never been around such massive beasts, and she found it reassuring that, despite their size, they were so docile.

Ian pulled her to a halt beside his mount. "Let me take this," he said, his hands sweeping the cloak from her shoulders. He tossed it over the saddle, then brought his hands to rest where the cloak had been.

Though she couldn't see him clearly in the faint moonlight, she could feel his gaze caress her face. She trembled in reaction.

"Are you cold?" he asked, leaning toward her to whisper in her ear. Another shiver coursed through her at the subtle movement of his lips against her skin, carrying fire in its wake. He slowly pulled her into his arms. "Let me warm you."

He surrounded her with his touch, his scent, as he brushed his mouth over her face and neck. His tongue darted out to taste the hollow of her throat, turning her knees to jelly. But he held her steady in his arms, lending her his strength.

Lily's hands had been loosely clenched at her sides, but she could no longer resist the temptation to caress him, as well. She cradled Ian's face in her hands, savoring the contrast of the rough stubble on his chin with the firm softness of his mouth. When she stroked his bruised lip, he captured her fingertip with his teeth and drew it lightly between his lips; she gasped as the sensation shot through her body to center deep within her.

He hadn't even kissed her—that was the act Sister Maud had warned her against, claiming it led to all sorts of licentious behavior—yet he'd catapulted her senses into complete confusion. The chills blanketing her body were not caused by cold, but by heat—a fire raging through her blood, bringing with it a burning ache only the Dragon could ease.

The darkness enveloped them in its embrace, adding a sense of illusion. Every movement seemed destined to bring pleasure—and a yearning for more.

Lily gave in to the unconquerable urge and raised her mouth to Ian's. She felt awkward, unskilled, but he gathered her closer in his arms and met her touch for touch, kiss for kiss. Only the strength of his embrace kept her from sinking to the ground in a heap of mindless pleasure.

Now she understood how easily a woman might be led to sin, how simple it would be to give in to these feelings. Her body ached for Ian's touch—in places she'd never imagined could feel such sensations. He hadn't done more than kiss her, and despite her ignorance of what came after kissing, she knew there was more—far more—to lust than **this.**

He pressed hard into the cradle of her thighs and groaned, then set her away from him so swiftly she would have fallen without his hand on her arm to steady her. But as soon as she found her footing, he turned away.

"Don't you know better than to tempt a man like that?" he snarled.

Her emotions already felt rubbed raw. His accusation poured salt on the wound and made her lash out. "Do you blame me for what happened?" Her voice sounded high with outrage. She sought to lower it. "I've never done these things before. I didn't realize where they'd lead," she added, not quite truthfully. She grabbed his arm and tugged until he spun around to face her. "Can you tell me *you* didn't know?"

Ian rubbed his hand over his face, then shook his head. "I'm equally at fault." He straightened and took her elbow in an impersonal grip. "Come. We must leave this place before that Viking bastard regains his senses—assuming he had any to begin with," he added wryly.

"He won't come to any harm, will he? He didn't hurt me. He was simply doing his duty." It seemed cruel, to leave Swen trussed up alone in the wilderness.

Ian snorted. "He'll be fine, except perhaps for a headache. I wouldn't worry about him, if I were you. He would have done far worse to you, if Llewelyn wished it." He hoisted her into the saddle, then climbed up behind her.

Her body tensed as she sought to ignore the warmth of him pressed close to her back. His hand on her shoulder urged her to turn and face him. "And don't call what he did duty, Lily. 'Twas for his own gain. Duty is when you hate what you must do, perhaps loathe what you've become—'' he nudged the horse in the ribs ''—but you do it anyway.''

Chapter Seven

Ian held Lily snug in his arms as they rode through the night. His comments about duty had silenced her completely, and once he settled his cloak about them, she soon fell into a sound sleep.

The fight and the usquebaugh, not to mention the kiss—and more—he and Lily had shared, left him feeling revitalized. The bruises he'd gained at Siwardson's hands were nothing, especially after the balm of Lily's touch. He wished he could push his mount to gallop, to carry them on their way with the speed of the wind. God only knew how much time they would have before Llywelyn sent someone after them.

At first he couldn't decide where to take her. If he left her at Saint Winifred's, her situation would be the same as before. He doubted she'd endure that for long before she found a way to escape. And as much as he'd love to go home, Gwal Draig wouldn't be safe. It might be a very long time before he returned there.

If he ever did. All depended upon Llywelyn's reaction to his disobedience.

He needed to find Dai, to learn if he'd discovered

anything useful at the abbey. Perhaps then the question of where to take Lily would answer itself.

Lily stirred in his arms as the colorful rays of the rising sun glowed on her face, then jerked upright. "Dragon?" she asked, her voice urgent.

"Aye."

Her body relaxed, and she nestled her head against his shoulder with a sigh. "What are we doing?"

Her trust in him was gratifying, though he didn't know that he'd done much to earn it. Perhaps she was always like this. He fought down a twinge of jealousy when he thought of her cuddled so sweetly in Siwardson's arms. Had she been?

"Lily. Wake up." He nudged her in the ribs with his fingertip. She squirmed, and a groan escaped her lips, before her eyes snapped open.

"I am awake," she said with a glare.

"Good. We've plans to make. I need you to think clearly."

"I always do."

Too bad he didn't, he thought, noticing that she wouldn't meet his gaze. Perhaps she didn't, either.

"Good." He scanned the area around them. "Do you need to stop?"

A flush tinted her cheeks. "Please."

Ian helped her down and held her arm until she seemed steady on her feet. "Don't wander too far," he cautioned as she headed for a thick clump of bushes. "I'm sure you don't want me to come looking for you."

He took care of his own needs, then removed a few handfuls of corn from his saddlebag for the horse. This mount was still new to him, a gift from his sister, Catrin, and her husband, Nicholas Talbot. Catrin had named it Mouse, of all things. He couldn't bring himself to call such a magnificent beast so ridiculous a name. He simply called it Horse, and would until he thought of something better.

On this journey, the stallion had proven himself the tireless destrier Nicholas had claimed. The Norman was accounted a good judge of horseflesh; evidently his skill extended to training, as well.

Ian rubbed down the horse with a clump of dried grass, lavishing him with well-deserved praise. When he stepped back to toss the grass away, he found Lily standing at the horse's head, stroking his nose.

"Have a care," he warned, moving quickly to her side. "He can be dangerous. He's not a pet, like a dog."

She smiled as she continued to rub the beast's velvety muzzle. "But he's so gentle. What is his name?"

Surprisingly, the animal seemed to enjoy her attention. Of course, he'd enjoy it, too, if she was stroking him like that. If the beast tolerated it, where was the harm? "It's ridiculous," he said wryly. "My sister named him Mouse."

"'Tis a good name," she said. She murmured to Mouse, too softly for Ian to hear, then looked up at Ian and smiled. "He likes it, I think."

Didn't she know anything about horses? Mayhap she didn't, he reminded himself. She'd told him that her entire life had been spent within the abbey. Most likely the largest animal she'd seen there was a cow.

But it was amazing to see her treat this war-beast as if he were as docile as some farmer's milk cow. Evidently the stallion's size didn't frighten her.

Did anything?

He'd be better off to stop wondering about her, thinking about her. But he might as well tell his brain to cease working. She'd managed to worm her way into his mind. He couldn't make her leave; in all honesty, he wouldn't have, even if he could.

"Come, we'll eat on the way," he told her. He rummaged in the saddlebag again and handed her a hunk of cheese and half a round of dark bread, then hoisted her onto Mouse's back.

Once they were moving, she broke the cheese and bread into pieces for each of them, then handed him his. "Are we going back to Dolwyddelan?" she asked before she bit into her share.

"Are you daft? Why would I free you from Siwardson, only to turn you over to Llywelyn again?" Didn't she realize who had ordered the Viking to take her away?

By Christ, he was an idiot! He should have discovered where Siwardson had been taking her. It wouldn't have changed his own plan—if he could call the unformed thoughts floating through his head a plan—but perhaps if he'd known, it would have given him a bit more information about Llywelyn's intentions. It was too late now.

Or was it?

"Did Siwardson mention where he was taking you?"

"No. Just that I'd be safe there." She munched on her food for a moment, then asked, "Why wouldn't I be safe in Llywelyn's keep—or anywhere else, for that matter? Safe from what? I almost wish I hadn't gone there." She looked up at him from beneath her lashes. "Almost."

Ian fought against the temptation to lose himself in the depths of Lily's eyes, instead forcing himself to scan their surroundings until she returned her attention to her food.

Silence reigned until they finished eating and he

nudged Mouse to a faster gait. "I believe that Llywelyn is trying to keep you away from me."

She turned to meet his gaze head-on, her green eyes assessing. "Are you a threat to me, Dragon?"

"I could be," he growled. "But I don't think that's why Llywelyn wants to keep us apart. There's something about you he'd like to keep hidden—from me, at least. He doesn't usually act this way with me, but I've seen him do it to others often enough to recognize the signs. I just don't know why."

"Whatever his reasons, I'm glad he didn't succeed. I didn't fear Swen, but I didn't trust him, either. I know you won't allow anyone to harm me," she said. "And I won't permit any harm to come to you."

Startled, he watched her expression. He could see that she meant what she'd said, although how *she* could protect *him*, he did not know. She'd heard his reputation—much of it exaggeration, true, but close enough to reality. "How is it you don't fear me?"

"You are a good man, Dragon." She met his skeptical look with a smile. "I'm not stupid. I realize you've done things that would make most people shake with fear. But you don't frighten me—I know there's more to you than the deeds you've done. You did them for a reason, I imagine. A good reason. Who am I to question your judgment?"

Ian glanced away first. How did she know these things? How did she know so much about him? There were times when he couldn't understand how anyone could bear to be in his presence, including his own flesh and blood. He didn't blame people for their reaction to him; he expected nothing less.

But Lily's unquestioning loyalty and trust made him quake inside. He didn't deserve it, nor her.

It was past time he reminded himself of that fact.

Perhaps he'd bring her to l'Eau Clair, he decided, though not immediately. Llywelyn might expect him to go to ground there with his cousin Gillian, or to Ashby with his sister Catrin.

But first he'd find a place to lie low for a while, until he had a chance to meet with Dai. Only when armed with more information about this mystery woman—this woman who made the powerful Llywelyn nervous— could he decide whether Lily might be a danger to the others.

The cave! Well hidden in the remote hills, yet not too far from Ashby, l'Eau Clair and his own manor at Gwal Draig, he could think of no better place. It had served Catrin and Nicholas well as a shelter after they were attacked by outlaws. He'd be able to track down Dai, and obtain supplies from home. Best of all, no one but his family knew of it.

Lily would be safe there.

Toad made his way through the passageway with ease, despite the lack of light. Dark or light, it mattered not. He'd traversed these hidden corridors and stairs so many times the past few months, every detail remained etched upon his brain.

He found it amazing how the mind and body could adapt themselves to any situation. When he considered the injuries that had resulted in his crippled state, he marveled that he'd survived at all. But the mind trapped within this hideous shell remained unchanged; if anything, it had grown sharper, more keen and alert.

Only thus could he endure this taste of hell.

He'd triumph in the end, show all his slow-witted kin how wrong they'd been to underestimate him. They were so stupid, they believed him dead. Couldn't they see what frequently stood right in front of them?

How he wanted to laugh when they walked by him, looked past him, turned away from the ugly thing he'd become.

He would laugh one day, when the tides of power turned and he regained all he'd lost—and more. Skulking through the walls like a rat, listening to Llywelyn's plots and dreams. For endless months he'd waited, at times impatiently, for the proper opportunity to come along.

And now he'd reap the rewards.

She was so beautiful, the girl called Lily. Far more lovely than the woman he'd nearly made his bride. He laughed, the near-silent sound rich with satisfaction. Aye, Lily would suit him better. Since she'd never left the abbey till now, he had little doubt of her purity. The Viking wouldn't touch her, for fear of Llywelyn's anger, and Toad knew well that the Dragon had little to do with women—other than his hell-born bitch of a sister.

If only he'd had a chance...

He shook off the old anger. It availed him nothing to think of what might have been. Instead, he must look to the future, to the girl Llywelyn had protected so well all these years. How the prince would howl when he learned his plans were all for naught.

Toad would have the last laugh, when Lily was his.

Swen awoke to find bright sunlight blinding him. He closed his eyes quickly, but it didn't seem to matter. His skull still felt as though it had been pierced by a razor-sharp dagger.

Probably his own.

His hand and feet were numb, and his backside was cold and damp. Where was he?

He forced one eye open a crack, just enough to catch a glimpse of his surroundings. What he saw made him damn the consequences and risk opening both eyes again.

It felt as if Thor's hammer kept pounding on his head, but he ignored the pain as memory came flooding back.

Lily.

And the Dragon.

Trust Lord Ian to truss him up like a holiday goose around a spit! He tested the bindings tied about his wrists and ankles. Aye, he could break them, but not without skewering himself a thousand times, at least, on the thorny bush he sat wrapped around.

Since he always appreciated a good joke, even when he was the butt of it, he had to chuckle at the picture he must present. He never would have imagined that the Dragon had a sense of humor. He hadn't seen any evidence of it in his time at Llywelyn's court.

Perhaps Lily made him laugh, made him more than a humorless man bent upon nothing but carrying out Llywelyn's law. From what he'd seen of the woman, she was worth fighting for. He flexed his aching jaw and grimaced. Hell, she was even worth a beating, when it came down to it. Clearly, the Dragon thought so; he'd taken his share of abuse in their battle.

He must care for the girl deeply, to go against Llywelyn's wishes. In his admittedly brief acquaintance with the Dragon, Swen hadn't seen any sign that the Welshman might defy his prince—or deny him anything.

Swen slipped his hands free of the cord that bound them, heaving a huge sigh of relief. Perhaps it was just as well that Ian had beaten him and taken the girl away. She would have remained safe in his care on their journey, but who could say what might have occurred once he handed her over at their destination? Llywelyn hadn't seen fit to share his plans for her with Swen—he'd simply taken advantage of a convenient ally to perform a messy job.

Look at the situation he'd gotten himself into! Llywelyn's promise of the trade concessions Swen had been seeking had sounded too good to be true. The "simple favor" the prince required of him in return had turned out to be anything but simple.

Swen had come to Wales at his father's behest, hoping for adventure; instead, he had discovered how slow and boring trade negotiations could be. Any chance that Llywelyn would uphold his end of the bargain had disappeared the moment Swen lost possession of Lily.

But he couldn't regret that he'd taken on the task. In fighting the Dragon, he'd finally gained what he'd wanted all his life.

Excitement. Challenge. Adventure.

All he had to do was convince the Dragon to take him on as one of his men.

Swen looked up, then burst into laughter again at the sight of his gear draped over the branches above his head. Evidently the Dragon didn't intend his escape to be too easy.

If Lord Ian wanted a head start on him, he had it. But in the long run, it would not matter. Swen would find him.

He trusted the Dragon to get Lily away, to keep her safe.

Swen had done as Llywelyn asked, so far as he was

able. But he had no intention of collecting on the debt Llywelyn now owed him.

Now he would do whatever he could to help the Dragon keep Lily safe.

From everyone.

Ian pushed Mouse as hard as he dared, considering that the poor beast carried a double burden. At times, rough terrain kept them to a walk, but they managed to cover a remarkable distance in spite of it.

He estimated it might be several days before they reached the cave, especially since he planned to avoid settled areas. The farther they remained from civilization, the better their chance of evading Llywelyn's men. Ian knew it was only a matter of time before Swen freed himself and returned to Dolwyddelan to report that he'd lost possession of Lily; even if the Viking didn't go to Llywelyn right away, there was always the risk that the prince might learn that Ian hadn't gone to Rhys's keep.

Ian looked down at Lily's hair, savoring the way the setting sun gilded the coppery stands. He dropped a light kiss on the top of her head—scarcely touching her—and settled her sleeping body more comfortably in his arms.

He couldn't imagine what it took for her to remain so uncomplaining. His sister Catrin would have harried him nigh unto death if he'd dared to drag her across northern Wales at this headlong pace, and he'd have deserved every word. He was no gentleman, he knew it well, but he did what he had to do. What good were courtly manners if you were dead?

Since the light was fading, he dismounted, carrying Lily with him, and placed her on his cloak under a tree while he tethered Mouse, then scouted the area for a spot to make camp for the night.

A stream flowed nearby, and deadwood enough for a small fire lay scattered beneath the trees. He gathered fir boughs and built a small shelter before Lily stirred.

She appeared confused for a moment, but then she caught sight of him watching her and smiled. "How could you let me sleep when there was so much to do?" she asked, attempting to rise.

One of her legs buckled beneath her, but she reached for the tree trunk beside her, pulled herself up and leaned back against it. "'Tis most unfair for you to do all the work. You must be weary. Sit and rest, milord. I'll prepare our food."

"There's precious little to prepare," he told her. He came to her side and urged her to sit, but she would have none of it. "I set some snares, so perhaps we'll catch a rabbit before we starve." He dropped down on the cloak, leaving plenty of space for her beside him as he lounged there. Though she appeared reluctant, she sat down on the edge of the material. "Come, I've bread and cheese."

She shook her head. "Nay, you eat it. I'm not used to eating much, anyway."

He picked up her hand and slapped a piece of bread onto it. "I was joking, Lily. There's nothing to cook right now, but we've enough food. You needn't go hungry," he told her, exasperated by her self-sacrifice.

She nibbled at the crust, but seemed uneasy. "What's wrong?" he asked. "Are you worried about spending the night here? I'll make sure you're safe."

Tossing aside the bread, she leaned toward him. "I made the trek from Saint Winifred's to Dolwyddelan by myself." The flush on her cheeks looked as hot as her voice sounded. "Do you think I'd be concerned about something so unimportant as that?"

He felt properly chastened. He hadn't meant to insult her courage. God knew, he'd seen evidence of it often enough. But it had been a valid concern.

"Then what is it?"

She reached out and placed her hand along his jaw, absently running her fingers over several days' growth of dark whiskers. He clenched his teeth against his body's immediate reaction, but he didn't push that caressing hand away. "I'm worried about you." She lowered her gaze to a spot somewhere in the vicinity of his chest. "You shouldn't have come after me, Ian. I must be exceptionally thick-skulled, for I didn't think of this till now. But Llywelyn will be very angry that you took me from Swen, won't he? That night in your room, I could see that he wanted you to have nothing to do with me."

He'd hoped she wouldn't realize that, at least not so soon. But he didn't regret a thing he'd done, nor a moment of the time he'd spent with her. "It's not your concern," he said evenly.

She straightened and moved her hand away from his face. "How can you say that? You should send me back to Dolwyddelan immediately, or at least take me back to Saint Winifred's. I cannot begin to guess what Llywelyn intends for me, but I don't want you involved. I don't want him to blame you for helping me. For some reason, he sees me as a threat. Why else would he continue to lock me away?"

"The first time was my decision. I could have lodged you in the keep, I suppose, though I really didn't have any place for you, but I sent you to the cell, as I would have a man who'd done what you had."

"I knew that. And I expected no less, when I decided to scale the wall." Her face looked soft and forgiving in the firelight. "It was a risk I chose to take. But the other time—we both know he was the one who sent me into the vaults." She slid closer and touched his face again. "And you cannot deny how angry he was, Ian. Although I'd never seen him before, 'twas clear to me he was not pleased to have you interfere."

Trying to ignore the heat flowing between them, he laid his hand over hers and held it still. Instead, she traced a fingertip over the outline of his lips.

He sat up swiftly. "Are you doing that on purpose?" he snarled.

"What?" She looked confused—and adorable.

"Touching me—tempting me." He grabbed her hand and held it tight. "Do you realize what it does to a man when a beautiful woman touches him, pets him?"

"I meant no harm—"

"The harm will be to you, Lily, if you continue. Do you think I'm made of stone?" he asked as he released her.

"You would never harm me! How dare you say that!" She reached out to him again, but didn't touch. "I thought you liked it when I touched you."

"Aye, I like it," he admitted. "Far too much." He took her hand in his once more. "Don't you understand what comes after the kissing, the touching? By Christ, Lily, if you keep that up, you're apt to find yourself flat on your back with me between your legs before you even realize what I'm about."

It was difficult to see her expression in the firelight, but he didn't think she understood. Otherwise, she'd have moved as far away from him as she could by now.

"I want you, Lily, as a man wants a woman. Feel

what you do to me.'' He pushed her hand down, pressing her palm over his swollen manhood. Perhaps this would shock her into keeping her distance.

If it didn't kill him first.

Ian knew he'd made a mistake even before she moved her fingers, shaping his aching hardness in an innocent caress. Innocent or not, that simple touch threatened to send him over the edge. He'd hadn't felt so near to spilling his seed with so little provocation since he'd taken his first woman.

"I didn't realize," she said, wriggling her fingers again.

He bit back a groan and pressed her fingers tighter about him.

Then, sighing in frustration, he shoved her hand away and turned his back on her, resting his forehead on his updrawn knees and gulping for air. "I must be mad," he growled.

Lily moved closer to Ian and laid her cheek against his bowed back. "I'm sorry," she whispered. Slowly, lest he push her away, she wrapped her arms around his torso and held him. "You must think me a naive fool."

He permitted her embrace; indeed, it seemed to her he welcomed it, for he brought his hand up to touch her arm where it wrapped about his chest. His breathing had slowed, and his body no longer felt rigid with tension.

"And now you know I'm a crude one," he said, turning into her arms. He drew back a bit, until their chests barely touched. "Forgive me. I just wanted you to understand how it is for a man—and a woman, too, I'd imagine."

Was that possible? she wondered. "Do you think so?" She cringed at the eagerness in her voice.

He must have heard it, too, for he looked her sternly

in the eye. "Perhaps. But don't ask me to show you, for I'll not do it. I don't know how I've withstood the temptation to make you mine."

She felt oddly pleased by his admission. And curious, as well. Just how much *could* he withstand? The question brought a flush to her entire body as she remembered the feel of him enclosed within her fingers. She'd never have imagined men were so very—so excitingly—different.

But now that she knew, he tempted her even more.

Ian rolled away from her and took up one of his saddlebags. "I'm going to sit in the stream for a while." It seemed a strange thing to do, and she wondered at the laughter she heard in his voice. "Perhaps 'twill calm me. Don't go anywhere," he ordered, heading into the trees.

Lily lay back on the cloak, absently drawing the edges about her. She felt cold now, without Ian beside her.

How could Ian think she'd leave, when she could imagine no place she'd rather be than with him?

Besides, where did he think she'd go?

She had no place to go to.

Chapter Eight

Lily and Ian traveled the next two days in near silence, separated by an unacknowledged, invisible wall. This journey passed much more quickly and smoothly than Lily's trek from Saint Winifred's to Dolwyddelan. She knew that Ian made certain she was as comfortable as he could keep her, under the circumstances. She couldn't fault him for that. She, in turn, labored hard to keep from inadvertently doing anything to anger him.

Or to tempt him.

With so much time to think, she turned the problem over and over in her mind, although continued thought brought her no closer to an answer. The question of why Llywelyn wanted to lock her away she pushed aside for the moment, since she had no way of solving it.

But Ian... Ian captured her thoughts constantly.

The longer she was with him, the more she found to admire. She enjoyed looking at him, 'twas true. His vivid green eyes and dark hair were a perfect foil for his strong, even features. But she loved his determination the most. No matter what obstacle fortune threw his way, he sought to overcome it with a single-mindedness she couldn't help but respect.

And he treated her with a consideration that she doubted she deserved, for compared to Lord Ian ap Dafydd, she was no one. No nobleman would want a woman of unknown origins, not for more than his leman. After a lifetime spent within the abbey, giving her body outside the bonds of marriage was not an option she believed herself capable of—unless it meant survival.

So, despite her growing admiration and yearning for the Dragon, she remained courteous but silent, and tried not to wish for more.

They reached the cave in the full, rich light of early afternoon. Ian emptied his saddlebags, placed their remaining stores inside the roomlike cave and gathered firewood, but didn't unsaddle Mouse.

"I have to go for more supplies, and for information," he told her. "Will you be insulted if I ask if you'll be all right here, alone?"

She shook her head. "Of course not, milord." He sent her a curious look—because of her formality? What did it matter? "Not so long as you return quickly."

"I'll return as soon as I can." His gaze searching, he stepped closer and handed her a dagger. "Don't be afraid to use this."

She accepted the knife and tucked it into her belt, patting the hilt for reassurance. "Be careful, Dragon."

He bent and brushed her lips with his. "Don't stray farther than the stream. It would be easy to get lost. I could be gone till after dark."

He swung into the saddle and set off down the hill without a backward glance. She stood in the entrance and waved anyway. "May God protect you," she whispered as he disappeared from sight.

* * *

Ian made good time on the familiar trail leading toward Gwal Draig. Finally he paused outside a cotter's hut on the fringe of his land, hailing the inhabitants.

In no time at all, a child had been sent on to Gwal Draig with a message for Dai, and Ian had filled his saddlebags with food enough to last them a week, if they were careful. The cotter's wife gladly accepted his coin in return for the supplies—and the promise of more once this was over.

An honest family, and loyal, in all likelihood they'd have done what they could for him without payment, but he refused to abuse their generosity. If he dealt fairly with them, so they would with him. It had always been his way.

The child returned just before dusk, bringing Dai with him. One look at his lieutenant's face in the fading light told Ian the man was fair bursting with news. After thanking the lad, they left.

He and Dai led their horses into the woods, not picking up the trail until they were certain they hadn't been followed.

"What do you here, milord?" Dai asked urgently. "I never expected to hear from ye so soon—nor to find you so close to home. I just got back here myself, just past midday."

"I had to leave Dolwyddelan sooner than I planned. You wouldn't believe how much has happened," Ian said, shaking his head. He swiftly outlined the events of the past few days, glossing over his growing attachment to Lily. But he didn't fool Dai.

"I knew you'd get dragged into whatever happened to the girl." Dai's lined face creased into a frown. "Christ, milord, just wait until you hear what ye've stirred up. 'Twas a surprisingly easy task to find out the information you wanted. The abbey was in a bit o' disarray. I managed to listen when they didn't think I was about, and then I was lucky enough to find an ancient boarder quite willing to talk—once I told her I'd come from Llywelyn," he added with a rueful smile. "Seems the abbess was afraid of what Llywelyn might do, since one o' the boarders came up missing."

"That doesn't surprise me," Ian said dryly. "Nothing would, after the things I've seen happen lately."

Dai snorted. "Oh, I think you'll be surprised by what I have to tell ye, milord. I couldn't have imagined the news I heard at that place, not in a hundred years." He pointed toward a tree trunk lying in the woods along the trail. "You'd best sit down to hear this tale, milord."

"Jesu, is it that bad?" Ian asked. Curiosity piqued, he tethered the stallion's reins to a nearby bush and took a seat on the log.

"It appears the prince has been doing a lot of lying these many years," Dai said. His gaze fixed on the ground, he hitched up his belt and toyed with the hilt of his dagger. Finally he looked up and met Ian's questioning look. "I don't know how to tell you this, milord, except to say it straight out. D'ye remember the Lady Lowri, Lady Gillian's mother?"

"Of course. I'm hardly likely to forget my own kinswoman, even if it has been years since her death."

"That's just it, milord." Dai cleared his throat several times before he got on with it. "She wasn't dead after all."

Ian surged to his feet. "What?" he roared. "That's impossible!" Dai must be mistaken—

"Sit down, milord, and be quiet." Dai shoved at

Ian's shoulders until he sat down again. "I'm not going to tell you another damned thing until you calm yourself. No sense hopping about. You'll be too busy stewing to hear a word I say."

Ian did feel ready to leap up and do battle, and Dai had barely begun. But what he'd said seemed too preposterous to be true. However, he knew Dai would never lie to him—especially about something as important as this.

Drawing a deep breath, he dropped back onto the tree trunk. "All right, I'll behave."

"You remember how Lady Lowri ran off from l'Eau Clair a short time after Lady Gillian was born?"

Holding his tongue with a patience he hadn't realized he possessed, Ian nodded.

"Who told Lord Simon his wife was dead?" Dai asked with a questioning look.

"Llywelyn." Ian began to see where this was headed, but he kept his mouth shut so that Dai would get on with it.

"Aye. Said they'd discovered her body in the forest near her parent's manor. Lord Simon grieved, and gave up his rights to his wife's dowry."

"Which the prince inherited, I believe."

Dai gave him a quelling look. "He did. But the truth of the matter is that the poor lady'd lost her wits. Your kinsman Llywelyn," he said with a glare at Ian, "found her wandering about, confused and ill, in the woods near his holdings. Instead of caring for her until she recovered, then sending her back to Lord Simon, he brought her to an abbey where no one knew her and convinced her that her husband and daughter were dead. After about six months, she gave birth to another child—"

"Lily," Ian said.

"Aye. The poor child's had a family all these years, milord, though she never knew it. She's your cousin."

"A distant cousin." This time when he stood, Dai didn't try to stop him. "This explains any number of things, except for one. Why?" His mind working furiously, Ian paced back and forth along the side of the trail. "Llywelyn destroyed an entire family, and for what? By Christ, when I think of the years that Simon grieved... And Gillian needed a mother so badly." He pounded his fist against a nearby tree. "And all this time she not only had a mother, but a sister, as well."

Dai plunked down on the log with a sigh. "From what I heard, Lady Lowri wasn't a mother, milord. 'Course, who's to say that would have been the case if she'd gone back to l'Eau Clair? Most of the time, she lived in a world of her own. Perhaps grief turned her mind. I don't know. But Lily—beg pardon, milord— Lady Lily didn't have anyone in that place, even before her mother died. 'Tis no wonder she left when she got the chance."

That certainly agreed with what Lily had told him about her mother. Poor child—and poor Lowri. Pawns in a game of Llywelyn's making.

But now the rules had changed, Ian thought with a surge of satisfaction. Lily was alone—and powerless— no longer.

"Has Llywelyn contacted the abbey?"

"He hadn't when I was there. But the abbess had just sent a messenger to tell him that Lady Lily was missing. Didn't want to admit they'd let her run off. I imagine he's heard from them by now, not that it matters. Of course, I doubt the abbess thought Lady Lily would run to the prince."

"I need to think about this, decide what to do." Ian stopped pacing and placed a hand on Dai's shoulder. "Thank you, old friend." He could see that Dai was drooping with weariness. "Go home and rest. I'll send word to you in a day or two, once I talk with Lily and figure out some plan. Right now, my head's in such a muddle, I don't trust myself to do much of anything."

Ian waited until Dai headed toward Gwal Draig before he mounted up and rode in the opposite direction. His mind was still whirling like a top. The news Dai had given him opened up a host of possibilities for Lily.

And it brought his own battered feelings to the fore.

He'd enforced Llywelyn's law, carried out Llywelyn's justice, for so long, he'd reached the point where he seldom considered the effects his actions had on others. As long as he worked toward his goal, he could close off the part of him he buried deep inside. The near-silent voice of censure, of caution, seldom made itself heard over the cry for justice that echoed through his brain.

It was his father's voice he heard calling for him to do all he could to stop the endless squabbling of the Welsh nobility, to carry out the work to unite them under one leader. Would that voice ever be silenced?

Would he ever be permitted to walk away and live his own life, his services no longer necessary?

Ian brought Mouse to a halt and sat, rubbing his hands over his face. 'Twas unlike him to question his duty, and selfish to wish for what he knew he could not have. He knew better than this. Straightening in the saddle, he shoved the traitorous thoughts deep, so that they could not rise to the surface of his mind to taunt him. This time with Lily was nothing more than a brief interlude in his life, a shifting of his obligations to his family, rather than his country.

And perhaps if he told himself that often enough, he might begin to believe the words.

Enough! He nudged Mouse into motion. He'd wait until morning to tell Lily her news, when his mind had cleared and they both had had the benefit of a decent night's rest. Craven behavior on his part, but he simply didn't know what else to do.

The moon had risen by the time he reached the cave and tethered his mount. The narrow doorway hid the fire within the chamber until he was nearly upon it.

Inside was snug, warm, welcoming. Lily sat beside the fire, picking at a small roasted bird. But she jumped to her feet and hurried to his side when he stooped to enter the low door. Dropping the saddlebags, he scooped her into his arms.

She stiffened, then relaxed in his embrace. It felt so good to hold her. The past few days had been a hell of their own making, of silence and careful avoidance. He'd regretted the distance they'd put between them every moment of the journey.

She clung to him for a moment, smelling of fresh air and woman. "You were gone so long," she murmured against his throat. "Is everything all right?"

"I'm sorry. I sent a message to Gwal Draig. I had to wait for an answer." He couldn't tell her more than that, not now. "I returned as quickly as I could."

She took his hand and led him farther into the cave. "Here, sit and be at ease," she said, pushing him down onto the cloak. "Are you hungry?"

"Aye." He settled himself more comfortably on the floor and accepted a mug of water from her. "There's food and other supplies in my packs."

She carried a saddlebag to the cloak and sat down beside him. "Shall I?" she asked, although she'd already lifted the flap. When he nodded, she began to unpack the bag.

She exclaimed over each item she removed, excitement bringing a sparkle to her eyes and color to her cheeks. Had there been so little joy in her life, that these simple gifts made her happy?

He knew when she reached the bottom from the way she pulled out the last item. She lifted the simple wooden comb from the leather pack as if it were a priceless treasure. "For me?" she asked, raising her other hand to smooth it over her tangled locks.

"Aye. Will you let me?" He held out his hand for the comb. Lily gave it to him and settled beside him with her back to him.

Surely this had to be a new temptation devised by the serpent in the Garden of Eden, Ian thought as he carefully worked the comb through her hair. She arched like a cat, the smile on her face bringing all kinds of lascivious thoughts to mind.

It seemed to take very little time to bring order to the shimmering mass, but he continued to draw the comb through it, letting the luxurious strands slide through his fingers. His battle-roughened hands seemed to have developed a new sensitivity. Each brush of her hair against his skin sent a jolt of desire straight to his loins.

Finally he had to stop, lest he lay her down and take her then and there. He gathered her hair together and draped it over one shoulder, then pressed his lips to her soft nape.

He drew in a deep breath when he felt her shiver at his touch. "Ian," she said, turning into his arms.

She seemed as hungry as he, her mouth greedy as

she explored his face. Her hands swept over his chest before coming to rest upon his heart. She smiled.

"Did I do this?" she whispered. Her fingers opened, as if to hold his pounding heart in her hand. Her other hand slid down his tunic until it hovered above his aching flesh. "And this?"

Groaning deep in his throat, Ian lay back on the cloak, carrying her with him. She was every temptation personified, the touch of her lips, her hands, the sweep of her hair over his neck and chest, combined into one irresistible caress.

But it was wrong, he knew it. And so would she, once she was thinking clearly. "Lily," he said against the tender skin of her throat, "sweeting—we have to stop."

She didn't seem to hear him. "Lily." He spoke more sternly, as he lifted her up off his chest and set her beside him.

A tide of pink swept up her throat and over her face. "I'm sorry," she cried, as she scooted backward away from him until her back pressed against the stone wall.

She looked stricken with guilt, though the fault was his. "No, wait," he said. "I'm to blame. I never should have touched you."

Her eyes downcast, she nodded. "Nor I you."

The change in her was startling. He couldn't bear to see her look so sad. Pushing aside his own cowardice, he held out a hand to her. "Come here."

Ian appeared distressed. Lily pushed aside her own discomfort—and guilt—and crept back to join him on the cloak. He need not know the comfort and pleasure she received simply from sitting near him. She felt his warmth beside her and sighed. With only this, she could be content.

"Dai has returned from Saint Winifred's," he said. Startled, Lily met his gaze. "He found out a great many things you wanted to know."

He took her hand in his, intertwining their fingers when she didn't resist. "I hadn't intended to tell you tonight, but that was selfishness on my part. I hadn't gotten over my own anger at what I heard. But how I feel isn't important. You deserve to hear this. It's your news more than mine."

Lily had never expected to hear so soon. Heart beating wildly, she reached up and smoothed his hair back from his forehead. "Tell me."

"I don't have many close relations, just my sister, Catrin, and a few cousins. But I have many more distant relatives, however, Llywelyn among them."

"The prince is your cousin?" She hadn't realized that.

"Aye, more's the pity. He's my least favorite, at the moment," he added dryly. "My favorite cousin, however, is a half-Welsh marcher baroness, Lady Gillian FitzClifford de l'Eau Clair. She's wed to a Norman knight who, fortunately for him, treats her as he should. Gillian's mother was a Welsh noblewoman, her father a Norman baron. When Gillian was naught but a babe, her mother ran away. Later, we were told she'd died," he added, his voice rough. Giving her hand a squeeze, he continued. "I remember Lowri well. She was very beautiful, and kind to a pesky little boy." He smiled in remembrance. "However, as it happens, Lowri didn't die, not for many more years—years she would have shared with her family, but for the lies of yet another kinsman."

"Llywelyn?" she asked. Why was he telling her so much about his family? What could it matter to her?

"Aye," he growled. "I don't know for certain why he did it. But I intend to find out. I swear to you I will." He took both her hands in his and held them tightly, his gaze never leaving hers. "Lowri had another daughter, Lily. You."

For a moment, Lily could not breathe, her shock was so great. She'd never expected this. But she found her voice—barely—to ask the question burning in her mind. "I have a sister?"

He nodded. "And a niece, a brother-by-marriage, and many distant cousins. Including me."

"Does my father still live?"

"He died two—no, three—years ago. Lung fever took him. He was much older than your mother. A good man, worthy of respect." And Ian *had* respected him, she could see it in his eyes, hear it in his voice. How she wished she could have known her father!

But she mustn't be greedy. Already she'd gained so much more than she'd ever anticipated.

A possibility surged to the front of her mind, demanding to be explored. "Was my father's name Simon?"

Ian looked surprised. "How did you know?"

A shiver passed through her. "My mother would ramble on sometimes, calling for people I'd never heard of, wailing as though her heart had been torn away. She called for Simon most often. And Gilly, too. I used to think she was trying to say Lily," she added.

"Damn Llywelyn," Ian muttered, cupping her cheek in his hand.

How she used to hope it was "Lily"—a sign that her mother remembered her existence. Lily set aside the old hurt; her mother's pain had to have been so much deeper.

"I thought 'twas all in her mind, for the sisters claimed she was quite mad. Most of the time, she simply stared at the wall. No one could reach her. Not even me."

Tears streamed down her face. Ian gathered her into his arms and held her as she sobbed against his shoulder. "I wanted a family so much," she whispered. "How dare he take that from me, from Gillian? How dare he send my mother into a living hell? She grieved all those years, and for what?" She took several deep breaths, then sat up.

Ian wiped away Lily's tears and smoothed her hair back from her face, but she derived little comfort from the soothing gestures. "It's no wonder he didn't want to see me. I wish I'd taken your dagger to him when I saw him," she snarled.

Her ferocity—and her insight—reminded Ian of her sister. He hadn't thought Lily would realize so quickly who was to blame for this tragedy. Or that there had to be more to the story. They needed to consider it all, to find a way to best Llywelyn. Otherwise, Lily would always be in danger.

"I believe I know why he did it," Ian said. He reached for the mug of water she'd given him and handed it to her, urging her to drink.

"What reason could he possibly have for this?" she asked, her voice bitter.

"Power."

"Doesn't he have enough power already?"

"He could always use more. And eighteen years ago, he hadn't yet gained what he has today. He has a vision, one we share, of a united Wales. We'll be better able to fight our enemies if we're not constantly battling each other. 'Tis a curse upon the Welsh people, I think, that we cannot agree with anyone about anything for long.''

"I don't understand, Ian. What does he stand to gain from this? From me?"

"You are the daughter of a marcher lord and a member of the Welsh nobility—kin to the prince himself. Your father's keep, l'Eau Clair, commands a fine piece of the marches—a Norman piece, for the moment. Although it is your family's only holding, 'tis an important one."

"But if my sister is Norman, she has no loyalty to Llywelyn. How—"

He waved her to silence as the pieces began to fall into place. "I believe I see it now," he told her. His lips twisted into a smile. "It all makes perfect sense, and explains any number of other events I didn't really understand."

Lily poked him in the chest. "Then explain this to me. I don't have a clue what you're talking about."

"Llywelyn is a crafty bastard, though I knew that already. But I never realized how far to the future he looks when making plans. Your sister is Norman, true, but she was an infant when Lowri left. And so far as I know, Lord Simon had no idea she carried another child. Life is uncertain, and Simon was already a man past his prime. Perhaps Llywelyn thought to gain control of l'Eau Clair."

"I still don't understand," Lily said impatiently.

"It could have happened several ways. If Llywelyn had possession of Lowri and Simon died, he could bring her back and control the keep—and the heir, Gillian—through her." His blood thrummed through his veins with growing anger as he considered it. "Once you were born, it added another possibility to the scheme.

If Gillian died, as well, or survived her father but refused to comply with Llywelyn's wishes, he still had you. You've been raised as a Welshwoman. Your loyalty should be to him.''

"It isn't now," she added darkly.

"Since you're a woman—a woman with little knowledge of the world, thanks to him—he could control you." He frowned as he considered another alternative. "Or wed you to someone he could manipulate."

"But if Gillian is married and has a child, he cannot use me for this."

"He could if they died." He took her hands again and gazed into her eyes, those eyes he'd thought seemed familiar. Now he knew why. "The past few years, since your father died, several very strange things have happened to Gillian. She was kidnapped twice by another member of our charming family. Steffan intended to wed her and gain control of l'Eau Clair. Her child would never have survived." He glanced away and sighed in frustration. "Llywelyn did nothing to him, despite the fact that he'd harmed a noblewoman—his kinswoman. The second time, Steffan tried to kill my sister, Catrin, too."

"Where is Steffan now? Could he be involved in this?"

"He's dead," Ian said, his voice rich with satisfaction. "My only regret is that Nicholas Talbot got to him before I could." He smiled ruefully. "Of course, Gillian's husband, Rannulf, would likely have stepped in before I got a chance. He had the right."

Lily stared at Ian, fascinated by the play of emotions across his handsome face. She still hadn't quite adjusted to the idea that she had a family after all—and what a family! Strong, powerful, and loyal to each other. She tried not to think about her other kin, the dangerous ones. She pushed the sadness of her parents' grief deep, and tried to focus on the present.

"There's so much I don't know. Will you tell me?" She rubbed at her forehead, but the ache growing behind her eyes refused to disappear.

Ian smoothed his hand through her hair and stroked the back of her neck in a soothing caress. "I'll tell you all I can, but not tonight. You look ready to drop." He turned her so that her back was to him and used both hands to rub at her tense muscles. "Rest awhile. Try to sleep. There will be time enough in the morning to talk again."

Lily wanted to continue the conversation, but she could see that Ian would not. He'd already given her so much to consider, she doubted she'd rest at all. But she settled herself more comfortably on the hard ground.

The last thing she heard before she drifted off was his deep, strong voice promising that he would protect her, no matter what.

Chapter Nine

A strange clattering sound jolted Lily from sleep. It seemed to rise from the earth itself, shattering the silence. She sat up and discovered that her skirts were tangled with Ian's legs.

He already had his sword in hand. He flipped her bliaut out of his way and stood. His booted feet made quick work of extinguishing the glowing embers, all that remained of their fire. In the near dark, he tugged his dagger from the sheath at his waist and handed it to her.

"No matter what, stay behind me," he whispered harshly as he crept toward the doorway.

The sound of hoofbeats stopped. She could just make out the brush of Ian's tunic against the rough stone wall of the cave, and then there was silence.

Her heartbeat echoed loudly in her ears, and she clutched Ian's dagger until her knuckles ached. Who would come for them in the night? Who even knew they were here?

"God damn it, Dai!" Ian cried. Rocks clattered outside the cave. "It's a wonder I didn't skewer you."

She could hear someone's gasping breath—Dai's,

perhaps—then the thump of running feet. "Lily, come quickly," Ian called.

Moving with care in the darkness, she left the cave. At least there was still moonlight outside, faint but helpful. Partway down the hill, Ian supported a slumped-over man. "Dai's been shot," he told her as she rushed to them. "Took an arrow in the shoulder. Come help me. We've got to get him inside."

Dai raised his head, moaning from the effort. "Nay, milord. You must go. Now. They'll be on your trail by morn. Don't worry about me. Somebody'll find me soon enough."

"Who did this?" Ian asked, ignoring Dai's instructions and half carrying him to the cave.

"Llywelyn's man. He's dead, but there'll be others." Dai coughed, and blood trickled from the corner of his mouth. "Go, damn you! Who knows what he'll do to you?" he gasped. "Or to her. Will you let him win?"

Ian brought him inside and struck his flint to a candle stub. Lily looked at the old man in the flickering light and knew he could not last. She met Ian's gaze. He knew it, too, though she could see he didn't want to accept the fact.

"Please, milord!" Dai cried, attempting to rise.

Lily shook her head sharply when Ian opened his mouth to speak. She grabbed his arm and tugged him to the mouth of the cave. "He's done for, Ian. There's no way you can help him but to do as he asks. At least he'll rest easy, knowing you escaped."

He closed his pain-filled eyes and nodded. "Gather our things, quickly, while I say goodbye."

She stuffed their possessions into the packs, with complete disregard for everything but speed.

"Lily, come here," Ian called as she closed the flap on the last bag.

He'd propped Dai up against the wall. He looked ghastly, his wrinkled face as pale as his linen shirt.

Lily knelt down beside him and took his hand. "'Tis good to see you, milady," he said. His voice sounded weaker than before. "Take care of the Dragon." When he met her gaze, she could see that he knew she cared about Ian.

Dai picked up Ian's hand and held it with hers. "And you take care of her, lad. You were meant to find her. I know you'll keep her safe."

As they watched, Dai's eyes drifted shut, and his breath eased away in a sigh.

Lily made the sign of the cross, and saw Ian do the same. His eyes shuttered, his face cold, he unbuckled Dai's sword belt and took it with him as he stood. "It was a gift from my father," he said quietly. "Dai wanted me to have it."

She drew Dai's cloak over his face as Ian shouldered the saddlebags. Then, giving Dai's body one last look, she snuffed the candle and left the cave.

Ian took her arm to help her over the loose rocks dotting the hillside. "Dai brought an extra horse. They're tethered with Mouse. We'll be able to make better time, with three mounts."

"Where will we go?"

"I'm not certain. Ashby might be best. It's close by, and since it's a Norman keep, Llywelyn doesn't have access to it without Nicholas's leave—which he will not get," he snapped.

"Nicholas is your brother-by-marriage?" she asked, gasping at the headlong pace he set. He grabbed her just as her feet slid out from under her.

"Aye." He slowed down a bit, a consideration she appreciated greatly. Her skirts hampered her; there was some advantage to men's garb, she thought.

"You *do* know how to ride?" he asked when they reached the horses.

"No. I'm sorry."

He began to curse.

"Mouse seems a gentle animal."

"He's a trained war-horse, Lily. A beast like this is quite capable of killing you where you stand—or unseating you and crushing you beneath his hooves. Don't let his name—or the fact that he seems to like you—lead you to believe him to be something he's not."

She swallowed the huge lump suddenly clogging her throat, but she stood her ground. In truth, it was the thought of sitting up so high by herself that she found frightening—a foolish reaction for one who'd climbed a castle wall, she knew. But a wall did not move.

However, she didn't want Ian to see her fear. "He's used to me. I could ride him." Still he hesitated. "What alternative do we have? I refuse to slow us down—I'm endangering you enough as it is. Either put me up on that horse, or go on alone." She folded her arms about herself for comfort. Both choices left her shaking like a leaf. "That would be best, anyway."

It was difficult to see in the moonlight filtering through the trees, but she thought Ian looked at her as though she were daft. Perhaps she was. However, he saddled Mouse and loaded the packs onto the spare horse.

He tossed her onto Mouse's broad back and handed her the reins without a word to her, though he stopped to murmur to the horse.

Swinging into the saddle, he wheeled his mount

around until it sidled up to Mouse. "Just let him do the work. Trust that he'll keep you safe." He leaned over and kissed her lips, hard. "Stay with me and be careful."

The terrain between the cave and Ashby Keep was rocky, hilly, and difficult to traverse. The mere sliver of moon hanging low in the night sky didn't do much to help light their way. At times they scarcely made any headway at all.

Lily clung to the saddle with one hand and the reins with the other, although Mouse seemed to manage fine without her guidance. Trying to ignore the way her heart raced at the remembrance of Ian's mouth upon hers, she turned her attention instead to staying in the saddle. For the first time on this journey, she rode astride, with her skirts all rucked up about her knees. The skin along the insides of her legs had begun to chafe already.

Ian halted beside her as dawn began to brighten the sky. "I don't believe we're being followed. Not yet, at any rate. We'll rest for a bit, eat, and let the horses drink." He pointed to a tiny stream.

He helped her down and held her steady until her legs stopped shaking. "Here," he said, scooping her up in his arms and carrying her to an area carpeted with dead leaves. "You rest, while I take care of the horses."

Though it went against the grain to sit and let him wait upon her, Lily accepted his help gratefully. Her legs felt boneless, and her thighs burned. She didn't think she could have been much help. So she spread out her cloak and basked in the wintery sunshine, letting it soothe her. So much had happened in the past few days, she felt battered and confused.

And now she worried whether her family would accept her.

What would Ian's sister, Catrin, think, when he rode in with her? They had been raised in a noble household. Lady Catrin would expect Lily to know all sorts of skills that Lily knew she lacked. She was unfamiliar with any other life but the cloister.

And her sister, Gillian. Gilly, her mother had called her. Lily fought back tears. How she wished her mother had lived long enough to see her husband and daughter again! Her grief must have run deep, at being told they'd died. Certainly she'd never recovered from the loss.

Llywelyn had deprived not only Gillian of a mother, but Lily, as well.

Her rage at Llywelyn grew every time she thought of what he'd done to her, to her family. Was the power he would gain worth such cruelty to his own kin?

And now Ian's man, Dai, lay dead. Another sin to place at Llywelyn's door, one she feared Ian would find difficult to forgive.

Despite the sun, she shuddered when she considered the things Llywelyn had done to her already. Being locked away in the vaults had been bad enough. She could only imagine what lay in store for her if he found her again.

She refused to consider that possibility. She'd rather die than live that way.

But if her family denied her sanctuary, she might not have a choice.

Perhaps Gillian was a haughty Norman lady. She might not wish to acknowledge an unknown sister, a potential usurper. Lily could not blame her if that was so.

But how she hoped she was wrong!

Still lost in thought—in worry—she didn't notice that Ian had rejoined her until he handed her a piece of bread. She accepted it with a murmured thanks and began to absently nibble on the crust. When he placed a water-beaded cup in her hand, she started, spilling the icy liquid in her lap.

She shrieked as the water soaked through her skirts, then began to laugh. "Did you do that on purpose?" Yielding to temptation, she tossed the dregs in his direction, catching him on the throat. The water ran down the neckline of his tunic.

"How could I?" he asked, brushing at the dampness. "You did it to yourself." But he grinned and, snatching up his own mug, flung the contents in her face.

She gave a muffled shriek again and, ignoring the water trickling over her cheeks, lunged for him. She caught him square in the chest, toppling him onto his back.

Before she could do more than gasp, he rolled her beneath him and licked delicately at her wet mouth.

The contrast between the cold air on her damp skin and the fiery heat of Ian's body covering hers made all her senses come alive. He traced her mouth with his tongue, over and over, until she knew no water remained on her lips, until she thought she'd weep if he didn't kiss her. She buried her fingers in his hair and clung to him.

Feeling quite daring, she darted out her tongue to duel with his. He entered into the play with enthusiasm, but he still wouldn't kiss her. Finally, when she thought she'd go mad with longing, she tightened her grip on his hair and tugged until he lifted his head.

He stared into her face for a long moment, his eyes

the color of emeralds. "What is it, milady?" he whispered against her lips. "Have I displeased you?"

"Kiss me...please."

"I was kissing you," he murmured. He smiled. "There are many kinds of kisses, sweeting. Would that I had time to show you all of them."

She reached up to trace his mouth with her finger. He grabbed it with his strong white teeth and nibbled, sending waves of heat throughout her aching body.

He soothed the tiny hurt with his tongue, then levered himself off her. "We both must be mad," he told her. He helped her up and brushed at the leaves clinging to her gown. "Every time we sit together, we end up writhing about on the ground like a pair of overheated snakes." He picked up the cups and shook out her cloak. "It's fortunate for us we'll soon be surrounded by our loving—and extremely inquisitive—family. I can guarantee they won't leave us alone together for a moment."

He sounded as though he didn't want her to draw any meaning from the attraction between them. It had been naught but a foolish dream. Embarrassed, Lily couldn't meet his eyes.

Ian cupped her chin in his hand and lifted her face. "I am honored by your attention, Lily, truly. You are beautiful and brave, and you could do far better than me. Don't waste yourself, your future, on a man with no heart to give."

Forcing steel into her spine, Lily stared back into his eyes and told herself his words did not matter. But they did. "I don't agree, milord. But I'll not embarrass you further." She shook out her skirts and walked over to her horse. "Shall we be on our way?"

How could she believe he didn't want her? Ian wondered, going over their words yet again as they plodded along. What she'd heard had not been what he'd said at all. Christ, how did any man understand a woman?

Mayhap the problem was, indeed, that they seemed to wind up on their backs every chance they got. It was difficult to think clearly when all he wanted was to bare her delectable body to his greedy gaze and make a meal of her. She only grew more beautiful the longer he was around her, until it seemed he had become the randiest fool in creation.

If he was to place her hand on his aching flesh now, he'd have her on her back with her skirts over her head before she realized what he was about. Hell, before *he* knew what he'd done.

They couldn't get to Ashby too soon for him. Tonight, he'd find a willing woman and exorcise this madness. Then, perhaps, he could look her in the eye and treat her like the lady she was, and not some wanton camp follower.

Thinking about her helped keep his grief over Dai's death at bay. He remembered what Dai had whispered to him as he lay dying. He'd claimed Lily was a fitting mate for him, even more so now, considering who she was. And with the Dragon as her husband, perhaps Llywelyn would leave her alone.

But he refused to think of it now, not when her immediate safety was all that mattered. He said a prayer for the loyal old man who'd been a second father to him, and pushed the other disturbing thoughts away.

They were almost there. When they broke through the trees and rode to the track leading up to Ashby, he heard Lily gasp. She halted Mouse in the middle of the road and sat staring up at the castle.

It was an impressive place, certainly, utilizing every Norman defense to intimidate. But compared to rugged Dolwyddelan, Ashby Keep appeared a pretty bauble.

"Are you afraid?" he asked her challengingly, much as he had when she clung to the curtain wall. The words had a similar effect. Lily cast a haughty glare in his direction and nudged Mouse into motion.

As he followed behind her, he admired the way the setting sun glinted off her unbound hair. It hung past her waist, invoking all sorts of fantasies in his mind.

It suddenly occurred to him that decent Norman women covered their hair. He didn't wish to fight some lust-crazed man-at-arms because Lily's hair had tempted the man beyond all reason. Ian rode up beside her and, ignoring her questioning look, reached over to tug up the hood of her cloak. Giving a nod of satisfaction—'twas the best he could do for now—he led the way into Ashby.

Lily stared about her as they passed over the drawbridge and into a bailey teeming with activity. Ashby seemed a prosperous holding, the people well fed and smiling, the land clearly in good heart. She focused her attention on little details of the sights surrounding her to distract her thoughts. Otherwise, she would turn into a nervous, blithering idiot.

Whether she'd succeed in that quest, she couldn't imagine.

A brawny man came forward and greeted Ian, his manner cautious but respectful. Clearly, the Dragon's legend was well-known—and believed—within his sister's keep.

Ian nodded to the man, then came to help her down, handing the reins to a waiting stable boy before he lifted her from the saddle. He'd no sooner set her on her feet than a woman's voice cut through the babble.

"So, brother. Finally you deign to answer my summons and grace us with your presence."

They turned together, then Ian stepped way. A smaller, feminine version of Ian stood before them. But that biting voice couldn't belong to this dainty woman, could it?

It did. Lily couldn't believe it when Ian's sister, after coming forward and embracing him tightly, stepped back and launched into a scathing harangue.

And she found it truly amazing that he did nothing more than laugh when Lady Catrin paused to draw breath. Which was the dragon in this family?

Or were they both, she wondered.

"Have done, wife." A tall, handsome blond man came up behind Lady Catrin and covered her mouth with his hand. She bit his fingers, but he appeared uncowed. "Where are your manners? Can't you see that Ian has brought a guest?"

Ian took Lily's arm and led her toward them, squeezing her arm lightly—no doubt because he could feel how she shook. She tried to smile at him, though her lips felt frozen in place. But she wanted him to know that she appreciated his support.

"May we go inside, Talbot?" he asked. "The news we bring you would be better said away from prying eyes and ears."

They followed their hosts up a spiraling flight of stairs to a solar atop the tower keep, Ian and his sister bantering lightly all the while. Though Lady Catrin never stopped talking, her curious gaze remained fixed upon Lily. But their conversation stopped when they entered the chamber. Ian waited until a maidservant had brought mead and closed the door behind her before he spoke again.

Lily wondered if Ian knew how close to collapse she felt. But as he drew her to stand beside him, he gave her a smile of support, lending her the extra strength she needed.

"Catrin and Nicholas, may I present a newfound cousin? Lily and I met at Dolwyddelan." He'd told them nothing startling, but still she watched them closely as he pushed her hood back from her face and hair.

She curtsied. "I am honored to meet you," she murmured, appalled at how weak her voice sounded. She hoped her manners weren't lacking.

Lady Catrin responded in kind. "As I am to meet you." She stared at Lily, obviously curious. "How may I address you? As cousin?" she asked, with a glare for her brother.

"My name is Lily, milady." She noticed Lord Nicholas eyeing her strangely, as if she were a puzzle he couldn't quite solve.

"Have we met?" he asked.

Ian laughed.

"Ian, stop your foolishness, if you please," Lady Catrin said tartly. "If you've some point to make, please do so. Otherwise, sit down and be quiet." She turned to Lily. "Forgive me. My brother frequently makes my manners—and my wits—go a-begging. Please sit and take your ease."

Lily took the seat—a real chair, she noted with amazement—that Lady Catrin indicated, and waited. Ian obviously had something in mind, something he hadn't seen fit to share with her.

Did he think to surprise them? Or did he simply intend to taunt Lady Catrin?

He took the goblet of mead his sister offered him and went to stand beside his brother-by-marriage. "Does she look familiar, Nicholas?"

"Nay, but there's something about her...."

"My reaction, exactly. Similar enough to pique your memory, but different enough to mystify."

"Jesu, Ian! We're both properly confused," his sister snapped. "Are you satisfied? Or must I beat the answer out of you?"

"My apologies, to both of you. I wanted to know if I was blind to the truth, or whether there truly was too little resemblance to notice. Of course, I'd no more reason to look for it than you have."

He moved to stand beside Lily's chair and, taking her hand, brought her to her feet. "She *is* our cousin. Lily de l'Eau Clair."

Swen heard the approaching horses long before they caught up to him. If he'd wanted to avoid them, he could have. But what would have been the sense? He'd bought the Dragon some time, although by now Llywelyn might know that his plan to move Lily had failed. But if these were the prince's men, perhaps he could glean some information. And if he was particularly fortunate, they wouldn't realize he'd failed to carry out Llywelyn's wishes.

It wouldn't be wise to make them suspicious.

If Llywelyn learned what he'd done, he would be fortunate indeed if he wasn't sent back to his father in pieces.

But Swen didn't care. He didn't know who Lily was, or why Llywelyn wished to lock her away. He simply knew that it was right for the Dragon to take Lily with him, wherever they were headed, and right for him to help them gain as much time and distance as they could.

As the horsemen came into view, he checked his weapons. The Dragon had left them all for him to find, with a bit of work. He couldn't blame him for that, nor for the scratches that covered his forearms. They didn't bother him one whit.

He looked on them as mementos of his brush with the Dragon; he wore them proudly, small though they were.

Swen smiled as the small troop caught up to him. It was a good day. He lived to fight.

But it soon became apparent that Llywelyn's men hadn't come to fight him. Indeed, they hadn't come for him at all. They'd simply recognized him and thought to ask him to join them.

"Got rid of your burden already, eh, Swen?" the leader, Sion, asked.

A decent fighter, Sion had a filthy mind, which bothered Swen not at all, and a filthier temper, which did. "Aye, Sion. I've been taking my time going back to Dolwyddelan. Many a lovely Welsh lass to be found in the hills to keep a man busy," he added with a wink.

"If ye're not in a hurry to get back, d'ye care to join us? The prince sent us to look for the Dragon. He's got important work for him, I guess."

Llywelyn wanted to know what the Dragon was about, more likely.

"I can't. I'd love to come with you, but I've got other plans." Swen grinned. "Can't disappoint a lady, now, can I?"

Amid jests regarding his prowess, Llywelyn's men rode away. Let them believe he had nothing more important on his mind than laying every wench in sight, he thought scornfully.

Join those fools? Not likely. The only man he planned to join was the Dragon, if he'd permit it. Swen turned his thoughts to finding the Dragon. It sounded as though he might need help.

Chapter Ten

Lady Catrin sat down on the bench behind her, reaching up to clasp Lord Nicholas's hand. "'Tis no joke, Ian?" she asked, her voice at odds with its former stridency.

He shook his head. "We've a tale to tell you, so unbelievable you'll think 'tis naught but fantasy—the dark, evil kind."

Lily watched her cousins. Lady Catrin appeared stunned, but not outraged. Perhaps that would come later, she worried. Lord Nicholas simply looked at her with his lips quirked upward in a half smile.

"You're Gillian's sister?" he asked.

"So the Dragon tells me."

Nicholas looked from her to Ian at that, his gaze weighing, measuring. She didn't understand what had prompted his scrutiny, but it seemed she'd passed some test, for he smiled again—it was more of a grin, really—then choked back a laugh.

"Are you taking her to l'Eau Clair?"

Ian tipped back his goblet and drained it before he answered. "Eventually. I'm not certain when. I believe we have Llywelyn on our heels—or will have soon."

He settled on a stool next to Lily. "It's not a pretty story. Let me tell you what we know thus far."

Lily derived great comfort from listening to Ian relate the tale, partly because she loved to listen to the deep, even tones of his voice. But most of the feeling came from the words he chose, and how he said them. She and the others couldn't possibly fail to see that he considered this his fight—their fight.

His words, his voice, his reassuring looks, told Lily that for the first time in her life, she wasn't alone.

She had gained not only a family, but a champion, as well.

The mead, combined with the warmth of the room and the comfortable chair, set Lily yawning. Lady Catrin rose and came to her side. "You look tired unto death. Will you permit Ian to finish without you?"

"Aye, milady," Lily replied, embarrassed to discover that she'd slipped lower in the chair, until she slumped into the cushions. She sat up, wincing as her back protested the movement.

Lady Catrin took her arm and helped her stand. "Then come with me now. I've no doubt my brother has dragged you across the hills with little rest and less food." She smiled, that quirk of the lips lending a teasing look to her beautiful face. "I can offer you a warm bath to ease your aches, food, and a soft bed."

"Go with her," Ian said. "I'll wait to discuss this further, if you like."

Lily shook her head. "No, please continue. I trust you, milord," she murmured.

He rose and took her hand. "Thank you. Nicholas and I have business to discuss, as well. There's no reason that should keep you from your rest." He brought her hand to his lips, his mouth warm upon her skin. "Sleep well, milady."

Lily hated to leave him, but she felt safe here. And she knew he would not go without her. Moving slowly, she allowed Lady Catrin to lead her from the room.

Ian waited until he heard the women's footsteps disappear down the stairs before slumping back onto the stool. "Take the chair, you idiot," Nicholas said, pouring more mead into their goblets. "You look so weary, 'tis a miracle you haven't slithered to the floor."

Ian flopped into the cushioned chair and sighed. "I am tired. I cannot think clearly anymore. These past few days have been strange, hectic. And the days ahead threaten to be far worse. Only God knows how this will end." He drank, then held the cool silver cup to his aching head. "I apologize for carrying trouble to your door."

"You did the right thing. Where else should you come, but to us? And where should you bring Lily, but to your sister?"

"I could have taken her straight to Gillian at l'Eau Clair."

Nicholas shook his head. "No. It would be too much for Lily to bear all at once. Despite the fact that she went to Llywelyn in search of her family, I doubt this was quite what she had in mind," he added wryly. He took a turn about the circular room before stopping in front of Ian. "You do realize you'll have to marry Lily, don't you? I can't see that there's any better alternative."

Heart pounding wildly, Ian shot to his feet and glared at Nicholas. "Are you mad?"

Nicholas returned to his own seat before he answered.

"Not at all. If *you* were thinking clearly, you'd see the sense in it. Perhaps you haven't considered all the possible ramifications of Llywelyn's scheme."

"What do you mean?" He thought he'd looked at it from every direction, but he might be wrong. Had he been naive all these years? He had known Llywelyn was capable of many things, not all of them good. But, God help him, he'd never suspected him of plotting and planning like this.

"So long as Lily is alive, Gillian, Rannulf and Katherine are in danger. All your damned princely cousin has to do is get rid of them and place Lily at l'Eau Clair—with or without a husband he can control. So long as that remains possible, Lily's very existence presents a threat to her sister—and to Gillian's daughter."

Ian nodded wearily. "I'd thought of some of that, but not all." He rubbed at the back of his neck, seeking relief—from the aches of his tired body, from the helpless thoughts circling round and round in his overwhelmed mind. "Thank God you know the situation well."

"I was Gillian's guardian for long enough to learn something about it." Nicholas laughed; Ian had to join in. Gillian had nigh made Nicholas daft, those months when she was unwillingly under his thumb. "And there are few secrets in this family."

"There are none at all between Catrin and Gillian, I think." Ian sighed and gazed into his cup. "As I'm sure you've learned, to your everlasting sorrow."

"Let's just say that it's a good thing I love Gillian well, or your sister would see I paid for my stupidity." Ian heard Nicholas shifting in his chair and looked up to find the other man watching him with a speculative light in his odd violet eyes.

"What is it?" Ian demanded. He set his goblet on the table beside him and waited.

"To get back to what I was saying—if you wed Lily, it would be the best solution. For a number of reasons," he added when Ian would have spoken. "Not the least of which is that you want her."

"Of course I do—I'm a man, after all, and not dead. You'd want her, too, I imagine, if you didn't have Catrin." The look he sent his brother-by-marriage said it had better not happen.

"Not the way you want her. Or the way she wants you, *Dragon*."

"There must be something wrong with your eyes, Talbot," Ian snarled.

"Or yours."

Ian prowled the close confines of the room, cursing his sister's predilection for cluttering up the space with furnishings. It made it damned difficult for a man to pace off his frustrations. Finally he spun and faced Nicholas. "We strike sparks off each other, 'tis true. But that doesn't mean I'd make her—or any woman—a fit husband. Besides, if she knew even half the things I've done, she'd never come near me again."

"You judge yourself too harshly, Ian. I think you always have."

"I do not. She was raised in a convent. Her mind is as ignorant of sin as any saint's." Though she wouldn't stay that way for long in his company, he thought as he turned to stare out the window at the dying sun. Try though he might, he could not ignore the insidious heat the mere thought of Lily sent running through his veins. "I doubt she has any idea what I'm capable of." He dragged his hands through his hair. He could not bear it if she allowed him close, then pushed him away.

How could he blame her if she did?

He knew better than anyone, save God himself, the darkness in his soul.

He heard Nicholas walk up to him, felt the other man place his hand on his shoulder for a moment. "She knows, Ian. But she wants you anyway. Take a chance on happiness, my friend. You deserve it."

Nicholas's words lingered in Ian's head long after he went off to rest and refresh himself. As he lay back in a tub of steaming water in his chamber, Ian closed his eyes and let the bath soak away his tension, his worries.

He'd nearly fallen asleep with his head resting back against the padded rim of the tub—perhaps he *had* been sleeping—when the sound of footsteps startled his eyes open.

"Need your back washed?" Catrin asked. Her lips curled into a mischievous smile as she clambered up onto the edge of the high bed. "If you do, I should go get Lily. I'm certain you would prefer her help over mine."

"No, thank you," he said evenly. "I'll manage just fine on my own."

Jesu, was his every thought and feeling written all over his face? Dai, Nicholas, and now Catrin—each of them seemed able to look into him and see far too much.

"Truly, Ian. Is there anything you need?" she asked, her voice serious. "You do know how glad I am to see you, don't you?"

He looked up and met her gaze. Her gray eyes held love and concern for him. Despite their squabbling, they were very close. They always had been, even before their parents' deaths at the hands of a rampaging warlord. The arguments and teasing were simply their way of showing their affection for each other. He trusted Catrin with more of himself than he did anyone else, although she'd never seen all the ugliness he tried to keep hidden from her. But deep down he knew that side of him would not matter to her. Her love was unconditional, and as necessary to him as breathing. He only sought to spare her grief, for he knew how she worried about him.

It occurred to him that perhaps she was more like him than he had realized. Last year, he'd discovered the secrets Catrin had kept hidden, from everyone, for many years. Those dark and anguished memories must have evoked feelings he would recognize all too well.

'Twas no use hiding anything from her now. Who better than his sister, the last of his immediate family, to understand his fears?

"I've been about the prince's business of late—too much, I think. Perhaps familiarity has blinded me to his machinations." He scooped water into his hand, then watched as it trickled through his fingers. He forced himself to look up and meet her gaze. "Dai is dead."

"No!" she gasped, pressing her hand to her heart. Tears filled her eyes, making him regret the abrupt way he'd told her. "How did it happen?"

"One of Llywelyn's men caught him on his way to warn us. He'd been shot. He was already past help by the time he reached us. I left him there, for he felt we needed to run."

How it galled him to have treated Dai with so little respect! Leaving his body there—unattended, unprotected—seemed to Ian a sacrilege.

Evidently Catrin could see how it bothered him. "Nicholas will send someone—"

"He already has," he told her. "I'm just sorry I didn't bring Dai's body with us."

Catrin climbed down from the mattress. "Would you like me to leave so you can get out?"

He shook his head. "I intend to stay in here until the water is stone-cold."

She gestured toward the kettle steaming on the hearth. "I could warm the water for you."

"No. The colder, the better." And even that wouldn't help.

"Ah." She rolled her eyes. "No wonder you don't want Lily to come wash your back." Her gaze settled on the fine carpet spread across the floor. "'Tis just as well. That rug is very valuable, I'm told, and I'm exceptionally fond of it. I'd hate to see it ruined by a flood."

He tossed the sponge at her. She batted it away with a shriek, eyeing the water dripping down her bliaut with a scowl.

"What do you think of your new cousin?" he asked, not even bothering to hide his interest in her response.

Catrin dragged a chair over to sit nearer the tub. "She's beautiful, sweet, biddable—"

Ian choked back a snort of laughter.

"Which part did I get wrong?"

"The 'biddable' part," he said dryly. "Although you're right about the others."

"That poor child—"

"Woman."

She sent him a triumphant grin. "That poor *woman* needs us to help her, Ian. I knew Llewelyn was capable of just about anything, but this... This truly enrages me.''

Ian stared down at the water's rippling surface. ''Do you have any idea the shame I feel?'' he asked roughly.

''There's nothing you could have done to stop this, Ian. You didn't know. None of us did. If we had known, it certainly would never have gone on so long.''

''I realize that. No, I mean shame for the things I've done.'' He looked up at her, seeking to make her understand. ''If this had been someone else, some other family, I would probably have praised Llywelyn for his impressive scheme. It is impressive—he is capable of a great and far-reaching vision. I have set his plans in motion, plans worse than this, I assure you. And I've gloried in the reputation I've gained for it. Llywelyn's Dragon! I would do almost anything for him, to advance the cause.''

''Uniting Wales is a noble cause.''

''But the things we've done to gain it are not,'' he said flatly. ''And I'm the greatest of hypocrites if I don't see that I've been no better than he.'' He scooped the cool water over his face and rubbed at his eyes.

He heard Catrin cross the room, then felt a stream of warm water splash over him. The kettle clattered to the floor, and then Catrin picked up the sponge and began to rub it across his back. ''Relax, Ian. Be at ease,'' she said soothingly. ''You've carried the weight of Llywelyn's plots and vengeance for too long. Let us help you, for a change. You can lighten your vigilance for yet a while. We'll allow no harm to come to Lily.''

He leaned his head forward and let his tension melt away beneath Catrin's ministrations. ''Aye,'' he mumbled groggily. ''For a little while.''

Despite his promise to Catrin that he'd lie down and

rest, sleep wouldn't come to him once she'd left. His body felt better once he'd bathed and eaten, but his mind refused to let him be.

He couldn't decide if what he felt was guilt or shame. But whatever the emotion, it surged unchecked though him. If he sat in this room, it would drive him mad.

He shoved his feet into his boots and slammed out of the chamber in search of action. He needed the cleansing release of a good, hard fight.

But he found himself standing outside Lily's door.

He hesitated to knock, in case she'd had better luck than he at falling asleep. She ought to be resting like a babe, he thought. Her conscience was clear, as clean as fresh snow. He didn't intend to do anything to change that fact, either, he reminded himself.

His fingers had already unlatched the door before he realized that was what he intended to do. Just to see her, watch her—watch over her—as she slept. Perhaps, in the presence of such purity, he could find peace.

He pulled off his boots and set them inside the door, then crept across the room to the bed.

His eyes swiftly adjusted to the faint moonlight as he gazed upon her. Her hair lay all about her like a cloak, covering her shoulders, but allowing him a glimpse of one silk-clad breast.

The fabric clung to her, caressed her flesh as his fingers itched to do. A sheet lay rumpled about her legs in complete disarray, as though it had taken her a while—a restless time—to find slumber.

A strand of hair clung to her lips. He brushed it away, his fingertips lingering for a moment. Perhaps he'd tickled her, for her mouth curved into a smile.

"Ian?" she murmured, eyes still closed.

He knelt beside the bed. "Aye, 'tis Ian," he whispered. He smoothed her hair away from her brow and pressed a kiss there. "Go back to sleep."

Though she never opened her eyes, her hand reached for his and found it with unerring accuracy. She brought his fingers to her mouth and pressed her lips upon the back of his hand, then curved his palm about her cheek. Her breathing settled back into the slow, even rhythm of sleep, her lips still curled in a smile.

He could not—nay, would not—leave this place for the promise of salvation. Never moving his hand, Ian shifted into a more comfortable position on the floor and rested his head beside her on the mattress.

Content at last, he let his eyelids drift closed, holding the image of Lily.

A hand rested beneath her cheek, but she knew it didn't belong to her. The short, wiry hairs along the back of it tickled her skin, and she opened her eyes.

Ian knelt beside the bed, his head nestled against her breast. She'd apparently curled about him in her sleep. For the first time in longer than she could remember, she felt warm, rested, content.

Although the position he was in looked far from comfortable, he seemed to be sleeping soundly. She didn't dare move, for fear she'd wake him from his well-deserved rest.

But it was torture to lie here like this, with his breath wafting over her nipple in a subtle caress. She reached out to touch the dark hair curling over his brow, and his eyes snapped open, fixing her in place.

"Good morrow to you." The husky rumble of his voice vibrating against her sensitive flesh sent an answering shiver through her.

"Is it morning already?" A stupid question, she realized as soon as the words left her mouth. The sun was streaming through the shutters, painting them with strips of light.

She could hear sound rising up from the bailey, but it was distant, remote. It seemed that she and Ian lay in a gilded cocoon, separate from the world—in their own world, where nothing of ugliness could touch them.

"Aye, milady." He moved his head slightly and, his gaze never leaving hers, pressed a kiss on the upper curve of her breast. 'Twas the exact spot where the silk of her shift gave way to her bare flesh; the silk slipped over her skin, intensifying the sensation.

Or perhaps his eyes, holding her captive, caused that melting feeling.

She was reluctant to break the spell, but still, she hadn't expected to awaken beside him. "Why are you here?"

He lowered his gaze, leaving her bereft. "I came to check on you in the night." He toyed with the strands of hair draped over her shoulder. "I needed to see you, to be near you, Lily. When I saw you resting so peacefully, I decided to stay for a while. I must have drifted off." He shifted against her, setting off more sparks. "You make a most comfortable pillow."

A battle raged within her as she watched Ian's face, watched the play of emotions she knew he didn't think she saw. He did need her—for comfort, at least, though he'd never call it that. Even if that was all he'd ever want from her, she'd give it gladly, in whatever form he wanted. She'd thought long and hard about it last night, when she could not sleep. Perhaps she'd come into his life to give him something. Certainly he'd already done so much for her, she could never repay him.

And she was selfish, she admitted to herself. He'd

aroused a host of foreign emotions within her, feelings she couldn't imagine exploring with anyone but him. Freedom came in many forms, she saw that now. It wasn't just the ability to leave one place for another. There were worlds to explore without ever going anywhere.

And she wanted to explore them with Ian.

She touched his cheek. "Will you think I want too much if I ask you to kiss me? I swear to you, I'll ask for nothing more."

His eyes darkened, the color drawing her in like the cool green depths of the forest, providing sanctuary. "I would be honored to kiss you, Lily."

He rose to his knees and rested his weight on one hand, brushing aside her sleep-tousled hair with the other. "Where shall I kiss you? Here?" His lips brushed over her brow as softly as a butterfly's wings. "Or here?" He raised her hand to his mouth and trailed his tongue over the sensitive skin of her inner wrist.

She would have closed her eyes to savor each new touch, every nuance, every feeling, but he held her gaze enraptured with his own. By the time he released her, her body felt weighted by a languorous spell.

He ran the tip of his tongue lingeringly up the length of her arm to her shoulder, leaving a path of liquid fire in his wake. "Or here, perhaps?" he asked, nuzzling the valley between her breasts.

Her breath left her in a sigh. "Yes."

He chuckled, tickling her. He drew back to watch her face, his eyes searching. "Which one?"

She stared, transfixed by the changes passion had wrought in his face. His features seemed sharper, more defined, and a flush rode high along his cheekbones.

Black curls tumbled over his forehead. His lips looked full and soft amid the dark stubble along his jaw.

And his eyes saw to her very soul.

"Any of them. All of them," she said with a sigh. His mouth closed over hers.

Yes.

Chapter Eleven

If he could keep his legs off the bed, Ian thought, he just might survive this torture without robbing Lily of her virtue. Though it would be a near thing. He desired her more than he'd ever wanted any other woman in his life.

Her hands were never still. She touched him constantly, running her fingertips through his hair and along the edge of his jaw, nibbling at his lips. She managed to untie the neckline of his shirt without his noticing until she ran her fingers through the hair on his chest.

Why did she permit him to kiss her so passionately? And why was she practically undressing him? She had to know where this would lead.

Even if she didn't, he did.

He broke off the kiss, lingering over it, reluctant for it to end. But this time, he resolved, this time they'd go from passion to reason without anger or hurt feelings.

Eventually.

"You smell so sweet," he murmured. "Like flowers."

"Lilies," she whispered.

"I love the scent of Lily." And he did—even better

than flowers. He nuzzled the soft skin below her ear, making her shiver. "Do you like that?"

"Yes." She sighed. "Can't you tell?"

"Aye. But I like to hear you tell me what you like."

Her eyes looked huge. "Tell you?" A tide of pink swept up her neck and into her cheeks. "I don't know if I can do that."

"I wish—"

The door creaked open, accompanied by the sound of Catrin singing. Ian grabbed the edge of the sheet and yanked it over Lily's body, pulling so hard it came untucked.

Catrin tripped over his boots and tumbled to the floor. She sat up, cursing, and tossed a boot aside.

"What are you doing here?" she demanded. "Lily, is he forcing his attentions on you? For if he is, I'll set Nicholas after him— No, I'll take care of him myself." She got up off the floor and straightened her bliaut, indignation written in her face and stance. "She's a decent lady, Ian. I'll thank you to—"

"Have done, Catrin." He remained kneeling on the far side of the bed, though he would have preferred to stand. However, that might prove embarrassing—to Lily, at least. His body hadn't recovered from her kisses. And he knew that despite his sister's protestations, nothing much shocked her. This was for Lily's benefit, not his.

He chuckled. "Is this turnabout on purpose? It seems to me that I walked in on you and Nicholas once. And you were doing a hell of a lot more than kissing, if I recall correctly." He stroked his fingers along Lily's flushed cheek. Catrin's face was nearly as red, he noted. "At least I had the decency to knock first. Can you say the same?"

Lily gently pushed his hand aside and sat up, tugging the sheet with her when she got off the bed. "I'm sure she never expected to find you here, Ian." Her eyes downcast, her face still delightfully pink, she picked up a robe from the foot of the bed and slipped it on, tying the belt before she turned toward him. "I was surprised to find you here," she admitted.

Catrin stood watching them for a moment, then picked up his boots and held them out to him. Seeing no help for it, he took them and slipped them on. "Lily and I have things to do," she told him. "I'm certain you can find some way to occupy yourself until dinner. Nicholas is waiting for you in the hall, I believe, if you'd care to join him."

It seemed she had the morning mapped out—for each of them. "Anything else?" he asked dryly. "Am I permitted to dress, or eat, before I take up my agenda?"

"Yes, milord Dragon," Catrin said, with a laugh and a formal curtsy. She turned to Lily. "You cannot allow him to go his own way too often. He becomes unbearable, awestruck by his own power."

He returned to Lily's side and laid his hand on her arm. "Don't let her bully you," he warned. He bent and kissed her softly on the lips. "She knows all about how power can corrupt, believe me." Scowling at his sister, he sent her a mocking salute. "Until dinner," he said as he left the room.

As soon as Ian left, Lady Catrin began to bustle about the chamber, a fact that Lily appreciated greatly. It gave her an opportunity to collect herself.

She'd been mortified when Lady Catrin entered the room and caught them. Her face still felt as though it were on fire. She didn't know how Ian could be so calm, so quickly. Perhaps he'd had practice, she thought with a frown.

"I trust it's not my brother who displeases you," Lady Catrin said, placing a bliaut and undertunic on the rumpled bed. "You must not take our taunting and teasing to heart. My brother is very dear to me, though he doesn't like me to show it. We snipe and jape, but it means naught."

"I understand," Lily said. But she wasn't certain she did. Such experience was far beyond her ken. She hadn't spent any time with people her own age. All she knew was the more impersonal, formalized ritual of the abbey.

"Tell me of your life at Saint Winifred's."

"There's very little to tell, milady."

"Please, call me Catrin. We are cousins, after all. And who knows, perhaps we might someday be more," Catrin said with an odd smile. Lily wasn't certain what she meant, so she smiled in return.

"Though I never intended to join the nuns, still my life at the abbey was very structured. It was an endless series of days, each like the one before." She finally felt comfortable enough to take a seat on the bed. "I've had more excitement in the weeks since I left than I had in the eighteen years I lived there."

"You must have been desperate, to leave the abbey on your own. You were fortunate to have made it to Dolwyddelan safely. 'Tis a dangerous world for a woman traveling alone." She looked away for a moment, her face sad. "'Tis dangerous for anyone."

Lily didn't know what to say in response. "Everywhere I went, people were kind. Of course, I wore a novice's habit for most of my journey. Evidently nuns don't make very good victims, since they have nothing to steal.''

"Weren't you concerned some man might try to steal your virtue?"

Lily had to laugh at that. "Milady, the only man who has even come close to trying is the Dragon. And he is too decent to take what he knows he should not have.''

Catrin snorted. "If you allow him into your chamber as you did this morn, your virtue won't last much longer. He's a man of deep passions, though from what I've seen, he doesn't usually pay much attention to *that* appetite," she said frankly.

Eager to change the subject, Lily picked up the lovely dark green undertunic, but she hesitated. She wasn't used to dressing in front of anyone.

"Let me help you," Catrin offered. "Sometimes the lacing can be difficult."

"'Tis not necessary. I'm used to doing for myself.'' Indeed, the idea of having servants—or anyone—help her with such basic tasks seemed foreign to her. But then, nearly everything about life in the outside world seemed strange.

Catrin sat down beside her on the bed. "You're not an anonymous boarder at Saint Winifred's any longer, Lily. You are the daughter of two noble families. As such, you must become accustomed to servants. You'll find that there are any number of duties and obligations to go along with the benefits of our station. One of those duties is to provide work for our dependents." She picked up the undertunic. "I came to help you today, instead of sending a maid, because I didn't think you'd be comfortable with a servant's help. But that will change, I am certain.''

What objection could she raise? Lily appreciated

Catrin's consideration. It would be churlish to refuse her help. Lily slipped out of the robe and allowed Catrin to assist her into the undertunic and bliaut. "You're right," she admitted once she saw the laces running from armpit to hip on each side of the bliaut. "I'd never be able to lace this up myself. The clothes I wore at the abbey weren't so complicated."

Her *life* hadn't been so complicated, she thought later in the day. She had accompanied Catrin as she attended to her morning duties. She couldn't help but be amazed at the number and variety of the details Catrin was responsible for. After visiting the kitchen and the infirmary, and inspecting the weaving, they'd met with the priest.

All before midday.

And Catrin had said they had far more to do in the afternoon.

The faster pace at Ashby frightened her. Was this how a noblewoman lived? Abbey life had not prepared her, but then, why would they have expected that she'd ever need to know how to manage a household such as this? Although she was surprised Llywelyn hadn't planned for that, as well.

They joined the others in the great hall as the gong called everyone to dinner. Seated at the high table between Ian and Lord Nicholas, Lily felt as though all eyes were upon her.

As Ian handed her the wine goblet they would share, she asked, "Is it always like this?"

"What do you mean?"

"Does everyone always stare?" She glanced up from their trencher.

"They'll likely stop, once they're used to you." He took her hand and raised it to his lips. "Did it ever occur to you that they might be staring because you're beautiful?''

"Me?'' She met his gaze. "Do you think so?''

Was she blind? The Norman style of dress, with its tightly laced overtunic and gauzy veil, became her well. The dark and light green silks brought out the reddish tints in her braided hair, and intensified the green of her eyes.

But the image that clung to his mind was the way she'd looked this morning. Her hair spread out over the pillows, her silk shift slipping off one lovely soft shoulder...

He picked up the goblet and drained the wine, hoping to cool his ardor. However, that wasn't likely to happen with Lily seated at his side, smelling of flowers and smiling at him.

By the time the meal was over, Ian feared he'd not be able to stand without embarrassing himself. Simply listening to the soft murmur of Lily's voice as she answered Nicholas's questions kept the fire in his blood simmering.

Perhaps 'twas time for this interlude to end.

They couldn't stay here. He doubted there would be any danger from Llywelyn, but it was a chance he'd rather not take. Especially since he'd learned that Catrin was carrying her first child.

The thought filled him with joy. For so long, her life had been dark with pain, until Nicholas had brought her into the light of happiness. For that alone, Ian would have liked the Norman lord. 'Twas good fortune, indeed, that Talbot had turned out to be a man he could both like and respect.

He'd not repay them by putting their lives and their home in jeopardy.

Once again Nicholas had brought up the subject of marriage. "She's beautiful, desirable, intelligent—What more could you wish for in a wife? And you'd be protecting her—and her sister."

Ian could see the benefit in it, to everyone else, but the person who might benefit least was Lily. He might be wrong about Llywelyn's intentions. Perhaps Lily could find a husband who would be to her liking and Llywelyn's.

And Nicholas might be wrong about Lily's feelings for him.

She desired him, to some extent. But as ignorant as she was regarding men and women, she might not recognize those feelings for what they were. She might, as many women tended to do, believe that lust was something more, the courtly love the French blathered on about.

How could he ask her to share his life, when he didn't know what that meant anymore? Depending on the degree of Llywelyn's anger with him, he might not have a life to offer her.

He took her hand in his to help her up from the bench. "Will you walk with me in the garden, milady?"

Lily looked surprised—at his formal tone, mayhap—but she nodded and let him lead her outside. Catrin had made a walled garden, dormant now, in a sheltered corner near the tower keep. They could speak privately there, without fear of being overheard.

Despite the sun, Lily shivered, so he wrapped his cloak about her and settled her on a bench. Too restless to sit, he stood in the path before her, fighting the childish urge to dig at the crushed stone with the toe of his boot.

He didn't know how to begin, but Lily solved that

problem for him. "Will we be able to stay here long?" she asked.

"I don't think so. Llywelyn will look for us here eventually. Unless we leave the area altogether, there are few places where his arm does not reach."

She glanced at the herbs scattered about the beds before settling her gaze on his face. "You should take me back, Ian. Make your peace with your overlord. I've gotten what I wanted. I know now who I am. And I've gained a family besides. Don't you know how happy that makes me? 'Tis more than I ever dared hope for." She laid her hand on his arm. "It grieves me to know what you could lose, because of me."

"I thought you wanted to meet your sister," he reminded her.

"Once some time has passed, perhaps it will be safe for Gillian to come to me, wherever he sends me. We'll have a chance to meet, to know each other."

"Not if Gillian is dead," he said flatly. He steeled himself against the pain that darkened her eyes. Better to be cruel now than to watch her grieve for Gillian later. "So long as you live, Llywelyn has a chance to gain l'Eau Clair. If I were to take you back, I can guarantee you'd be wed in no time—a matter of weeks, at most. And the man will be of Llywelyn's choosing, not your own. He'll want someone loyal only to him. If you're lucky, the man could be fairly young, and not too stupid, although I wouldn't count on that."

Tears filled her eyes, tears he knew she would not allow to fall. "Why are you doing this, Dragon?"

He winced. For the first time, she said the name with the same degree of fear—or was it loathing?—he heard in others' voices when they spoke of him. He felt lower than a snake, but that didn't matter.

Lily was all that mattered now.

If he knew she was safe from Llywelyn's plots and schemes, he didn't care if she loathed him. So long as she did not fear him.

That he could not bear.

"In all my years of carrying out Llywelyn's vengeance, I never stopped to consider those I might have hurt. But I cannot harm you, Lily. And if I take you back, fall in with his plan, I will." He turned his back on her and stared at a withered shrub. "There is only one way I can think of to protect you and Gillian." He whirled to face her, pinning her with his gaze. "Marry me, Lily. As your husband, it will be my duty to keep you from harm. And Llywelyn will learn that even *I* have limits to what I will do for him."

He looked and sounded so torn, Lily could not bear it. "Ian, please." She held her hand out in supplication. "Sit here with me, so that we may talk."

Reluctantly, it seemed, he joined her on the bench, his shoulders hunched forward—though not against the cold. She could see the fire burning in his eyes.

But who was he angry with? Her? Llywelyn?

Or himself?

How could she let him face life alone? He considered himself unworthy of happiness, of a life of his own. Her heart began to trip faster as she examined the opportunity fate had given her. She wanted his happiness, more than her own. She would find a way to give Ian what anyone else would consider his right.

A home, a wife, a woman's heart.

Could love tame a dragon?

She smoothed her hand over his back and shoulders in a soothing motion, until she felt the muscles beneath her palm relax. They sat there for a time in silence, the twittering of birds and the muted sounds of Ashby a restful accompaniment to their thoughts.

Finally Lily could see that Ian's face had settled into its usual lines and color had returned to ride along his sharply defined cheekbones. She watched his face, seeking knowledge of the man she would join her life with.

He lifted his gaze to her face and caught her staring, sending a wave of heat over her face and neck. His emerald eyes, dark and intense, inspected her as carefully as she had him.

His fingers crept up and stopped the restful movement of her hand, capturing her fingers and slowly carrying them to his lips. "Have you decided?" he asked, watching her over their linked hands. He pressed a lingering kiss on her fingertips. "Will you be my bride?"

"Are you certain you wish it?"

He nodded.

"And you won't regret it?"

"Never."

That one word, so earnestly said, gave her the strength to decide. "Yes, milord Dragon, I will wed you." A surge of excitement fired her blood. "Whenever you will."

His eyes never leaving hers, Ian lowered his head and brought his lips to bear ever so gently upon hers. His kiss was a solemn vow, sealing their agreement with an irrevocable bond. Lily felt her flesh tingle where they touched—their mouths and the fingers of one hand—and felt an answering spark deep within her. She moaned from the intensity of it.

"Will you be my wife in all ways?" he whispered. "Will you let me make you mine, in truth?"

Beyond speech, beyond thought, she nodded.

"Will you wed me now, Lily? Before God and my

family? Talbot's priest will marry us, so long as you're truly willing."

He kissed her fingertips once again, his lips lingering as his eyes made promises of passion barely checked. She allowed him to lead her from the garden to go in search of his sister.

They found Catrin and Nicholas in Catrin's solar—waiting for them, it seemed.

Lily watched as the two men exchanged glances. Nicholas nodded, looking satisfied, then came forward and took her hands in his. "Are you sure, Lily?" Startled, she glanced quickly at Ian.

"He knows already, Lily," Ian said. He wouldn't meet her eyes. "'Twas his suggestion."

She felt her heart plummet to her toes, taking with it all her hope and joy. Marrying her was another duty to him, little more. She could accept that he did want her—her body—but as for anything else...

She'd be a fool if she looked for more.

Resolution stiffened her spine—and her resolve. She wanted Ian. She wanted to tame the Dragon, she thought, savoring the frisson of excitement dancing over her flesh. And if this was the only way she could get him, then so be it.

She could be patient. She'd make him want more.

"Aye, milord. I'm sure 'tis what I want," she said, smiling reassuringly at Nicholas. She was surprised by the approval she saw in his unusual violet eyes. He appeared to be genuinely happy for them.

Catrin embraced her brother, then came forward to wrap her arms about Lily, as well. "When will you do it?" she asked. "The priest is willing, once he's reassured himself that you're not forcing Lily into this."

"Will there be any trouble because she has no guardian?" Nicholas asked. "Or is she Llywelyn's ward?"

Ian frowned. "I hadn't thought of that. I suppose there's no problem, so long as the priest's not loyal to Llywelyn."

"I'll stand as her guardian," Nicholas offered. "Since she's Catrin's kin, that should satisfy the legalities. If it doesn't, Rannulf should agree. He's her brother-by-marriage, after all."

"So long as the marriage is legal and binding," Ian said. "Otherwise, 'tis all for naught. Llywelyn cannot be permitted to overturn it."

Catrin took Lily by the arm. "Come along, then, Lily. I've the perfect gown for you to wear. We'll meet you in the chapel before sunset," she told the men. "See that you're ready."

The thunder of feet pounding on the stairs heralded a furious knocking at the door. When Catrin pulled it open, a breathless man-at-arms nearly fell into the chamber.

"Milord! 'Tis a company of Welshman, a dozen or so, fast approaching the gates."

"Do they look as though they've come to visit, or to fight?" Nicholas asked.

"Fight, milord."

"Damnation," Ian snarled, striding over to the window and peering out. "Damn me for a fool. I thought we'd have more time."

"Gather your things. Quickly," Catrin said, heading for the door. "I'll collect some food," she told Nicholas.

Lily watched everything unfold in silence. They'd been so close! But she couldn't allow this to go on. "Wait!" she cried. "We cannot run forever. I'm sorry,

Dragon.'' She met his gaze. ''I cannot marry you. I can't ruin your life this way. If I go back with them, they'll leave you alone.''

Ian shook his head sharply. ''It won't matter, sweeting.''

Strong arms wrapped around her from behind, pinning her arms close to her body. Nicholas cursed when she drew back her heel and kicked him in the leg. How could they do this? ''Ian!'' she shrieked, before a callused hand covered her mouth.

Ian reached out and touched her cheek lightly. ''I'm sorry, Lily. But I will not give you up.''

Chapter Twelve

Cursing himself for a fool, Ian took Lily from Nicholas's hold and, keeping one hand over her mouth, pushed her down into a chair. "If you promise to be quiet, I'll take away my hand." Her eyes flashed angrily, but she nodded. Placing his hands on the arms of the chair, he loomed over her. "I will not allow you to sacrifice yourself for me. Do you understand?"

"But you're doing the same for me."

He glared at her. "Nay, I am not. It is my choice to marry you. No one is forcing me to. You gave me your solemn oath you would marry me, Lily. Will you deny me, and be forsworn?"

Although she glared at him still, she shook her head.

He stepped back from the chair, but stood close, lest she take it into her head to run. "Then come with me now. We can be away from here before they've made it to the gates, if we hurry. Believe me. I'll keep you safe."

Catrin rushed into the room and thrust a cloth sack into his hands. "'Tis all I could gather so quickly, but it should see you to l'Eau Clair."

A servant brought in Ian's saddlebags and weapons.

He accepted them gratefully, buckling on his sword belt and carrying Dai's scabbarded sword.

Catrin embraced Lily. "Don't worry, cousin. It will be all right."

Ian leaned down and kissed his sister's cheek, then grabbed Lily by the hand. "I'll send word," he called as they hurried from the room after Nicholas.

He led them into into the master's chamber. He dragged a curtain aside, the rings clattering on the rod, to expose a garderobe. Ian helped him lift out an armload of clothes from the hooks on the walls.

Lily looked at Nicholas as though he were daft. "We're not going down the privy shaft—"

"Nay," Nicholas said, laughing. "There's another opening in the wall, parallel to the waste shaft. You will slide down that into a tunnel beneath the moat. Ian knows the way from there."

"'Tis a pity we won't have the horses," Ian said, frowning. "The journey to l'Eau Clair will take forever on foot."

Nicholas smiled. "There are mounts waiting for you. Once you reach the forest, go to the manor farm—you know the place."

Ian nodded. He'd been there before.

"Tell Alfric you're ready to leave. He knows which mounts will serve you best. 'Tis already arranged."

Trust Talbot to think of a way out, in case they needed it. He reached out and clasped Nicholas's hand. "Thank you."

He could see that the other man knew exactly what he was thanking him for. "You'd have done the same," he said.

Nicholas turned to Lily and kissed her cheek. "Take care of him. And give Gillian a kiss for me. Go with

God,'' he told them, tugging a board from the wall and exposing the passageway door.

Ian went first. The copper-lined passage sloped downward gradually, allowing him to control his descent. So long as he kept the swords tight against his side, he had no difficulty. He landed on his feet in a dark, damp pit, their bags sliding down the chute behind him.

He'd no sooner moved out of the way than Lily popped out after him. "Are you all right?" he asked as he felt for her hand.

"Aye," she said, sounding breathless. She pressed a candle and flint into his hands. "Nicholas said to give you this."

The candlelight illuminated a narrow corridor, not quite high enough for him to stand upright. Their clothing brushed against the damp stone walls.

Ian felt like a packhorse with his saddlebags and the sack of food slung over his shoulders. He carried the candle and crept forward, Lily clinging to his belt like a leech.

"I hate these dark, close places." Her voice was faint and quivered slightly. "I've spent a lot of time in them since I met you. They must be part of the Dragon's lair," she said, giggling.

She had to be terrified, he thought with concern. She didn't seem the type of woman to giggle. He picked up the pace, moving as swiftly as possible. He'd be glad to get out of here, as well. He felt like a crab scuttling along.

Finally they came to a metal-banded wooden door, laying on a slant above them. He snuffed the candle, reached back and pried Lily's fingers from his belt and handed the stub to her.

"Keep this," he said.

Then, throwing his weight into it, he pushed on the door until it gave, swinging upward with a faint squeal of the hinges. Light poured into the tunnel, temporarily blinding him.

"Not too bad for a bolt hole. But I hope there's no one waiting out there for us. I cannot see a thing." He blinked until his eyes could focus again.

Praise God, they were alone. He levered himself out of the hole, then reached down and hauled Lily up beside him.

He framed her face with his hands. "I may need to order you about quickly, if there's danger. Promise me you'll do whatever I tell you."

She pressed a kiss into his palm. "I promise," she said, her eyes solemn. "And I'm sorry for what I did back there. 'Tis just..."

"I understand." He did. He'd have done the same for her. He smoothed back the strands of hair escaping her braid; she'd lost her veil in the passageway. But he also knew he could not permit her to fall into Llywelyn's grasp again.

He adjusted the packs and took Lily's hand. "Come on. It's a bit of a walk to the farm." He cast a measuring look at the sky. "We'd best be going."

They left the farm at nightfall. Ian took only one horse. Lily had done well with Mouse on the journey to Ashby, but he truly believed it was only because the stallion had taken a liking to her. The mount he had chosen now looked to have the stamina they'd need, but it was clear he also had a nasty disposition. And the terrain was difficult in many places, far worse than the route they'd traveled to Ashby. He didn't doubt Lily's courage, but her lack of skill could have dangerous consequences. Better to have to rest more often than to worry that Lily's horse might run off with her, or harm her in some way.

Besides, on this leg of their journey, endurance was more important than speed. Especially since he intended a detour on the way to l'Eau Clair.

There was a small, out-of-the-way village he knew of, a village whose priest owed the Dragon an enormous debt.

Before they finished the journey to L'Eau Clair, he intended to collect.

Toad took up his usual position in the wall near Llywelyn's chamber, his body fairly quivering with excitement. He'd learned that some of Llywelyn's men had returned to Dolwyddelan, and the Viking's name had been mentioned. Now, perhaps, he'd be able to discover where Siwardson had taken Lily.

He'd overheard little of importance the past few days—save that the Dragon evidently hadn't gone to Lord Rhys's keep, as he'd been ordered to by the prince himself.

The question was, where had he gone instead?

Toad eased his aching shoulder against the wall. All this skulking about in the passageways took its toll on his poor, broken body. He'd wondered, as he lay near death with his limbs twisted all awry, if it would be worth it to survive. He had been a handsome man once, his body strong and well formed, in the full flower of his manly vigor. It had never been difficult for him to find willing vessels for his passion; women had always fallen into his grasp with a gratifying willingness, eager to satisfy his needs.

All women except one.

That woman he had wanted with a desire that far outstripped the puling lust he felt for the others. She could have given him power, lands, and a connection to the Norman king—as well as strengthening his ties with his kinsman, Llywelyn. The fact that she was related to him, as well, added a delicious twist to an already perfect situation.

Now the only outlet for his lust was vengeance. He savored his desire for revenge with every bit as much enjoyment as he'd ever found within a woman's body.

The men who had done this to him would pay indirectly for their crimes, once he regained the power and position he had lost.

Soon, he told himself, his crooked face twisted into a smile.

Soon Lily would be his, and his life would begin anew.

He pressed his ear to the wall as the level of noise in the room beyond increased. "Sit down and stop babbling," he muttered. He could hear the sound of a deep, booming voice—Siwardson's, he hoped—but he couldn't understand the words.

Then, suddenly, the volume increased. Tamping down his excitement, Toad pressed his ear to the wall and settled down to listen.

Llywelyn stood before the fire in his chamber, a goblet of wine in his hand, and surveyed the motley band he'd sent out in search of the Dragon. They hadn't brought him back with them; that much was obvious. But he wasn't surprised. Few men had the courage to stand up to Ian. However, that did not mean their journey had been a complete loss. Perhaps they knew where he'd gone.

Their leader, Sion, stood tall and met his master's questioning gaze. "No, milord. We didn't see a sign of the Dragon anywhere. We ran across the Viking, though, a day's ride from here."

"Did he have the girl with him?" Llywelyn asked.

"Nay, milord. Must have handed her over already. You'll not be troubled with her now," Sion added with a dismissive shrug. "But here's what we did to try to find the Dragon...."

Llywelyn listened as the man outlined in boring detail every place he'd searched for Ian.

"We even went to his sister's keep at Ashby, milord," Sion said. "They hadn't seen him there."

"And how do you know that?" Llywelyn asked. "Did they allow you inside, give you an opportunity to ask questions, search for information?"

"Nay, milord. 'Tis a Norman keep. Lord Talbot spoke with us at the gate, but he wouldn't let us in. But he said that he hadn't seen his brother-by-marriage in months, that the Lady Catrin was ready to slay her brother for ignoring her for so long."

"That I could believe," another man put in. "The bitch would do it, too, given half a chance."

Llywelyn crossed the room in two strides and knocked the man to the floor. "Lady Catrin is my cousin, and a noble lady. Watch how you speak of your betters." Fools! He returned to his chair and flung himself into it. "Take your friend out of here before I decide to do worse to him," he told Sion. "I'll speak with you later." He drank deeply of his wine as the men hurried from the room.

Llywelyn slammed the goblet onto the table in frustration. Where was Ian? And why hadn't Siwardson returned?

He had hoped the message he'd received from Saint Winifred's was a mistake, that the Viking and the messenger from Sister Maud had simply missed each other. Now, however, Siwardson's absence took on a more ominous tone.

After all the time the Viking had spent at Dolwyddelan, waiting for a decision regarding those damned trade negotiations, he should have returned to the keep by now.

Unless he lay dead somewhere. Given the man's size and strength, that seemed unlikely.

Had the bastard reneged on their bargain, perhaps traded the girl to someone? The Vikings were known for trafficking in women, and Lily was a beauty.

Or had he sold her to the Dragon?

By Christ, he couldn't trust anyone.

Not even the Dragon.

Ian had spoiled him. The Dragon had been the most dependable man ever to serve him. At least until Lily arrived at Dolwyddelan.

He poured more wine. He would never have guessed that a woman would prove to be Ian's downfall.

But sooner or later, his men would run the Dragon to ground.

And when they did, Llywelyn would show him who was master.

Toad bit at his hand to keep from screaming his rage. He still didn't know where the girl was! Evidently Siwardson had not returned. But Sion might know where the Viking had been taking her. Damnation, why couldn't Llywelyn keep his temper long enough so that he could learn what he needed to know?

He could go to Sion and ask, but that would likely

solve nothing. The days when Llywelyn's men-at-arms had given Toad what he sought were long past. Sion would probably kick him down the stairs or knock him across the room for daring to approach him. Everyone else did.

His only options seemed to be more eavesdropping outside Llywelyn's chamber, or finding the Viking and following him about in the hope that he'd lead him to her.

Or perhaps he should head for l'Eau Clair. He had the feeling that the Dragon—and Lily—would find their way to Gillian's keep eventually.

He'd do it, he decided.

What did he have to lose?

It took a day's hard riding to reach the village of Llanrhys. Lily remained virtually silent on this leg of the journey. Ian welcomed it, for he wasn't in the mood to discuss his plans—despite the fact that they involved her. The less she knew at this point, the better; he was already amazed that her acquiescence had lasted this long.

He had plenty of opportunity to ponder the course he would take. He'd never thought to marry, but for some reason, the thought of marrying Lily did not bother him—much. His reservations all centered around the feeling that he was about to do her an enormous disservice. He would gain a lover, a wife, while she stood to lose what she had so recently gained—her freedom.

He only hoped she did not come to regret her decision.

But she didn't seem hesitant, just quiet. Since it served his purpose, he let her be.

They didn't arrive in Llanrhys until well after dark.

Ian tethered the horse in the trees a distance from the tiny church and led Lily by the hand through the shadowy town.

They entered the church and crossed the sacristy to a door beyond the altar. Ian tapped upon the panels, then waited impatiently until he heard the sound of shuffling feet. The door opened a crack.

"Who is there?"

"Take a look, old man," Ian said, pushing the door open wide.

The short, scrawny priest hitched up his robes and snatched a candle from the wall pricket. Holding it high, he stepped from the room.

"Good eventide to you, Father," Ian said, his voice polite. He smiled, the Dragon's smile, all teeth and vengeance.

He could tell the exact moment when recognition dawned. The priest made the sign of the cross, his eyes wide. "Lord Ian." He bobbed his head and, reaching behind him, tugged the door closed.

"Why are you here, milord? The prince hasn't..." He shook his head. It was more of a twitch really. "No, he couldn't know about that." He looked up at Ian, eyes pleading. "Could he?"

Ian snorted; he actually wanted to laugh, but that was hardly likely to further their ends. He would rely on intimidation alone to get what he wanted. No sense in frightening the worm to death, at least not till he'd done the deed. "Nay, Father. He doesn't know." He took a step toward the door. "However, that could change— very quickly, as I'm sure you know."

The priest bobbed his head again. "Thank you, milord, thank you. What brings you to Llanrhys, then, if not the prince's business?"

Ian drew Lily forward. "Marry us."

"*Now*, milord? In the middle of the night?"

"I know of no better time to make her my bride," he said, allowing his gaze to travel in a slow, purely sensual foray over her body.

"Indeed." The priest stared at her more closely, until he caught sight of Ian's glare. "I understand, milord."

Ian ignored the frowning look Lily sent his way and drew her toward the crude altar. "A true wedding, Father, binding before God and man."

"Aye." The priest bustled about behind the altar. "We'll need a witness, milord," he added nervously. "Perhaps 'twould be best to wait till morning."

"I'm certain whomever you have warming your bed will do nicely," Ian remarked, grinning when Lily gave a shocked gasp.

The old man hurried into his chamber, emerging a few moments later with a young woman of incredible endowment. She finished tugging her gown up over her breasts, then looked at them and smiled.

"Is it your wish to wed this man?" the priest asked Lily. She nodded. "He isn't forcing you?" he added sternly, surprising Ian. He hadn't thought the licentious fool would care.

"No, Father," Lily replied, sounding shocked. "Of course not."

"Then let's get on with it," he said, moving behind the altar.

In a matter of moments, the ceremony was over. They were wed, Lily thought, shoving aside a feeling of disappointment over the circumstances. What difference did it make that they'd been married in a tumbledown church by a lecherous old priest who evidently owed Ian a favor?

She certainly didn't expect romance.

Until yesterday afternoon, she'd never expected to marry at all.

The deed was done. She'd bound herself to the Dragon, casting aside all her dreams of freedom in a moment.

But she couldn't find it within herself to mourn their loss.

"Thank you, Father." Ian took the piece of parchment containing their marriage lines, then placed something in the priest's hand—surprising him, to judge by his startled look. The old man smiled and moved his hand, making the coins jingle merrily.

Ian took her by the hand. "Come along, wife. Time to go."

She let him lead her through the town in silence, but when they reached the trees, she jerked her hand free. "I don't suppose you'd care to tell me what that was about back there?"

He untied the horse and turned to lift her into the saddle. "No."

"No, what?" She took a step back, intent on eluding his grasp until she got an answer.

"No, I'm not going to tell you," he replied in an even voice. "'Tis old business, and nothing to do with you. Wife." He backed her toward a tree.

She spun away, careful of her footing in the faint moonlight. But he caught her anyway, and held her close. "If I promise to tell you, will you get on the horse?" he asked, his voice husky with laughter.

'Twas more than she'd expected.

Lily nodded and allowed him to assist her into the saddle.

Once they picked up the trail again, however, she nudged him with her elbow.

"What?" He twitched away from her arm, but she knew she hadn't hurt him.

"You promised you would explain," she reminded him. Another thought occurred to her. "And why were you laughing back there?"

He grinned and shook his head. "It seemed ironic. Newly wed, and already making demands."

"I wasn't..." She thought back over what she'd said—and how she'd said it. "I was," she admitted. "But you tell me next to nothing. I've never liked to be ordered about and expected to blindly obey."

He nodded. "And I'm not used to explaining myself to anyone. Not even Llywelyn himself."

Ian was a true storyteller, reminding her of a bard she'd heard once at the abbey. She found his grasp of human nature remarkable. He kept her entertained with a variety of tales as they traveled through the night.

For the first time, the darkness didn't seem like her enemy, but rather like a comforting cloak, binding them together—alone.

Perhaps their marriage would work out better than she'd thought. He seemed at ease in her company, far more than she had ever noticed before. In truth, they scarcely knew each other.

Although there had been times when Lily felt she'd always known him.

"I know so little of the world, Ian. Will you answer my questions, even if they seem foolish?" she asked. "I won't expect you to tell me things all the time."

He sighed. "I will try, Lily. It could take some time for me to grow accustomed to not being alone any longer. But I will try."

It was more than she'd expected. Lily vowed she would take what he offered, and not press for more.

She tried not to notice the way the greedy little voice inside her head laughed.

Chapter Thirteen

Lily wondered about many things as they rode along, searching for a hut or some other shelter where they might spend the remainder of the night. Not the least of which was whether her husband intended to truly make her his wife. The details of how they'd go about that process were still somewhat vague in her mind, but she couldn't help feeling curious about it.

And what he planned to do.

That was one question she couldn't ask him. It seemed too bold, too frightening. Her curiosity kept nagging at her, but she refused to give in to it. She could only hope he would answer that question without being asked.

It began to rain soon after they left the church, and she felt thoroughly chilled, despite her cloak and Ian's shared warmth. Even the fire in her veins at the thought of Ian's kisses could not warm her. He'd told her there were all sorts of kisses; she hoped that once they got wherever they were going, he'd show her.

If they didn't fall asleep first.

Lily wrenched her thoughts away from indulgence to more serious concerns. Even now, Llywelyn's men might be on their trail. But she didn't really fear that they would catch them. Her trust in Ian was absolute.

They'd scarcely rested in two days. She only hoped that exhaustion didn't destroy Ian's vigilance. She'd do what she could to help him, but she knew she hadn't his skill. He was the Dragon; she didn't doubt he could go on for days with little rest, without its affecting him. But he did look tired.

She sat up with a start when Ian halted their mount outside a tumbledown hut. It had begun to rain, a misery in the cold mountain air. She knew they were fortunate to have found any shelter at all.

He tethered the horse beneath a thick stand of firs, then asked her for the candle they'd had in the tunnel. He left her waiting under the shelter of the trees while he investigated the hut.

He returned almost immediately. "It's little more than four walls and a roof—which leaks—but 'tis better than staying out here. And there's some wood inside. I'll be able to make a fire."

The flames lent a cheerful glow to the hut, disguising its dilapidated state. Lily spread a cloth and laid out bread and cheese, and a skin of mead. They hadn't eaten since midday, and she was starved. Ian fell to with a hearty appetite, but despite her hunger, Lily found she couldn't eat much. Curiosity about what Ian might expect of her made her nervous.

He noticed at once that she only picked at her food. "Here, try the mead. Catrin makes the best mead I've ever tasted. Perhaps it will stir your hunger."

She drank, savoring the honeyed sweetness and the hint of spice. When she lowered the skin, she found Ian watching her, his eyes dark. Her heart paused, then pounded furiously, at the longing in his gaze.

He took the mead from her and brought it to his lips, then leaned close and captured her mouth with his. His lips skimmed hers, teasing, taunting her with the barest hint of passion.

Groaning, he tossed the drink aside and buried his fingers in her disheveled hair. He tasted of honey, a sweetness she shared as he plunged his tongue deep to toy with hers.

He nibbled at her lips, then worked his way down her throat, teasing and licking the sensitive places he found along the way. She felt his fingers at her ribs, tickling her as he struggled with the laces of her gown. Cursing, he tore at the strings, still kissing her all the while.

Finally the laces gave, and he tugged at her bliaut, pulling it up and over her head, leaving her still clad in her undertunic and shift. But the loose garments made her feel free, relaxed.

Lily wanted to touch his skin, to smooth her hands over the warmth of his lean, well-muscled body. She tugged without success at his tunic. "Let me," he murmured against her throat, gently brushing her hands aside. Rearing back, he pulled his tunic and shirt over his head and tossed them over his shoulder.

A mat of dark curls covered his chest, tempting her fingers to explore. Simply touching him set her blood to simmering in her veins. She raked her nails from his collarbone to his waist, glorying in his reaction. He leaned back on one elbow, breath hissing through his teeth. But he did not stop her.

He lay there for a time, allowing her to learn him as she stroked his darkly tanned skin. But he was hardly a passive participant. He undid her braid and swept the long fall of hair over her shoulders, combing his fingers through it as he drew her toward him. "Kiss me, wife," he growled, his gaze never leaving her as she moved closer.

Ian's mouth on hers spread fire over her entire body, sending more heat spiraling through her. It was a wonder she hadn't burst into flames. He stroked his hands the length of her body and back again, kneading and shaping her flesh until she arched like a cat in his arms.

She ached to feel his fingers touch her skin, and he must have sensed. He found the hem of her undertunic and began to inch it upward, dragging his fingertips in a tortuous path along her inner thigh.

She clamped her legs together, fighting the urge to let them fall open wider, to invite his touch. But Ian would have none of that.

His hand firm on her knee, he said, "Nay, love, let me touch you. Here." He traced the back of her knee, then smoothed his palm along her calf until she relaxed, savoring the caress.

He eased her back onto the cloak, maintaining the soothing, yet exciting, motion of his hand. "I want to kiss you," he whispered. "But you're wearing too many clothes."

What did clothes have to do with kissing, she wondered, but she helped him remove her undertunic. When she sat up, she ran her hands over his chest again, reveling in the way his eyes darkened even more.

Ian leaned over her and nudged the sleeve of her shift over the curve of her shoulder, making the neckline drape low over her breasts. He nipped at her neck, sending a shiver of delight down her spine.

"You're so lovely," he said, staring into her eyes. Moving slowly, he slipped the shift down to her waist.

But before she had the chance to feel exposed, he

covered her aching breasts with his hands. He continued to watch her. The combination of his hands slowly moving over her sensitive flesh and the seduction of his gaze made her body feel heavy, languorous.

Ian could have gotten lost in her eyes, could have drowned in their soothing green depths. He saw each tiny play of emotion reflected there, her reaction to the touch of his hands against the pebbled hardness of her nipples making his mouth yearn to taste them.

Her flesh was soft and sweet, a delight to his senses in the flickering light. The low moan she made when he took the rosy tip into his mouth sent a renewed surge of vigor to his already throbbing manhood.

With her attention focused on what his mouth was doing, her legs had fallen open, allowing him access to her sweetest flesh. He slipped one hand up beneath the rumpled silk of her shift and cupped her soft curls in the palm of his hand.

She arched off the cloak, hands clutching at his back. Sweat beaded on his face as he drew her nipple into his mouth, scraping his teeth gently over it as he stroked the damp petals of her womanhood.

"Ian," she moaned. She shoved at the waist of his braes, then tugged on the string until it came untied. Pushing at the loosened fabric, she managed to bare him to the knees. Keeping up the rhythmic caress with hands and mouth, he somehow got the leggings off.

His reaction when she tentatively stroked his aching flesh wasn't very different from her own. Jesu, he thought he'd spill his seed into her hands. She was ready for him, he could feel it. He didn't know if he could wait much longer.

But he had to be certain that this was what she wanted.

Pressing his hand over hers to halt the mind-stopping caress, he sat back on his heels and moved her hand away. "Lily, sweeting, look at me," he commanded softly. Her eyes drifted open, widening when she swept her gaze over his erect shaft.

She smiled.

The effect on his body was nearly as strong as if she'd put her hand upon him again.

"Do you want me? Do you want to make love with me?" he asked, his voice taut with desire.

Still smiling, she sat up and touched her fingertip to the end of his staff. "Yes." She leaned closer, dragging her hair across his thighs, the cool strands a sensuous contrast to his burning flesh. "Yes," she whispered, drawing her fingers over his chest.

When she nuzzled through the dark curls and swept the tip of her tongue over his nipple, he could endure the torment no longer.

Pulling her beneath him, he set about making her his.

Lily welcomed him with an enthusiasm that surprised him, given her inexperience. Her gaze never left him as he moved between her legs and settled into the cradle of her body, allowing her to adjust to his weight atop her. "Don't make me wait, Dragon," she whispered as she pulled him closer.

"Sometimes 'tis better to wait," he said teasingly. "I'm not through kissing you yet."

He closed her mouth with his, the rhythm he set as he thrust his tongue into her mouth echoing that of his body rubbing against hers. Her fingernails scraped along his ribs, digging in when he tore his mouth free and began kissing and licking his way down her body.

She watched him curiously as he cradled her hips within his hands and nuzzled the damp curls at the juncture of her thighs. But she was writhing wildly in his arms in no time, her voice a keening sigh as she called his name.

Ian slipped into her as her body began to spasm with satisfaction, easing his way into her grasp. Lily wrapped her legs about his hips and held him tightly, her anchor in the swirl of passion he'd begun, swiftly matching his rhythm, until she plunged with him into the throes of completion.

Lily lay pressed beneath Ian's weight, unable—and unwilling—to move. She'd never felt so tired or exhilarated in her life. She burrowed her face in his tousled curls and smiled.

"I must be crushing you," he muttered, his voice sounding as weak as she felt. He levered himself up and settled alongside her, wrapping his arm about her waist and cuddling close.

Now she knew, Lily thought. Her ignorance didn't matter after all; if anyone had tried to describe love-making to her, she never would have imagined this. And there was so much more to it than the physical actions, she realized. The sense of closeness with Ian, the yearning to be one with him—those feelings were as amazing as the explosion of sensation that still echoed through her body.

Eventually the sensations subsided. Lily stared past Ian's shoulder into the dying flames, tired, but not yet ready to sleep.

"Is this what the priest and that girl were doing?" she asked. She could feel a blush sweep over her at the thought.

Ian laughed. "Most likely. I told you before what he's like, the lecherous old bastard. He's certainly not much of a priest, though he served us well. But the last

I knew, priests were not supposed to partake of the sort of activities we just indulged in.''

He turned her to face him and kissed her lips softly, slowly. ''Enough about him. Marrying us was assuredly the best deed he's performed in a very long time. Now we're wed, we're free to indulge as often as we like. If it pleases you,'' he added. Taking her hand in his, he nibbled at her fingertips, renewing the echoes of passion lingering in her body. ''Did you like what we did?'' he asked, his gaze assessing.

What a stupid question! ''If I liked it any better, I would probably be lying here unconscious,'' she told him. '''Tis no wonder the Church tells us 'tis a sin. Once indulged, I think this appetite must become stronger, never to be satisfied.''

''Hungry again?'' he asked, his lips quirked upward in a devilish smile. ''If you're not, what tidbit might I give you to whet your appetite, milady?''

Lily ran her glance over him from head to toe, taking her time and enjoying every detail of the journey. It appeared that even her eyes' caress had an effect upon him, bringing his manhood erect and making the pulse in his neck throb faster.

'Twas a powerful feeling, to know she could cause such a reaction without even laying a hand upon him. It made her wonder what he would do when she finally did touch him. Smiling, she decided to find out.

Fingers digging into the dark curls on his chest, she pushed him back on the cloak they used as a blanket. He folded his arms behind his head and smiled. ''Do with me whatever you wish,'' he told her. ''Our bodies hold a wealth of pleasures. Explore them with me. I promise I won't mind.''

His eyes hinted at delights she had yet to experience.

His face and body dared her, tempted her, to partake of them with him.

Uncertain where to start, Lily placed her open hands upon the corded muscles of his chest and kneaded the hard planes of his stomach with gentle strokes. Firelight flickered over his body, painting him with its warm glow. Dark hair curled around her fingers, the crisp texture making her breasts tingle in remembrance of that wiry mat rubbing against her nipples.

She covered his face with kisses, enjoying the sound of his indrawn breath whenever she did something he liked. And it seemed to her that he liked practically everything she did.

He lay there and allowed her to explore his body, satisfying her curiosity—and increasing her own desire.

Finally his hands snaked out from beneath his head and, grabbing her about the waist, he set her atop him. "Take me now, Lily," he groaned.

Curious about this new position—and aching for his possession—she sank down upon his shaft, delighting in the fact that she was in control. Now was her chance to make him squirm.

But the sensations were too intense to endure for long. Much too quickly, it seemed, pleasure overtook her, and any sense of control disappeared. Moaning, Lily slumped over Ian as he, too, surrendered to passion.

Lily fell asleep still atop him, and awoke to find him staring up at her. A faint trace of sunlight crept beneath the flimsy door.

"Good morrow, wife," he whispered, drawing her down for a kiss.

He held her attention quite thoroughly with his lips,

and she felt herself start to drift into the fog of passion she'd inhabited the night before.

But they didn't have the time to indulge themselves now.

"Shouldn't we be going?" she asked when they paused for breath.

"Regrettably, yes," he said with a sigh.

Lily tried to roll off him and discovered that she could scarcely move. Ian assisted her in sitting up. She realized she was sore in many places. She hadn't hurt when he made her his, but she hurt now. Sitting atop the horse today would be painful, she could tell that already. Still, she smiled. Last night had been worth every twinge.

"Are you all right, sweeting?" Ian asked, scooping her into his arms and setting her on her feet.

"Just give me a little time to move about and I'll be fine," she told him as she clung to his arm.

He watched her closely when she stepped away from him and bent to pick up her undertunic. "I apologize," he said. "Here, sit. I'll get everything ready to go." He knelt down beside her. "I shouldn't have been greedy," he said. "I didn't realize how sore you'd be."

"I'll be fine, Ian, once I get moving. We cannot stay here," she pointed out. "If the men who came to Ashby were truly looking for us, we need to get to l'Eau Clair soon."

"I know." Although his voice seemed calm, normal, she could see concern in his eyes, and his face was set in stern lines.

He helped her dress, then offered her food and mead. She accepted the food eagerly, for she was hungry after their exertions of the previous night. Once he'd smothered the dying fire, they went on their way.

Ian tried to make it easier for her, but even though she sat pillion before him, cushioned on a folded shirt, every jolt of the horse brought a new twinge of discomfort. Finally, in an effort to distract her, Ian began to sing in a low voice.

Most of the songs were lewd, probably worse than they sounded. She didn't understand half of the words. Many of the things she did understand sounded physically impossible. She asked him to explain some of the songs, and he soon had her doubled up with laughter.

"You're jesting, aren't you?" she asked after he told her what one song meant. "People don't really do those things—" she gazed up at him through her lashes "—do they?"

"Certainly they do," he said, eyes twinkling in return. "Would you like to try—"

"No!" She poked him in the ribs. "You aren't serious, are you?"

He loved how huge her eyes became when she couldn't decide if he was joking. She knew so little of the world; he could see that some of the songs shocked her, though they weren't shocking at all. Many were soldiers' ditties, true, but others were sung in noble households.

He wondered yet again if he'd done her a grave disservice by wedding her so soon after she emerged from the abbey. What if she came to regret marrying him after she became more accustomed to everyday life? What of his duties for Llywelyn? Assuming the prince would allow him back into favor, Ian knew he might have to do things that would disgust Lily. How would he bear it if she turned away?

Already he couldn't stand the thought of leaving her. If their lives ever returned to normal, he'd have to leave

her on occasion, whether on the prince's business or on
his own.

Simply thinking of it made him ache with loneliness—he who had never minded being alone.

And what would he do if the prince refused to allow
him back into his service? That Llywelyn would be angry over this, Ian had no doubt. Clearly, he'd intended
Lily's existence to remain a secret until he had need of
her.

'Twas no use thinking of it yet again. He'd only grow
angry himself—again. He'd be better served to make
certain that he and Lily arrived at l'Eau Clair as soon
as possible. Gillian's keep was located more toward the
English side of the marches—hence its strategic importance to Llywelyn. They'd be safer there, while they
decided what to do next.

Ian scanned their surroundings. When they left the
hut this morn, the sun had been out, although there had
been numerous patches of fog to obscure the way. But
the sun had disappeared by noon, leaving the day
shrouded in gloom. He had the feeling that it would
start to rain again soon, and he knew of no place in this
area convenient for shelter.

Although Lily hadn't complained, she had to be dam-
nably uncomfortable. But she kept it hidden, laughing
at his songs, asking him about his sister and Nicholas,
making the time pass quickly for both of them. She
carried such joy within her, and she was unstinting
about sharing it with him.

He'd remember their first night together for the rest
of his life. Lily had given him a gift, a feeling he'd
never before shared. In the past, lovemaking had been
an urge to be satisfied, like hunger or thirst. But sharing

passion with Lily had been different from anything he'd felt before. Already he yearned for more.

They crested a steep hill and stopped to rest the horse before venturing down the narrow path on the other side. He dismounted and turned to help Lily from the saddle.

Suddenly her welcoming smile changed to an expression of horror. "Ian!" she screamed.

He jerked his sword free as he whirled and they fell upon him.

Four men, well armed with swords and daggers—and the element of surprise. Ian kicked and slashed, dodging many, but not all, of their blows. Rocks clattered down the slope, striking one of the men a stunning blow.

So now there were three.

Suddenly hooves thundered down the path and into their midst. His horse leaped into the thick of the fight, feet flying. The stallion kicked out, scattering the men straight into a hail of stones.

Lily knelt above them, shrieking abuse as she pitched rock after rock down the slope. Most of them missed their targets, but she kept at it.

Ian took the opportunity afforded by her harassment to continue his attack. Between the rocks, the horse and his sword, eventually the band of attackers were subdued. The last man surrendered with a whimper, once he saw that he faced the Dragon alone.

"There's rope in the saddlebag," he called to Lily after he calmed the stallion and discovered that the packs had fallen off the saddle, halfway down the hillside. "Can you find it?"

She scrambled about on the loose rocks, then flopped onto the grassy verge to dig through the bag, grimacing as she squirmed. She tossed the rope down to him, and he jerked out of the way just in time.

All four men had injuries, but none appeared life-threatening. He trussed them up and left them sitting alongside the path. Their weapons he pitched over a nearby cliff.

"Who sent you?"

"'Twas Llywelyn, milord. Said as how you'd gone missing, along with something he values greatly. Offered us a reward if we brought you back to him. Said you're an outlaw now."

By Christ's bones! He hadn't thought it would come to this. He'd underestimated his overlord greatly, it seemed. They had to get moving. Now. There was no telling how many others Llywelyn had sent after them.

"Someone will travel this track eventually," he told them, his voice as cold as ice. "You'll survive till then, I imagine." He whistled the horse over and checked the saddle. "If some animal doesn't get to you first."

He lifted Lily onto the saddle carefully, but still he couldn't miss the fleeting look of pain in her eyes. Swinging up behind her, he scanned the sky. Heavy black clouds scudded across the heavens, and lightning flashed and thundered in the distance.

He spurred the horse on, hoping to reach lower land before the storm reached them. These hills were dangerous under the best of conditions, and in a storm they could be deadly.

Lily clung to the saddle as the stallion slid down the rock-strewn hillside. Sensing the oncoming storm, the animal rolled his eyes wildly. Ian had his hands full keeping the beast from bolting when thunder boomed nearby.

The rising wind was strong, blowing sticks, leaves

and dirt into their faces and making it difficult to see. "We've got to find a place to wait this out!" he shouted to Lily. She nodded and huddled deeper in his arms.

They reached the small valley at the bottom of the mountain just as the clouds opened up and sent a torrent pouring over them. It had gotten so dark, especially down here in the glen, that he could scarcely see ten feet before them.

The stallion plodded on, head hanging low as he forged through the wind. Ian wrapped himself about Lily, protecting her as best he could.

He didn't know how long they traveled thus, plunging into the darkness for want of a place to shelter. It had obviously been too long, for he could have sworn he heard snatches of song in between the near-constant rumbling of thunder.

Flickering light shone up ahead, and Ian headed for it. Before long, he realized they were moving toward the mouth of a cave.

A fire burned merrily under the overhang, flaring up when the wind gusted. Ian halted the horse and slipped from the saddle, then pulled Lily into his arms.

A figure walked toward them from inside the cave, a dark shape silhouetted against the fire. Ian couldn't distinguish more, but friend or foe, they were going into the cave.

The man stepped out into the light.

Lily gasped and clutched Ian's shoulders tightly.

He started to laugh when he saw the man's face.

It was Siwardson.

Chapter Fourteen

"Dragon, Lily. Well met. Come, join me by the fire." Siwardson reached out to take Lily, but Ian had no intention of handing her over to him.

He nodded to the Viking as he walked past him into the cave, then knelt to lower Lily onto the ground near the leaping flames. The icy rain had soaked her cloak, and she'd begun to shiver. Her teeth chattered hard. He had to get her warm—quickly.

Siwardson rummaged through a bundle leaning against the back wall, then brought them a blanket. Ian stripped away Lily's sodden cloak and wrapped the blanket about her, then sat behind her and drew her into his arms to give her his warmth, as well.

Siwardson's face, as always, looked cheerful. Ian couldn't tell what went on behind those pale blue eyes, a fact that infuriated him.

But he'd take it as a good sign that he hadn't seen Siwardson's infamous knife yet.

Still, it wouldn't hurt to question him, see if he could discover what the Viking was doing out here. 'Twas far too coincidental, under the circumstances.

"Tell me, Siwardson—will I have to fight you again anytime soon?"

"Nay, Dragon, not at all." He grinned, his teeth flashing white in the firelight. "You won. It was a fair fight. And I like your sense of humor. I hadn't realized before then that you had one."

Sense of humor—?

"'Twas a good trick, tying me up that way. I'd never have thought of it, myself. The scratches are nothing now, though they stung like the devil at the time. But it took a while to untangle myself from that bush. Excellent idea," he added, his deep voice warm with admiration.

Ian shook his head. He couldn't understand Siwardson. It probably wasn't worth it to try.

"Are you like the others now, out to capture the Dragon and claim the reward?" Ian asked. "Or do you seek revenge upon me?"

Siwardson snorted. "Don't include me with the idiots your prince sent out looking for you. He declared you outlaw soon after I left. I haven't been back. I didn't want to be there once he realized that I'd handed Lily over to you, not the abbess." He poked at the fire with a stick, staring into the flames. Then he looked up suddenly, snaring Ian with that icy gaze. His eyes were bright with humor. "I didn't want to tell him that I'd handed her over to *you*."

"Why?" Ian truly didn't understand. "And why did you allow me to take her?"

He shrugged. "She belongs with you. I could tell that from the start. And a woman like Lily should not be locked away as a pawn in a game not of her making."

Ian was impressed. The Viking was obviously much more intelligent than he let on.

"You were correct. Lily does belong with me, in the eyes of God, at least. We were married last night."

"Good, good," Siwardson said, nodding. "Perhaps now Llywelyn will think twice about locking away the Dragon's mate."

"If you left before Llywelyn named me outlaw, how did you know about it?" Ian asked, puzzled.

"Once it stops raining, I'll show the source of my information. You might be able to learn something of value from them, as well."

"More men from Dolwyddelan?"

"Aye. Four of them. There were five, but one died," Swen said in a matter-of-fact voice. "I left them trussed up out there." He motioned toward the forest beyond the cave. "I didn't feel like looking at them."

Lily stirred within his arms.

"Are you getting warmer, sweeting?" Ian asked. He moved the blanket away from her face. Her skin was pale, except for the two spots of bright color riding high along her cheekbones. But she'd stopped shaking.

Her eyes drifted open. "Did I hear Swen?" she asked, her voice husky with sleep.

"Aye," Ian murmured near her ear.

She wriggled about, trying to escape the constricting folds of the blanket. "We must go!" she cried. "He'll try to take you back to Llywelyn—"

"Hush, 'tis all right."

She stared at Siwardson, clearly attempting to judge the threat he posed. But, as usual, the Viking just grinned. She wouldn't be able to tell much from that.

"Swen, do you swear you're not here to take us back?" she asked, her voice gaining strength with every word.

He nodded, hand over his heart. "I have no intention of doing such a thing."

"Then why *are* you here?" She sat up straight, not leaning her weight so heavily upon Ian. He tightened his arms about her, unwilling to release her just yet.

Siwardson picked up a metal cup set near the fire and brought it to her. She accepted the warm drink—ale, from the smell of it—and sipped at it, waiting patiently.

Siwardson's face settled into sober lines, the rare serious expression lending an entirely different cast to his attractive features. He looked dangerous now, Ian thought. He looked deadly.

He'd known the man as a decent fighter, but despite that, and his great size, he'd not considered him a threat. He would have to revise his estimation of him now.

"I could stay at Dolwyddelan no longer," Siwardson said. "What Llywelyn wanted me to do felt wrong, and I owe him no allegiance. I came here to negotiate trade between my father and the prince, not to help him as he carries out some vengeance upon you." Disgust colored his voice, lending it a sinister air. "I don't make war upon women. Whatever you did, I cannot believe you deserve to be locked away in an abbey. It would be a terrible waste."

Ian and Lily shared a look; then they both laughed. Ian wondered what reason Llywelyn had given Siwardson for sending Lily to the convent. Whatever the reason, it obviously hadn't mattered to him.

"Were you taking me to Saint Winifred's?" Ian could feel Lily shaking again, but he didn't think it was from the cold. It was probably from laughter, or disbelief.

Siwardson nodded. "'Tis a damned shame to lock

away a beautiful woman like that,'' he said, clearly angry. "It would be an outrage.''

"I thank you for saving me from that fate. But if Ian hadn't arrived and fought you, where would you have brought me?''

"I hadn't really decided. Probably to my father's home in the North Lands.'' His face creased into a smile again. "But I knew the Dragon would find us before then.''

"How could you know that?''

He shrugged again. "I just knew.'' He rose and searched through his pack, then returned with food. They accepted it with thanks.

He did not join them. "What did you do, Lily, to anger Llywelyn?'' he asked. "It must have been something terrible.''

"She angered him by escaping the abbey,'' Ian said.

"You'd been there before?'' he asked, surprise coloring his voice.

"I lived there all my life.''

"Then why—?''

"I have only myself to blame for everything that's happened,'' Lily said. "I came to Dolwyddelan in search of answers, answers I believed only Llywelyn could supply. But he didn't want to tell me. He didn't want me, or anyone else, to know.''

"We've spoiled a scheme he's nurtured for almost twenty years,'' Ian added. "He'll not forgive us—especially me—for that.''

Siwardson appeared more confused than before, but Ian didn't intend to tell him anything further at this point. He still wasn't certain he could trust him, not since he'd seen the man behind the mask of humor.

"May we stay here by your fire for the night?" he asked.

"Of course. You are welcome."

Ian noticed that Siwardson held his dagger in his hands. He was toying with the weapon. Ian thought the man looked nervous. It must be a trick of the light, he decided. Siwardson didn't strike him as the type of man to become nervous about anything.

"My father will be enraged when he hears that I have angered Llywelyn," he said, staring at his knife. "He wanted to set up a trade route with the Welsh very badly. I'm sure that will be impossible now." He finally looked up and met Ian's gaze. "I wish to join your household, Dragon. If you will allow me to."

"Why?" Could Llywelyn have sent Siwardson as a spy? Everything he said might be true, but how did he know the Viking had really fought men who were after him? It might be a lie, and this might be a trap.

Still, the man was a bold fighter. If he was loyal, it would be an asset to have him on their side.

"You are a warrior," Siwardson said. "I respect that, and I admire your courage. Few men would be willing to risk what they already have to do what is right. And it is a fine thing to go into battle at a warrior's side." His mouth quirked up into a smile, different from his usual mirth. "Besides, I like your sense of humor."

"I will think on it," Ian told him. He didn't need to decide tonight. He would have been vigilant, staying here with Lily, even if he knew he could trust Siwardson. There would be plenty of time to ponder it, while Lily slept.

Despite her protests, Ian carried Lily to a place along the wall and lay between her and the entrance to the cave. His sword within easy reach, he kept watch over her.

Sometime during the night, Swen rose and left the cave. Ian feigned sleep until the other man left, then followed him outside.

It seemed he'd only gone to answer nature's call. Ian stayed far enough away to give him privacy, but he refused to simply accept what he thought to be true and go back into the cave.

Siwardson came up beside him. "I thought you were awake," he said quietly.

Ian scanned the trees surrounding them, although it was virtually impossible to see far. The rain had died down to a drizzle, but once again fog shrouded the land.

The flesh on the back of Ian's neck tingled. "Something's not right here," he murmured. He tightened his grip on his sword.

Siwardson looked back the way he'd just come, his face uneasy. "I went to check on the men I left out there. Two more have died—the others were sleeping. I feel it, too—like someone is out there. And it's not those men."

A rustling in the bushes startled them both, and they leaped forward, until a rabbit came bounding out of the trees. "Jesu," Ian snarled, heart thundering in his chest.

"Amen," Siwardson agreed.

Suddenly there was movement and noise everywhere.

Two men jumped from the overhang above the cave, while an unknown number swarmed from the trees and headed for them, weapons flying.

"The fire!" Ian cried, whirling to douse the flames. The light shone like a beacon in the darkness, marking where they stood as clearly as any banner in battle.

Siwardson laid about him with his sword and knife,

kicking and dodging and laughing like a lunatic. Ian stomped out the blaze, sending sparks flying into the air and singeing his clothes in the process.

In the last flare of light, he spied Lily, crouched in the back of the cave, both hands wrapped about the hilt of Dai's sword. Her hair swirled all around her, giving her the look of an avenging angel in the dying light.

He kicked dirt over the last embers, plunging them into darkness.

He couldn't worry about her now, he told himself as he jumped into the fray. He and Siwardson would survive, and so would Lily.

But to ensure that, he needed to keep his mind upon his work.

A glorious surge of battle lust roared through Ian's veins, lending him the strength and agility he needed to vanquish these foes. They had the advantage of numbers, plus the element of surprise in the dark, but he and the Viking were clearly the superior fighters.

The darkness sharpened his senses so that he felt where his opponent would be, heard the sounds of his breathing. Instinct took over.

He wound up back-to-back with Siwardson as they finished off what seemed to be the last two attackers. Afterward, they leaned against each other for a moment, catching their breath.

Ian realized he heard nothing from the cave. "Lily?" he called. She didn't answer. He headed for the cave, while Siwardson quickly stirred up the embers. There was enough spark left to kindle a stick. He didn't wait for the light; with the other man trailing behind him with the torch, he turned to where he'd left Lily.

He found her slumped over a body. He grabbed the torch from Siwardson and shoved the end of the stick into the ground. Then, grasping her about the shoulders, he lifted her away from the corpse.

Blood covered the front of her gown and dripped from her hands, but she appeared unharmed. "I killed him!" she sobbed, holding her hands out before her, horror in her eyes as she stared at them.

She had pierced the man straight through the chest with Dai's sword. He was amazed she'd been able to drive the heavy weapon with such force; the blade had passed straight through.

Siwardson joined them. "Good work, milady," he said cheerfully as he surveyed the scene.

She snarled and reached for him with her bloody hands. "I killed a man. You call that good work?"

He evaded her grasp. "Aye. Otherwise, 'twould be your bloody corpse lying here. Which would you prefer?" he asked pointedly.

She met his gaze for a moment, then lowered hers to her hands. Picking up the hem of her gown, where the blood hadn't reached, she began to wipe her hands.

"Are you hurt?" Ian asked. He felt shaken, looking at the body and Lily and thinking of how it might have turned out. He sat back against the wall, suddenly grateful for the support.

"No. 'Twas just the one." She looked up from her skirts. "And you?"

Swen grabbed Lily's victim by the heels and dragged him out of the cave, then returned with Dai's sword, wiping the blade clean on a scrap of material. "The Dragon is as skilled in battle as I had heard. I wish there had been light, so that I might have seen him better."

Ian snorted. "You were busy enough yourself. If you'd stopped to watch me, we'd be laying out your body come morning."

Ian's words sank into Lily's still-stunned brain. He could have been killed—they all could have. It amazed her that they had survived, while apparently none of the others had. It was a testament to the skill of both men—and perhaps herself, she thought with a swift glance at the puddle of blood in the dirt.

How had they known, she wondered? She hadn't suspected an attack in the night, during a storm. And she hadn't heard a thing until the battle began.

She knew that the sound her attacker had made as the sword blade slid into his body would haunt her dreams. And even though she was glad she'd survived, still it was no easy thing to take someone's life.

In truth, taking a life *was* easy; 'twas living with what she had done that would prove the most difficult.

Now that the battle was over, she felt drained, exhausted. Her entire body ached and throbbed with pain. She'd been through so much in the past weeks, both physically and emotionally, that she couldn't think clearly.

But she didn't regret a moment of it. She shook her head. Not so long ago, she'd believed that she would need to travel to foreign lands to find adventure.

God help her, 'twas all she could do to survive right here at home.

At first light, Ian roused Lily from sleep with a steamy kiss. "Come with me, wife. I've a gift for you."

Curious, she dragged her aching body off the ground and tried to stand. But her legs refused to cooperate, and she slumped against Ian, groaning.

"No matter," he said as he swept her into his arms and carried her from the cave. "Your weight's not like to cripple me."

She poked him in the ribs, and he swooped his arms as if to drop her. Smiling, she clung to his broad shoulders and kissed his stubble-covered cheek.

The sun shone down on them as brightly as if yesterday's storm were nothing more than a dream. Ian carried her away from the cave and into the trees, which had been washed clean by the rain. The air smelled fresh, scented with pine.

Although morning's chill lent a bite to the air, it wasn't unpleasant.

They broke through the trees into a small glade. A waterfall splashed down onto moss-covered rocks, and mist rose from the surface of the pool.

It looked to be a place of magic, set here among the craggy hills.

Ian lowered her to her feet next to the pool. "Would you like to bathe?" he asked with a glance at her blood-stained clothes.

She found the thought appealing, though the water was bound to be cold as ice. Still, it wouldn't do to arrive at her sister's gates in her present state. There was little enough she could do about her clothes, but at least she would be clean.

She bent and trailed her fingers in the pool, gasping in surprise at the warmth of the water. Ian watched her, clearly enjoying her reaction. "Now what do you think of your gift?" he asked, grinning.

"It's wonderful," she said, grinning. "I only wish I had a gift for you."

His fingers toyed with the laces of her gown. "You do."

She looked at him questioningly.

He leaned down and captured her lips in the softest of kisses. "You."

"What if Swen should come while we're here?" she asked, eyeing the pool longingly now. She could already imagine the warm, soothing water caressing her aching body—and Ian's hard, callused hands working their magic upon her, as well.

"He's already been here. He found it yesterday, when he was looking for a place to put Llywelyn's men. He's agreed to stand guard, lest more fools come in search of us." He knelt and slipped off her shoes. "No one will see us here," he assured her as he removed the rest of her clothes.

Still uncomfortable about Ian seeing her nude, Lily sank into the pool's warm embrace and watched him disrobe. Sunlight highlighted the muscular planes and whipcord leanness of his body. The warmth she felt now had little to do with the water, and everything to do with her husband.

He joined her, scrubbing playfully at her hands, then urged her to stand in the waist-deep water while he moved his ministrations to the rest of body. In turn, she ran her hands over him in a teasing foray. She captured his swollen shaft beneath the water, cupping him in her hands with a boldness that surprised her.

His tongue darted out to capture the stray droplets scattered over her shoulders, then followed the water's path down over the curves of her breasts. Never ceasing her own caresses, she used her free hand to press his head to her bosom as he suckled her aching nipples.

He licked his way back up her body, then melded his mouth to hers in a sipping, tasting kiss. Placing his hands about her waist, he drew her into deeper water, then lowered her onto his shaft.

Lily moaned at the onslaught of sensation flooding her. Ian's heat within her, the warm water caressing them, and the delicate mastery of Ian's mouth on hers, swiftly sent spasms of release flooding through her. His mouth tight against hers, Ian groaned as he joined her in satisfaction.

Arms and legs still wrapped about Ian, Lily slowly returned to an awareness of her surroundings. The air was cold now on her wet flesh, and she felt exposed, self-conscious.

"What is it?" Ian asked. He kissed her tenderly and held her more tightly when she clung to him.

"I feel strange here...like this," she mumbled against the brawny curve of his shoulder. "May we get out now?"

His gaze searching, Ian examined her face and stared into her eyes. "I didn't hurt you, did I?"

"No. 'Tis just that I feel so exposed, out here in the open. What if more of those men come here looking for you?" she asked, her voice shaking.

He carried her from the pool and wrapped his shirt about her. "We'll be all right, Lily. Don't worry." He rummaged in the pouch on his belt and pulled out her comb. "Just concentrate on where we're headed. We'll be at l'Eau Clair before nightfall."

She took the comb and worked it through her tangled hair as Ian rinsed the blood from her bliaut and wrung it out. "You'll have to wear just your shift and undertunic for now," he told her. "But perhaps by the time we're close, this will be dry enough to put on."

The bliaut bore little resemblance to the lovely gown she'd put on at Ashby. Faded, bloodstained, wrinkled and torn beyond repair. She'd look an impressive sight to meet her sister, she thought with dismay. Yet it wasn't anyone's fault—and she hoped it wouldn't matter to Gillian. It was only a dress.

She could blame Llywelyn, she supposed, though that would grow old quickly. She held him responsible for much of what had happened of late.

Still, they would triumph over him, of that Lily had no doubt. Neither she nor Ian was a person to give up easily. For something as important as this, they'd never give up.

Wearing his braes and boots, Ian came to retrieve his shirt and help her dress. "You are so lovely," he whispered against her cheek. He smoothed her still-damp hair away from her face. "I am the most fortunate of men."

Lily couldn't help wondering, as they headed back to the cave, why Ian's words had held the sound of good-bye.

Chapter Fifteen

The rest of the journey to l'Eau Clair passed without further attacks, but it was still a hellish trip. The previous day's storm had washed out the trail, leaving mud and rocks for them to navigate as best they could. And Swen insisted on bringing his two remaining prisoners, which slowed them even more.

Lily's first sight of her sister's keep took her breath away. Silhouetted against the setting sun, l'Eau Clair looked beautiful—and powerful. Like Ashby, it was a true Norman stronghold, a symbol of Norman might perched upon the Welsh frontier.

The village appeared newly built, the freshly thatched cottages laid out in a neat pattern of straight streets. "The town burned to the ground last year," Ian told her. "'Twas another of our kinsmen who was responsible for it." Hatred echoed through his voice. "You may find that belonging to this family is more than you bargained for."

The guards at the gate knew Ian. They were admitted to the bailey—almost empty of people, since it was nearly suppertime—and swiftly brought into the keep. A deferential manservant led them to Gillian and Rannulf's private quarters, then excused himself with a bow.

Ian had sent the two prisoners to the captain of the guard, and Swen had come into the keep with them. Lily knew that Ian had been suspicious of Swen, but evidently the Viking's actions during the battle last night had convinced him of Swen's sincerity. She doubted Ian would have brought him into l'Eau Clair, otherwise.

They stood outside the closed door for a moment. "Are you ready?" Ian asked, his eyes searching her face. For the first time since their lovemaking this morning, his gaze held warmth, concern. All day she'd been treated to the Dragon's impersonal care, but now, it appeared, Ian had returned.

She smoothed her hands down the front of her rumpled bliaut, then decided to pull her cloak closed over the much-abused gown. She admitted to herself that she was trying to hide within the cloak's voluminous folds. But she could not hide forever.

She appreciated Ian's support, though she'd have managed without it, if she'd had to. She nodded, and Ian knocked on the door.

"Come in," a woman called.

Ian opened the door and motioned for Lily to precede him and Swen into the chamber. She stopped just inside the chamber, scarcely leaving enough room for the men to enter.

Lily paid them no mind. All her attention was focused on the scene before her.

A finely dressed woman sat in a chair beside the hearth, some sewing in her lap, her head thrown back in laughter as she gazed with obvious affection upon the chubby infant sitting astride a man's back as he crawled on hands and knees across the rug-strewn floor.

The woman looked up at the sound of the door swinging closed. "Ian!" Tossing aside the sewing, she ran across the room and launched herself into his arms.

"Rannulf, do get up," she called. "Ian is here."

She kissed Ian on both cheeks, her hands touching his arms and shoulders as she stepped back a pace and looked him over from head to toe.

"You need rest, I can tell. You haven't been taking proper care of yourself. What have you been about?" she asked.

The man reached around and swung the child up in his arms as he came to his feet. "Perhaps if you'd stop chattering like a magpie, my love, he could tell you." He tugged his shirt collar out of the baby's mouth. "He's brought guests." He stepped closer to Lily and held out his hand to her. "You'll have to excuse my wife—she hasn't seen Ian in months. Please, milady, come in and be comfortable."

She placed her hand in his and allowed him to lead her to a seat by the fire. She felt as though she were watching everything through thick glass, the colors vivid but remote, distanced.

Dear God, Gillian looked like their mother, startlingly so. Her coloring was similar, down to the dark, coppery braids draped over her shoulders.

But she'd never seen that expression of contentment on her mother's face.

Gillian released Ian and smoothed her hands over the skirt of her dark green gown. A tinge of pink stained her face. "I beg your pardon. Ian, please introduce our guests."

"Rannulf, Gillian—this is the newest member of my

household, Swen Siwardson,'' he said, motioning Swen farther into the room. A typical grin on his face, Swen came forward and made his bow, lingering over Gillian's hand until the blush of color on her cheeks deepened.

Lily cast a quick look at Gillian's husband—her brother-by-marriage—to gauge his reaction to the flirtatious Viking's attention to his wife. She was pleased to note that he simply smiled at the byplay. He'd obviously taken Swen's measure already.

Ian then crossed the chamber and stood at Lily's side. He reached down and slipped the hood back from her hair, draping the material over her shoulders. She leaned into his touch, grateful for it now, when her nerves felt so raw. Her stomach had been twisted in knots ever since l'Eau Clair came into view; it was a struggle to keep from simply giving in to the urge to jump up from her seat and race from the room.

Courage, she told herself. She'd faced down the Dragon himself, more than once, and survived to tell the tale. She felt Ian's gaze upon her face and glanced up to find him waiting patiently. She reached up and touched his hand before he spoke again. He squeezed her fingers reassuringly. "And this is my wife, Lily.''

Rannulf immediately swept into a bow, graceful despite the child clinging to him. "I am honored, milady.'' He took her hand again, this time raising it to his lips. "Welcome to the family.''

She could see why he hadn't seemed to find anything amiss in Swen's greeting. His own manner charmed her, the expression on his handsome face making her feel special. Lord Nicholas had been the same; perhaps it was a Norman trait, or else they simply had more refined manners than the few Welshmen she'd met.

"Trying to entice my wife with your courtly ways, FitzClifford?" Ian asked dryly.

"'Tis the least I can do, considering the greeting you received from my wife when you walked through the door," Rannulf retorted, laughing. "She didn't even notice anyone else was here."

Lily stood when Gillian approached her, dropping into a deep curtsy. "'Tis a pleasure to meet you at last," she told Gillian. "Ian has told me much about you."

"Then you have the advantage over me, milady," Gillian said, her eyes questioning as she examined Lily's face.

Whatever she found must have met with her approval, for she nodded once and smiled. "When did you marry, Ian?" she asked, her gaze still fixed on Lily's face. "And why were we not invited?"

Ian nudged Lily to sit, then stood behind her chair, his hands resting on her shoulders. She reached up and touched his hand once again, gaining comfort from the contact.

She didn't know what to say, what to do. Ian hadn't told them anything, and Gillian continued to observe her. Mayhap she would be thus with any woman Ian brought to them; from their surprise, it seemed he'd never brought anyone here before.

"'Tis a long and strange tale," he said. "It could take a while in the telling."

"Then sit and be comfortable," Rannulf said. He went to the door and called for the child's nurse, then sent a servant for food and wine.

They spoke of inconsequential things until the supper arrived and everyone had been served. Then Rannulf motioned for Ian to begin.

"What I'm about to tell you might be difficult for you to hear, Gillian," Ian said.

She sent him a questioning look. "I thought 'twas your tale, and Lily's."

"It is. But it begins before our marriage. Indeed, it begins before Lily's birth."

Ignoring the food before him, Ian stood and prowled the room with a restless gait. Lily met his gaze and smiled reassuringly. Smiling in return, he appeared to steel himself for the task ahead, taking up his goblet of mead and drinking deeply of the brew.

"Lily and I met when I discovered her clinging to the curtain wall round Dolwyddelan."

Gillian gasped; Rannulf looked interested. Swen, as usual, just grinned.

Lily stared down at her hands, clasped nervously in her lap. She didn't want to watch their faces after all, she decided. 'Twas too difficult to try to interpret their reactions.

And what if she saw disgust in their faces?

"After I pulled Lily the rest of the way up the wall, she told me—eventually—her reason for attempting such a desperate feat. She needed to see Llywelyn. When she couldn't get in to see the prince by more conventional means—such as through a door," he added with a wry smile, "she thought to climb in and find him herself. She's fortunate she didn't get herself killed."

"Sounds like something you might try, my love," Rannulf said to Gillian, grinning when she sent him a disgusted glare.

"I locked her up in a cell, since she appeared to be so dangerous." Ian paused behind Lily's chair and bent to place a kiss on the top of her head. "I went to

Llywelyn and told him what Lily sought, why she'd been so desperate to talk with him. He seemed completely uninterested in her tale, and claimed he knew nothing about her."

"But what did you wish to know?" Gillian asked. "What was so important you were willing to risk your life to gain it?"

Lily looked up. "I wanted to know who I am."

Gillian seemed puzzled. "Do you mean to say you've lost your memory? I've heard of such. 'Tis a terrible thing!"

"Nay, milady. It's just that I've lived all my life behind the walls of Saint Winifred's Abbey. I knew nothing of where I'd come from, or who I am. I escaped that prison to seek the answers to those questions, and to see something of the world."

Ian placed his hand on her shoulder. "I helped Lily to find the information she sought. What we discovered will be important to you, Gillian, as well as to Lily."

Lily felt as though someone were examining her. Scanning the faces surrounding her, she found Rannulf gazing at her, then his wife, with a curious expression on his face. When she offered him a slight, nervous smile, he stared more intently at her.

"Get on with it, Ian," Rannulf said, his voice vibrating with suppressed excitement.

Running his hand through his already disordered dark curls, Ian sighed. "I don't know any other way to tell you this but straight out. Gillian, when your mother left here all those years ago, she did not die, as Llywelyn told your father. Instead, the prince took advantage of her confusion at the time, and told her that both you and Simon were dead. He took her to live as a boarder at Saint Winifred's Abbey. Your sister was born there six months later.''

Unable to resist, Lily watched Gillian's face as Ian told her. She saw confusion give way to anger, then dawning recognition. Scarcely daring to hope that it was acceptance she'd seen, Lily stood and waited until Gillian rose from her chair and came to stand before her.

''You are my sister,'' she said. She touched Lily's cheek with a gentle hand and examined her face carefully. ''She has the eyes, don't you think, Ian?'' She looked up at him. ''They're from the Welsh side, I believe, for yours are very similar.''

Rannulf stood. ''There's more to the story than this, unless I miss my guess.''

''Aye,'' Ian agreed. ''Thus far, I've only told you the happy news. Unfortunately, there is much more, and little of it good.''

Gillian drew a chair nearer to Lily's and sat beside her, glancing over at her as though to reassure herself that Lily was real. ''We have much to talk about, you and I,'' Gillian said. ''There are many years to make up for.'' She gave Lily's hand a squeeze.

Ian took another turn about the room, paused to poke at the fire. ''The information I've learned gives an entirely new meaning to several things that have happened to members of our family these past few years. I believe that Llywelyn, despite his protestations of familial loyalty, and his professed outrage over Steffan's despicable actions, has instead been doing his best all these years to gain possession or control of l'Eau Clair.'' He laughed, but it was a mirthless sound, and his face was cold, bitter over this betrayal.

''If he were the force behind it, much begins to make sense,'' Rannulf said. ''When Simon died, Llywelyn never came to Gillian's aid, despite her pleas—but Steffan did arrive here and try to gain access to the keep. And the times Steffan abducted our women—he escaped punishment for that, as well, until we meted out justice.''

Ian nodded. "I'm so suspicious now that I could even believe Llywelyn set events in motion for Simon to find Lowri wandering, injured and confused, in the forest near here. The fact that they married has certainly served him well. He's had a direct connection to a powerful marcher lord and his keep."

Gillian shuddered, and Lily noticed that her face had gone pale. "I always wondered how Steffan, that slimy worm, managed to avoid paying for his sins. Llywelyn never could give me an answer to that." Her eyes flashed angrily. "Now I know why. Damn him!"

Rannulf's handsome face was set in stern lines. "And I can just imagine how this all goes together. Quite an elaborate scheme, I've no doubt. Tell me this, Ian—are Gillian and I, and our daughter, meant to survive?" Lily heard Gillian gasp. "Or do you think some disaster will befall us, leaving the way clear for Simon's other legitimate heir to step in and take up the reins of l'Eau Clair?"

"With Llywelyn's blessing," Ian said evenly. Then he smiled, a dangerous dragon's smile. "But we have beat him at his own game, I trust. A plan such as that depends upon Lily being wed to someone Llywelyn can control. It's too late for that now," he said, voice rich with satisfaction. "She's my wife. I have absolutely no intention of leaving her a widow." He stared into Lily's eyes as he said the words, words that had the sound of a vow.

Lily felt her heartbeat quicken at the promises he made with his intent gaze.

"And that's why you wed Lily?" Gillian asked. Lily thought she heard disappointment in the question.

She awaited Ian's answer even more eagerly than Gillian appeared to.

Ian drew his finger over Lily's cheek. "'Tis one of the reasons. One of many."

She felt a flush creep over her face and neck at his caressing tone. It made her remember this morning at the pool, and the things they'd done together.

Her face burned even hotter.

Gillian glanced from one to the other, her expression one of amusement—and understanding. She stood, garnering their attention. "I'm certain the remainder of this discussion can wait until everyone has had a chance to bathe and refresh themselves." She turned to Swen, who sat observing everyone throughout the conversation. "I'll call a maid to assist you, sir," she told him.

Lily nearly laughed at the way his eyes lit up. Swen Siwardson was a rogue, she thought to herself. 'Twas a good thing he'd never tried to work his wiles on her, for she doubted Ian would stand for it. Of course, Swen was an intelligent man. He likely knew who he could safely flirt with, and who he'd do better to avoid.

And Ian had made it very clear that he trusted Swen now, since the Viking was now privy to all their secrets.

The maid who came to lead Swen away was a comely young lass. She seemed very pleased to be of service to Swen—he was a very attractive, brawny man, after all—and he followed her from the room with every sign of eagerness.

Ian shook his head after Swen left. "Like a lamb to the slaughter." He laughed. "Women fell all over themselves to get at him at Dolwyddelan. You'd best watch your maidservants,'' he warned Gillian, ''else you'll reap a crop of young Vikings nine months hence.''

She joined his laughter. ''Don't worry. Ardyth is known as the biggest tease in the entire demesne. She's saving herself for one of Rannulf's soldiers, who's off at FitzClifford at the moment. However, that hasn't prevented her tying nearly every male over ten and under eighty into knots.''

Rannulf came up behind her and enfolded her in his arms. ''I'm glad you qualified that,'' he said. ''You'll give your sister a bad impression of me, otherwise.''

Lily could see that they were very much in love, a fact that surprised her. From things she'd heard—admittedly, not much—she'd formed the impression that the English, the Normans, did not marry for love, but for land, power, position. Or, as in her case, for protection.

At least that was the reason Ian had wed her. He was a truly honorable man, more than willing to do whatever he must to help her.

She only hoped he'd never regret his decision.

That, she could not bear.

Gillian led them to a spacious chamber and arranged for a bath to be set up in front of the fire. Lily nearly swooned at the thought of such luxury, though she doubted that this bath would be anything like the one she'd taken that morning.

Unfortunately.

Ian stepped out into the hall for a moment to speak with Rannulf, leaving Gillian alone with Lily.

''I'll have some clothes brought for you,'' Gillian

told her. "We're close enough in height that my gowns should fit you."

Indeed, Lily stood only an inch or so taller than her sister, tall for a woman. "Was our father a big man, or was he short?" Lily asked. "Our mother was tiny. I never understood how I ended up so tall—too tall, I've always felt."

"Father was tall, with a sturdy build. He was old when I was born, nearly forty years, but he still was an imposing figure and a fearsome warrior."

Lily sank down on the bed, suddenly ready to drop with weariness. She yawned. "I beg your pardon," she murmured. "These past weeks have taken their toll." She pushed her hand experimentally into the pillowing softness of the mattress. "I never slept in a bed such as this until we stayed at Ashby a few days ago. 'Tis decadent—and delightful."

Gillian smiled. "You'll become used to it in no time, I'm sure. Ian's keep at Gwal Draig isn't as grand as this, but 'tis a comfortable manor. And Catrin trained the servants well. It hasn't been long since she was mistress there, so I doubt they've forgotten their duties."

Lily frowned. "I don't know that Ian will be able to return to his home anytime soon."

"What do you mean?" Gillian asked.

"It wouldn't be safe. Even though Llywelyn can't possibly know that Ian and I are married, evidently he suspects that Ian has been helping me to stay away from him."

Gillian looked at her, puzzled. "I can see that I should have waited to suggest leaving, until Ian told the rest of the tale. I'm confused. Why should you need to stay away from the prince?"

"He held me prisoner at Dolwyddelan. Indeed, I first

met Swen when he smuggled me away from the castle to remove me from Ian's influence—at Llywelyn's request.''

"And you brought the Viking with you? Are you mad?"

Lily held out a cautioning hand. "As Ian said, there's more to the tale. Believe me when I say that Swen is no threat to either of us. He truly admires Ian and wishes to serve him. Indeed, if he'd done as Llywelyn ordered, I'd be back within the walls of Saint Winifred's Abbey. I doubt that even the Dragon would wage war on a convent," she added dryly.

She stood and wandered to the window, absently staring down at the shadowed bailey. "No, the threat to Ian is from someone he ought to be able to trust."

"Who dares to threaten him?" Gillian demanded.

"'Tis Llywelyn," Lily told her. "He has declared Ian an outlaw."

Chapter Sixteen

An army of servants streamed into the chamber, bringing with them a bathtub and buckets of water. Lily could almost find it within herself to be grateful for the interruption. So tired she could scarcely think, she didn't feel ready to carry on a conversation with Gillian.

Especially when the topic was Ian.

Gillian gazed at Lily's face, then reached out to place a comforting hand on her arm. "Forgive me. You look nigh ready to drop with weariness, and yet I've done naught but question you."

"Nay, milady, it's all right. I know you care for Ian. Please don't apologize for your concern." Lily dredged up a smile. "I'm sure we both have questions—and many things to discuss. But I am tired, 'tis true. We've had little rest the past few days."

Gillian gave Lily's arm a squeeze, then stood as the last manservant closed the door behind him. "I can imagine. From the sound of it, you haven't had a moment's peace since you left the abbey. But you needn't worry now. L'Eau Clair is a Norman keep—Llywelyn has no power here. You and Ian are safe within these walls. Rest here awhile, spend time with your new husband," she added with a mischievous grin. She glanced toward the fire, where the bath set up before it sent up a fragrant cloud of steam. "We'll see that you have a chance to relax, to decide what to do."

Lily eased herself off the bed. "Thank you. Perhaps once I've slept, my brain won't feel so muddled."

"We'll talk again when you've rested," Gillian said, kissing Lily's cheek. Her gaze never left Lily as she walked from the room and shut the door.

How different the Normans were from the Welsh! Their clothing seemed brighter, more elaborate, of better quality—even the men's hair was different. Nicholas and Rannulf wore their hair cropped to the nape, unlike Ian's shoulder-length mane. They were both attractive men, rugged and masculine in appearance. But to her, the style looked tame.

Perhaps it wasn't the hair, but the man, for Ian possessed an untamed quality totally in keeping with his appearance.

Lily sank back onto the bed, running her hands over the silken coverlet and allowing her gaze to caress her surroundings. Since she'd been exposed to the fine furnishings and way of life of the nobility, she'd discovered a new aspect of herself. She enjoyed the soft, colorful fabrics used so lavishly at Ashby and l'Eau Clair, savored the sweet smell of herbs scenting the air, relished the feel of soft carpets beneath her feet.

After a lifetime spent within the austere confines of the abbey, Lily found it very easy to grow accustomed to luxury. Surely it must be a sin, to enjoy these fine surroundings so thoroughly.

She'd been taught that much in life was sinful, not least the sins of the flesh.

If that was the case, she had already passed beyond redemption.

Lily rose from the bed and walked to the tub, absently unwinding her braid. She hadn't bathed as much in the past year as she had in the past few days—another pleasure she'd come to enjoy.

But none of these luxuries meant as much to her as Ian. Though they had spent their wedding night in a crude hut, it did not matter. That night would stand out in her memory as the richest of delights. The joy of Ian's touch required no other embellishment.

He was everything she could ever have wished for. Brave, determined, kind. Although she knew he was capable of violence, she also knew he possessed a precise sense of justice. He did nothing without a reason.

And his loyalty was beyond question.

Add to that the fact that a mere glance from his deep green eyes made her heart beat faster, that his touch sent fire pulsing through her veins, that the sound of his voice made her shiver deep inside, and she knew she was blessed to have captured the attention of the Dragon.

For however long it lasted.

But at what cost to him? She feared he'd pay dearly for his gallantry in marrying her. If what he—and the rest of her family—suspected was true, Ian was a far cry from the type of man Llywelyn would have chosen to be her husband.

Clearly, even Llywelyn could not control the Dragon.

What if the cost of Ian's disobedience was their lives?

Only Ian's skill as a warrior—and a measure of luck in finding Swen—had prevented her becoming a widow already. They could not hide behind the walls of l'Eau Clair forever. Eventually they would have to leave—to go where, Lily had no idea—and Ian's life could once again be forfeit.

They could not live that way for long.

Lily sank down onto the carpet before the fire and covered her face with her hands. She could not bear to lose Ian, not now. Not after all he'd come to mean to her.

But if she had to, she would give him up.

What would a broken heart matter, if it saved his life?

She heard a sound at the door and sat up, swiftly wiping away her tears on the trailing hem of her sleeve. Ian entered the room and closed the door, then turned the key in the lock.

Cursing her sore muscles, Lily struggled to her feet, drawing Ian's attention. "Why were you sitting on the floor, when there are plenty of more comfortable places?" he asked, glancing about the room.

She didn't want him to know she'd been crying, so she turned away to trail her fingers in the still-hot water of the tub. "The rug is comfortable. But I forgot how difficult it would be to get back up, 'tis all."

Ian crossed the chamber to the fire. "Why aren't you in the tub?" he asked, his voice slow and deep. "Were you waiting for me to join you?"

Tears forgotten, she spun to face him, drawn by his teasing tone. "In there?" He grinned at her. "We wouldn't both fit in that tub," she scoffed. "It's impossible."

"Don't you know by now that you should never tell me something is impossible?" He sauntered closer, a devilish gleam in his eyes. "I cannot resist a dare."

Lily stepped back, coming to a halt when she bumped into the rim of the tub. "'Twas a comment, nothing more." She held her hand out to ward him off, but he ignored the paltry gesture and swept her into his arms.

"You dare me every time you look at me like that," he murmured in her ear.

"What do you mean? I don't look at you any differently than I do anyone else," she protested, fighting the insidious heat pouring through her as his lips brushed the sensitive flesh beneath her ear.

"But you do." He nuzzled her neck. "You look at me as if you want me as much as I want you. Do you know what that does to me?"

She didn't, but perhaps he'd tell her, if she asked. Feeling bold, she turned her head until she could see his eyes. "How does it make you feel?"

Ian sat down upon the carpet and held her nestled in his lap. "As though I'm the only man in the world. You make my heart quake with longing—and with fear."

He stroked her lips with his fingertip, sending a shiver of longing down her spine. She struggled to find her voice. "What do you fear?"

"Do I please you?"

Lily raised her hand to cup his cheek. "You know that you do."

"But I don't know that, unless you tell me," he said.

"Can't you tell—" she lowered her gaze, uncertain how to go on "—when you've pleased me?"

He rubbed his bristly cheek against her palm. "I know when your body feels pleasure." He stroked her mouth again. "But I don't know if I've pleased *you*."

Did he want her to tell him what she felt when he touched her, caressed her, joined his body to hers?

She could not. A flood of heat washed over her face, leaving a fiery blush in its wake—her skin burned with it. She had been far too bold already; despite her inexperience, he must think her wanton, the way she'd caressed him, stared at his body, welcomed him into hers with such ease.

Lily hid her face in the crook of Ian's shoulder as she recalled how very daring she'd been.

"Come, sweeting, you cannot claim shyness now," he teased, cupping her chin in his hand and turning her face toward his. "What you and I have shared, I've never had with anyone else. I know 'tis the same for you."

Lily still refused to meet his gaze. "But must we talk about it?" She brushed her nose along his jaw. "I was taught that *doing* those things is a sin. I cannot imagine talking about them is much better," she said dryly.

"You are my wife, Lily. Doesn't the Church also tell you to 'cleave unto your husband'?" He held her more firmly within his arms. "Besides, if you truly believed that what we've shared is a sin, I doubt you would be sitting here with me now—like this."

"I know 'tis not a sin, Ian." She raised her head to watch his face, his eyes. "But I cannot say that I'm comfortable talking about it, either."

She could not think clearly with Ian surrounding her with his body, his presence. 'Twas too distracting. She placed her hands upon his and slipped free of his grasp to stand beside him, then took a deep breath. "So much has happened to me, to us, so quickly. Please understand when I tell you I need time, to become accustomed to our life together, to my family," she pleaded.

He rose to his feet, as well, but turned his head away. "Do you wish to put me aside?" he asked, his voice flat.

"Nay, Ian." She reached over and framed his face with her hands, forcing him to look at her. His eyes were dark green, their turbulent depths at odds with his coldness. "You are my husband. I swore an oath before God—I swore to *you*—that I would be your wife. I will not break that vow." She stroked his cheek. "All I ask you for is time, enough time to understand everything that has happened."

"Will you leave me, then, until you're ready?"

Would it matter to him if she did? Lily wondered. His voice sounded detached, dispassionate. But she refused to believe that he did not care for her—a little, at least. Even the Dragon would not carry devotion to duty so far as to marry a woman he didn't want.

Would he?

"I will never leave you, Ian," she said, the words a vow. "Although you'd be better off if I did. Perhaps then Llywelyn would forgive your disobedience."

Ian covered her hands with his and drew them from his face, weaving his fingers together with hers and holding them tightly. "Are you mad? You are my wife—you are *mine*. No man forces me to give up what is mine."

He raised her hands to his lips. "Perhaps you've forgotten the promises I made to you, my lady wife. 'With my body, I thee worship.'" He nipped delicately at her fingers, then drew his tongue the length of them, setting her pulse to pounding, despite her efforts to remain unaffected. He leaned so close, his lips nearly touched hers, and his gaze held her captive. "'Tis my right—my duty—to partake of the delights you offer," he whispered.

She closed her eyes, but she could not shut him out. "Ian, please—"

"You may have all the time you need," he told her,

his voice rough with some unknown emotion. "But you may not refuse me this."

Why couldn't he understand, give her the distance she sought? If he kept up this sensual assault, she didn't know if she could bear it if he ever pushed her away. She had fallen into loving so easily; it seemed the most natural feeling in the world to share the delights of the body with Ian. But she knew they needed to share more than that.

Heart pounding a frantic rhythm, she started to pull away.

Ian held her captive, his fingers pressed to the pulse at her throat. "Please, Lily. I need you." She opened her eyes at the unexpected plea. "Not only with my body, but here..." He took her hand in his and laid it over his pounding heart. "Please, at least let me give you this."

How could she refuse him, when she needed what he offered, as well?

Beyond speech, she nodded, then buried her face against his shoulder as he swept her up into his arms. He carried her to the bed and placed her carefully upon the coverlet, then spread her unbound hair wide across the pillows. His touch was tender, deliberate, and he watched her all the while, as though gauging her reaction to each caress.

He lay beside her and bent to kiss her lips. His mouth brushed against hers in a butterfly touch, teasingly light, heart-stoppingly beautiful. When she tried to rise up and deepen the kiss, Ian eased her back and framed her face with his hands, gently refusing her request.

"Let me, sweeting," he murmured. "Take this gift from me."

Though she found it nearly impossible to simply accept Ian's touch without touching him in return, every time her hands crept close or she reached out to caress him, he gently pushed her hands away. But she could not seem to stop.

Finally he grasped her hands and held them, bracketing her wrists with his long, callused fingers. Her initial frustration at not being able to touch him in return gave way to a growing lassitude as he slowly deepened his kisses and pulled her farther into the web of passion he wove so skillfully about her.

She'd never thought she'd enjoy relinquishing control, but she found she didn't mind—for the moment, at least. Ian lifted her up to unlace her bliaut and slipped it over her head, then tugged off her undertunic, as well. Clad only in her silken shift, Lily lay back and watched as he quickly shed his own garments.

Her blood quickened at the sight of him, gilded by firelight. She yearned to smooth her fingers over the hard, lean planes of his body, to stroke the sleek hardness of his manhood.

But as soon as he joined her on the bed, he captured her hands in his once again.

"You are beautiful," he whispered. He kissed her shoulder, then began to nudge at the neckline of her shift. The fabric moved so slowly, Lily thought she would scream in frustration before he bared her shoulder. Her flesh was burning for his touch by the time he slid his tongue over her silk-covered breast.

Releasing her wrists, Ian cupped her breasts in his hands and stroked her through the thin material. The heat of his flesh burned through the cool silk, the contrast bringing her nipples to aching hardness.

Lily arched her back, trying to deepen the caress, but Ian would not be hurried. "What do you want, Lily?"

he asked, sitting back on his heels and caressing her with his gaze. "What would you like me to do?"

All her inhibitions seemed to have flown away. And she knew that, unless she told him what she wanted, he'd probably leave her lying there, aching.

She reached for his hands and placed them on her shoulders. "I want to feel your hands on my skin." She swallowed, then slid his hands beneath her shift. "Here."

He nudged the fabric down over her breasts, stroking his way along her skin until he settled his callused hands where she ached the most. "Is this what you wanted?" he asked as he shaped her flesh with his fingers.

Swallowing a moan, she nodded.

"Your skin is as soft as a rose." He nuzzled along her collarbone, then moved his hand and took her nipple into his mouth. By the time he released her, Lily felt as though her heart would bound from her chest, it pounded so hard. "You taste sweeter than mead, more fiery than usquebaugh."

He sat back and met Lily's gaze. "Am I pleasing you, milady?"

"Aye," she whispered. "Will you let me please you?"

"You are. Watching your pleasure pleases me, sweeting." He tugged her shift down her body and tossed it aside, leaving her sprawled across the silk bed cover. "Seeing your beauty makes my heart thunder and my body ache for you."

The fabric felt cool beneath her, a stark contrast to the heat of Ian's gaze as it roamed over her.

Since it was the only way she could touch him, Lily indulged herself with the pleasure of watching him—

his body, his face—as closely as he watched her. A dark flush rode high along his cheekbones, and his eyes looked as avid as a hawk's.

"What would you have me do?" he asked. "How shall I touch you next?"

Lily shook her head slowly. 'Twas beyond her to think, to decide anything. "However you wish, Dragon."

Ian climbed off the bed and stood next to it, then slid Lily along the smooth silk to the edge of the mattress. Her hair lay spread all about her, brushing against her skin in a subtle caress.

She watched Ian, curious. She could not imagine where this might lead.

He draped her legs over the side of the high mattress, then gently moved her thighs apart and stood between them. Placing his hands beneath her knees, he began to inch his thumbs up along the sensitive flesh of her inner thighs, not stopping until he reached the heart of her desire.

Lily felt a flush rise from her neck to her face. The way he looked at her, watching, waiting for her reaction, made her blood flow hot through her veins. "I wish to taste your desire, love." He moved his thumbs up, until he cradled her most sensitive flesh within them. "May I?"

Beyond speech, she reached up to him and drew him toward her.

Ian dropped to his knees beside the bed and gently caressed her. He slid his hands up her body to her hands, watching her all the while. "Show me where to touch you," he murmured against her skin, his voice rough.

She moved his hands to her aching breasts, pressing them there with her own.

Soon Lily was aware only of Ian's touch, his low-voiced words of praise, as she climbed toward the precipice. His attentions intensified, hurtling her over the edge, into a maelstrom of fire.

She reached for Ian. "Look at me," he said. She forced her eyes open as he stood and grasped her legs, drawing them about his waist. He pressed into her still-throbbing flesh slowly, his eyes possessing her even as his body did.

Lily cried out as passion consumed her again. But this time she rode the crest with Ian, his voice joining hers as he slumped over her body.

Lily fell asleep almost as soon as Ian slipped from her body. He gave her pleasure, he noted with satisfaction. She slept so deeply that she didn't stir when he gathered her into his arms and placed her under the bed covers.

He banked the fire for the night, casting a rueful glance at the tub of cold water beside the hearth. He considered climbing in, hoping to chill his still-fiery blood, but he decided against it. He didn't want to wash away the scent of Lily.

He snuffed all but one of the candles and climbed into bed with his wife. She nestled close when he took her in his arms, cuddling against him with a sweetness that warmed his heart.

But Ian could not rest. Lily's words haunted him. She gave herself to him completely in passion; he could not doubt she wanted him—and the pleasure he brought her. However, it seemed to him that she was unsure about the other parts of their life together.

Did she mistrust him, or herself?

If Lily wanted him to leave her, to step away from their marriage, she would be sorely disappointed. He had no intention of that.

He only wished he knew how she felt about him when they weren't lost in the throes of passion.

Despite the short time they'd known each other, she must have some idea what she felt for him. It had been time enough.

He had no doubt about his feelings toward her.

Although Ian was not ready to give her the words for what he felt, he knew them.

Indeed, they were burned across his very soul.

He hoped she never tried to leave him, for he did not know if he could ever give her up.

Ian had heard it said that the Dragon had no heart, that he could carry out Llewelyn's vengeance because he felt nothing.

Once, Ian might have believed that, too.

But no longer.

Lily had found the Dragon's heart, and taught it to feel again.

Joy, love, hurt, pain.

So many emotions, so vivid, so real, after being locked away for years.

She could not teach him to feel again, and then leave him to experience those feelings alone.

Chapter Seventeen

The next afternoon, Ian headed for the practice field, intending to work off his frustration with life in general, and his wife in particular, by taking on anyone who wished to fight. His blood was up, and he knew he'd be of no use to anyone, including himself, unless he wore himself out with battle.

Evidently dueling with Lily wasn't enough to cool the fire in his blood—or perhaps 'twas what made it run so hot. He didn't know. But whatever the reason, if he didn't do something about it soon, he'd go mad.

As he had suspected, Swen was eager to oblige. He and Rannulf joined Ian in the bailey, stripped down for hard fighting. In no time at all, a crowd had gathered, intent on watching the entertainment.

The Viking knew some moves Rannulf hadn't seen before, so he took him on first. Ian watched with interest as Swen, sword in hand, swiftly laid out their host in the straw-covered mud, much to the amusement of the audience. Rannulf was good, but it appeared Swen was better—or his style was very different, at any rate. Siwardson could give Ian just what he sought. Swen accepted the cheers of the crowd with his usual good humor, then urged Ian into the fray.

Ian didn't care what type of weapon Swen wanted to use—he was quite willing to fight him bare-handed, if need be. Actually, he thought as he and Swen circled each other, each armed with a sword, that might be best of all.

He tossed his blade aside. "We don't need them," he said in answer to Swen's questioning look. With a nod, the Viking handed his weapon to Rannulf and stripped off his tunic, throwing it to a comely wench.

"Are you looking to draw blood, Dragon?" he taunted. He stepped forward, fists raised, balancing on the balls of his feet.

Ian feinted with his left fist, then drove the right into Swen's gut. The other man didn't even flinch. "I'm looking for a challenge," Ian replied. "Can you give me one?"

"Aye," Swen said, grinning. "You've come to the right man."

Ian smiled grimly in return. Swen had no idea what he'd gotten himself into.

Gillian invited Lily to her chamber, ostensibly to find suitable clothing for her sister to wear. However, Lily knew there was more to it than that. Ever since they'd arrived at l'Eau Clair, Ian hadn't seemed willing to leave the women alone together. While she knew his interference was well-intentioned, she felt stifled by it. She and Gillian needed to become acquainted—without a nursemaid.

Gillian had given Rannulf strict orders to keep Ian busy—elsewhere—for the afternoon, at least. Lily had to laugh at the way Rannulf teased his wife, calling her his "dread overlord," before he left the two women together.

Lily sat on the bed while Gillian dug through the contents of several coffers. The chests were huge—and heavy, judging by the groans of the two men who had carried them up the spiral staircase and into the chamber.

The sweet scents of roses and lavender wafted through the room as Gillian laid several garments upon the bed. She stroked her hand lovingly over the soft wool of a dark green bliaut. "I wore this for Rannulf when first we met," she said, her voice soft with remembrance. "The embroidery design comes from a circlet he gave me years before, when we were naught but children." She looked up at Lily. "It would go well with your coloring. The fabric matches your eyes. Here, try it on."

"I couldn't, Gillian. It obviously brings back wonderful memories. You cannot give it away—it wouldn't be right."

Gillian chuckled. "I could not fit into the bodice of that tunic unless I were trussed up like a Christmas goose! Since Katherine's birth, I've become much more—" she wriggled her eyebrows "—motherly. Unfortunately, no amount of lacing will make this—" she gestured toward her ample bosom "—fit into that gown. You must try it on. It would please me to see you wear it."

It would be churlish to protest further, and the gown *was* beautiful. Lily stood and, with Gillian's assistance, removed her bliaut and underdress.

They went through the clothing in the chests slowly, taking their time, for they had many lost years to make up for.

"Did you ever miss our mother?" Lily asked curiously.

Gillian shook her head. "I missed having a mother, but I don't remember her. When she left, I was but an infant. What was she like?"

"She was very beautiful—like you. But petite. Other than that, you resemble her closely. But her sorrow weighted her down. 'Twas the terrible lies Llywelyn told her, no doubt, that buried her in grief. She was as lost to me as she was to you," Lily said, fighting tears.

Gillian clasped her hand for a moment as they shared their loss. "Our cousin has much to answer for," she said. "I don't know that I can ever forgive him for taking her away." She squeezed Lily's hand. "Or for keeping us apart."

She looked so sad. Lily set about bringing back her sister's smile. "Ian said you were raised like a boy until you were nearly a woman grown. That cannot be."

Gillian chuckled and wiped her damp eyes. "I was one of the roughest lads here," she agreed. "I could fight, spit, curse and ride with the best of Father's pages. The first time I met Rannulf, I nearly bested him at swordplay—in front of Lord William Marshall himself."

"You're jesting," Lily protested. Gazing at her sister, the epitome of all that was womanly, she found such a scene near impossible to imagine.

"I'm afraid not. I was twelve at the time, and looked quite like a boy in my tunic and hose, with my hair tucked up under my favorite cap. 'Twas great fun, though by then I'd begun to long for more. Fortunately for me, Lord William—he's my godfather, you know—convinced Father that I was desperately in need of a woman's teachings, and left Lady Allyce to help me."

Sadness tinged her voice. "She was very much like a mother to me. I miss her still. She died shortly after Father did."

She rose and took a turn about the room. "But despite Lady Allyce's affection, I did miss our mother, or rather, I missed having a mother."

Lily joined her by the window. "She never forgot you, or our father, either. She called for you—spoke to you—until the day she died." She made the sign of the cross. "But in all those years, I never knew you were real. When she'd call out to Simon, or Gilly, the sisters told me she saw people in her mind, people who didn't exist. Mostly she just sat staring at the wall. I believe she grieved for you both, always."

Gillian laid her hand upon Lily's arm. "And did she know you were real?" she asked, her voice kind. "Did she know you were there?"

Lily swallowed the lump of sadness that rose, choking, in her throat. It was an old pain, one that shouldn't have had the power to hurt her any longer.

Yet it still did.

"Sometimes she knew. And sometimes she'd remember me." She blinked away her tears as she recalled how lonely her life had been. "But, mostly, she didn't."

Gillian wrapped her arms about Lily and held her. "Poor child," she murmured. "Damn Llywelyn!"

All the tears Lily had never cried sought their release now. Her sister held her as she sobbed, washing away the years of resentment and sorrow.

"You are alone no longer, Lily," Gillian told her. "You have a family now, people who care for you. We—and Ian—will keep you safe."

Finally Lily lifted her head from Gillian's shoulder, spent. There had been such comfort in Gillian's touch, in her understanding. And she felt as though her sister, her family, had accepted her already. She had gained what she'd always wanted.

But Lily hadn't realized, before, the price she might have to pay. She'd wanted a family, a place to belong, people to care about her. However, she was trapped within that web of caring in return.

She would do whatever she must to keep them safe.

There was a comfort in belonging, a sense of peace she'd never known. It made it possible to forgive her mother's neglect; she had not understood what it was to care so deeply. But now she knew.

"We both lost when Llywelyn put his scheme into motion," Gillian said. "Although you got the worst of the bargain. At least I had Father." She reached over and wiped at Lily's wet face with her sleeve. "But that is in the past. We have each other now, and you have Ian. He won't permit Llywelyn to harm you again."

"But what if Ian cannot stop him?" Lily cried. "I fear Llywelyn will continue to send men after him. Eventually one of them will succeed in killing him—or taking him back to Dolwyddelan as a captive."

"Do you truly believe that our noble cousin wishes Ian dead? I do not. I think, rather, that he seeks to punish him for his disobedience." Gillian poured spiced wine into two goblets and handed one to Lily. "He needs the Dragon, Lily, for his plans to succeed. I would imagine he has plots in motion that make this one seem like child's play in comparison."

"But he still believes I'm free to bring back under his dominion," Lily protested. "And what if something were to happen to Ian? Life is uncertain."

"Drink your wine and listen to me," Gillian said, urging her to sit on the bed. She sat beside her and lowered her voice. "Rannulf has heard rumors of an attempt to bring our king under control—my overlord, King John. Perhaps if Ian were to volunteer to go to London with the others, to represent Llywelyn..."

Toad eased open the door and peered into Gillian's chamber. He could not believe his good fortune. Gillian and Lily in the same chamber! They sat together on the bed, their backs to the door.

He had made it into l'Eau Clair so easily last night, slipping in with a band of wandering peddlers, that he expected the rest to be simple. It had turned out to be very difficult to find them together, without the damned men in attendance. Nearly impossible, in fact. By Christ's balls, didn't they have anything more important to do than follow the women about like damned French courtiers?

He patted his waist, reassured by the feel of his dagger belted there. He would get no better opportunity than this. No one had come down the corridor since the two servants had carted up those chests.

Taking a quick look over his shoulder once more, he darted into the room, carefully closing the door behind him.

He wasn't as fortunate when he turned the key in the lock.

"Who's there?" Gillian called sharply.

Damned faithless bitch!

A tide of anger, red and hazy, flowed over Toad's mind. He couldn't think clearly, but that didn't matter.

He knew what he'd come here to do.

Find Lily.

Take her with him.

Make her his wife.

Gillian turned and spied him standing on the opposite side of the bed. "Mary save us!" she gasped, clapping her hand to her breast. "You startled me!" She stood and began to walk around the bed, but Lily reached out a hand to stop her.

"Stay, sister," she said quietly. "I fear he means you harm."

"Do you know him?" Gillian asked, never taking her gaze off him.

Toad smiled. "Aye, that she does. So do you, though I don't believe you'll recognize me now." He laughed at the confusion on her face. "You should listen to her, madame—but then, you were never very good at that, were you? As it happens, however, I don't intend to harm you—as long as you do as I tell you."

He drew the knife from its scabbard, the blade gleaming with beauty in the sunlight pouring through the window slit.

It had been many years since he'd been inside this keep, but it looked much the same. He'd coveted l'Eau Clair, desired it—and its mistress—with a white-hot passion that the passage of time had done little to quench.

But now his desire was for her sister, for through her, l'Eau Clair could be his. He'd make Llewelyn see the beauty in his plan—not so different from the prince's, after all—and he would finally attain his heart's desire.

"Come here, Lily," he said, motioning with the knife.

Lily stood, but remained rooted to the spot.

He glided closer to Gillian, the dagger held threateningly toward her, then lunged and grabbed her by the arm.

"I suggest you do as I say, Lily." He brought the tip

of the knife up and held it firm against Gillian's throat. "Else your sister, so newly discovered, will not remain long of this world." He pressed harder, until a trickle of blood oozed from beneath the blade. Whipping a length of cord from his belt, he wrapped it around Gillian's wrists and bound them together behind her.

Ah, the pleasure in this! He had wanted Gillian within his grasp for so long. Toad drew the tip of the blade along Gillian's skin, marking a crimson trail along her alabaster cheek. The hatred in her eyes...

He permitted himself to revel in her beauty for a brief moment more, then motioned again with the knife. "Come along, milady," he said to Lily.

Lily moved slowly around the end of the bed, then stood there, waiting.

"Very good," he murmured. "Now, madame—" he nudged Gillian with his foot "—you'll help me leave this keep with your sister. Don't think I won't use this knife on you—on your face, perhaps." He raised the blade to her cheek again, then lowered it to her throat. "I've dreamed of this for a very long time, you faithless bitch. I wonder how FitzClifford will like that?"

Gillian closed her eyes briefly, then opened them to stare into his eyes. "Steffan," she hissed. "We thought you were dead."

"Then you must be very surprised to see me." He laughed. "I'm sure you forgot all about your dear cousin—who would have been your husband, if you hadn't betrayed me with that Norman bastard. It's time for you to pay—and if I gain l'Eau Clair in the process, then that's justice, is it not? It should have been mine to begin with."

"How will you win l'Eau Clair if I go with you?" Lily asked, her beautiful face clouded with confusion.

He smiled. He didn't mind if she knew. Actually, this made it even better, for Gillian to know what she'd lost—and stood to lose.

"When we wed, I'll ask Llewelyn to give this keep to me. He owes it to me. He should have done more to help me win it before, but he was afraid Ian would find out what we planned. Llewelyn is a craven bastard—" he spat "—with all his secrets."

Lily stared at Toad, her head awash in startling revelations. He must be the cousin Ian had told her about, the one who had tried to marry Gillian, then attempted to kill Catrin. He'd burned the village, too.

He must have been a madman before.

What did that make him now?

He looked even worse than when she'd seen him at Dolwyddelan, if that was possible. Although she had to admit he didn't smell as bad. All that rain the other night must have rinsed him off, she thought with a strange burst of humor.

Obviously he didn't know that she and Ian were wed. She'd probably be wise not to mention that to him. She intended to do nothing that might set off his temper while he held his blade to her sister's throat.

"What do you want me to do?" she asked him.

"We're going to go out of the keep and through the bailey. There's a postern gate. I'm certain Gillian has the key—don't you, my dear?" When Gillian nodded, Steffan smiled.

At least she thought that was what he did. She found it difficult to read the expressions on his misshapen face. But his dark eyes glowed; he looked as though he were enjoying this, very much.

Her mind working furiously, Lily tried to remember the route they'd have to follow to leave the keep. If she found any place where she could try to disarm Steffan, she'd do whatever she had to, if it would prevent his plan from succeeding.

She doubted he intended to let Gillian live.

"You go ahead of us," Steffan told her, "but not too far. I don't want to give you a chance to warn anyone what I'm about."

As Lily passed by them, Gillian met her worried gaze with a slight smile, and the acknowledgment in her eyes that they'd try something—anything—to stop him.

Lily crept down the stairs, her attention more on the couple behind her than on what was ahead. It was a miracle she didn't pitch headlong down the spiraling flight of stairs, and even more of a wonder that Steffan didn't accidentally slit Gillian's throat, considering his uneven—and unsteady—gait.

She met Gillian's gaze once again. This was likely the only place, the only chance, they'd get to stop him. Thinking quickly, she decided what she would do.

Lily stopped dead in the middle of the stairs, throwing them all off balance. Gillian tripped, then doubled over and shoved at Steffan while he was in midstride. His weight shifted onto his crooked leg and he pitched forward, taking the knife with him. Lily pressed herself flat against the wall and Steffan tumbled past her, making a horrible, keening wail. He landed against the wall at the bottom of the flight.

"Gillian!" she cried, turning and gathering her sister into her arms.

The two women clung together on the stairs, Gillian gasping for breath, as a crowd of people came rushing into the stairwell. One of the men bent over Steffan's motionless body and felt his neck. "He's dead, milady."

Gillian carefully eased out of Lily's grasp and rose to her feet. "Good," she said firmly.

One of the maids gave a shocked gasp. "Milady!"

"Enough. Have done, Ella," Gillian said, her voice tart. "This man just tried to kill Lady Lily and myself. Since he didn't succeed, a certain amount of rejoicing is in order, don't you think?"

Lily stood, as well. Taking up Steffan's knife, she untied her sister. Arms about each other for support, she and Gillian descended the stairs.

"Your face and neck, milady!" someone gasped. "You're covered with blood!"

"Who was he, Lady Gillian?"

"My cousin Steffan." Gillian scanned the group crowded into the foot of the stairs. "I'm certain you all remember him," she stated, "since his men attacked this keep and took me captive." She leaned over him and felt his throat herself. "May God have mercy on his miserable soul," she said, making the sign of the cross. "But not too much. He deserves to suffer, after all the evil he did."

Completely ignoring the cut on her neck, which still oozed blood, Gillian stood and began to make arrangements for the removal of the body.

Once the crowd had thinned, Lily stepped to her sister's side. "The things he said make sense to me now," Lily said thoughtfully.

"What he said to us upstairs?"

Lily shook her head. "No. I'd seen him before, at Dolwyddelan. When Llywelyn had me locked away in the vaults, that vile creature came to visit me. He smelled even worse than he does now, if you can imagine it, and he said many strange things that I didn't understand at all. I simply believed him a madman."

"He was that," Gillian agreed. "Even before he fell over that cliff. Until he abducted me, I had never realized such ugliness existed. And it was hidden beneath the veneer of a handsome—"

"Handsome?"

Gillian nodded. "Aye, a very handsome face, and a body to match. He was something of a courtier, in the French fashion—fine clothing, the best horses. Most Welshmen would rather be dead than trussed up in fancy garb. But Steffan always wanted more than he already had. I suppose there's nothing wrong with that, so long as you don't try to rob others—including your own kin—to get what you want." She turned away as two men picked up Steffan's limp body to cart it away.

"He told me to call him Toad," Lily said, shuddering as she remembered those horrible hours of darkness. "The name fit him, I must admit. He said the man he'd been was dead—for the nonce. He must have planned this even then," she said, shaking her head in bemusement.

"Come, let's return to my chamber," Gillian said, her voice suddenly shaking. "We both need to sit down and try to forget we ever saw him."

"Don't you think that will be a bit difficult?" Lily asked as she turned to follow Gillian.

"I said we'd try," she said. "I don't know that we'll succeed."

The thundering sound of running feet echoed through the hall and up into the stairwell. Ian led the way, with Rannulf and Swen right behind him.

Ian grabbed Lily about the waist and pulled her into a rib-crushing embrace. "He didn't harm you?" he asked. His gaze swept over her.

Rannulf elbowed his way past them and hauled his wife into his arms in a similar fashion.

Then Lily didn't see anything but Ian's face as he stared into her eyes, his own dark with panic.

"He made a cut on Gillian's neck, but no, he didn't harm me," Lily murmured against his cheek. "He just frightened me."

"I knew we should have made certain he was dead, Ian," Rannulf said, his voice cold as ice.

Ian and Lily looked up. Rannulf slumped down on the stairs, tugged Gillian onto his lap, wrapped his arms about her and buried his face in her hair.

"How could we have known?" Ian asked. "No one should have survived that fall. And I can't imagine how he got out of that valley, injured as he must have been."

He clutched Lily close, and she burrowed against his strong body for comfort. "He was very bitter," she said. "When he spoke to me at Dolwyddelan—"

"You saw him there?" he asked sharply.

"Aye, in the cellars. He said he'd heard about me and wanted to see me for himself. I thought he was mad. I didn't know who he was until he came to us in Gillian's chamber."

Lily watched as Swen sniffed the air, then stalked back into the hall.

His roar filled the hall. He walked into the stairwell again, pausing beside Ian and Lily. "You should kill me now, Dragon," he said, his tone serious for once. "Here, use my knife." He took his knife from his belt and held it out to Ian, and stood with head bowed, refusing to meet their eyes. "I knew he'd been following me about before I left Dolwyddelan, skulking in the shadows, but I thought no more about him once I left. I never imagined he would follow me. He didn't look as though he could do any harm.'' Swen looked earnestly up at Gillian. ''I beg your forgiveness, milady.''

'' 'Tis not your fault, Swen,'' Ian assured him. ''If he knew who Lily was—'' Lily nodded her head ''—then he had to realize we'd come here eventually. He probably came here on his own. Believe me, he's been here before, the bastard.''

A servant paused before them. ''Lord Rannulf. What should I do with that?'' he asked, pointing back toward the hall.

Rannulf raised his head and stared down at the man. ''Send him back to Llywelyn, with my compliments.''

Chapter Eighteen

Ian carried Lily up to their chamber. He couldn't believe how badly shaken he felt at the realization that Steffan might have harmed her. How was it that goodness never lasted, but evil seemed to linger on forever?

Slamming the door shut, he set Lily on her feet and gathered her into his arms. She felt solid and vibrant pressed up against him. He stared into her eyes for a long moment, warmed by the softness he saw there, then lowered his mouth to hers.

Any thought of giving her time, of holding back, he forced from his mind. His body throbbed with the need to pillage, to take her mouth with all the depth of emotion roiling through him, but he feared he'd do her harm, so intense were the feelings.

Mayhap the battle lust he'd felt earlier still raged through him, despite Swen's efforts to beat it out of him. But he didn't really believe that. Steffan's attempt to take away Lily had outraged his sense of possession. And it had made him realize how much he'd nearly lost.

He savored every inch of Lily where they touched, the sweet, flowery scent of her, the reassuring sound of her breath whispering across his skin.

Someone pounded on the door.

Ian dragged his lips from hers. "What?" he snarled. He felt like taking his sword to whatever fool stood outside the door, to let him experience the wrath of the Dragon.

Taking a deep breath, he stepped away from Lily and struggled for calm. He doubted Gillian would appreciate it if he murdered her servants.

"Lady Gillian said as ye'd be wantin' a bath, milord," the man said. "Can we open the door?"

Ian tugged Lily loosely into his grasp and rested his forehead against her brow. "Fine," he called. Though he was sorry they'd been interrupted, a bath posed some interesting possibilities. He knew of no reason why he could not make love to his wife in the tub. For make love to her he would.

As soon as they had some privacy.

He seated Lily on the edge of the bed—he could feel how she still shook from her ordeal—and opened the door. The servants carried in the tub and water in record time, spurred on by Ian's impatient glower.

Finally they were alone.

He raised Lily from the bed and wrapped her in his arms. "How do you feel?" he asked, running his hands slowly, soothingly, up and down her back. "Are you certain he didn't harm you?"

"He never touched me, Ian. But he frightened me. I know he intended to kill Gillian," she said, her voice quavering.

"Steffan will never harm anyone again," he reassured her. "He is finally, truly, dead—God be praised."

He held her close, savoring the way she nestled into him. She felt so good in his arms. When he considered what might have happened to her...

"I could have lost you," he said, closing his eyes against the thought.

Lily stroked her palms over his shoulders and smiled reassuringly. "He wouldn't have harmed me, Ian." She shuddered. "He wanted to marry me."

"That would have been difficult, since you have a husband already," Ian said dryly. "Although Llywelyn would have approved. He certainly allowed Steffan enough opportunities to wed his way into l'Eau Clair."

Ian scanned Lily's face, not pleased by her continued pallor. He forced his lips into a bracing smile. "Come, sweeting. Enough of such thoughts. We are together, our family is well, and so far as we know, Llywelyn isn't lurking outside the gates." He led her toward the tub. "We'll help each other forget about the world outside this room for a time."

Lily looked into his eyes for a moment, her gaze assessing, then nodded. "I would like that, husband. What shall we do, I wonder?" She glanced down at his hands as he worked to the laces of her bliaut.

"Are you still sore from our travels?" he asked.

"No." A lazy smile on her lips, she leaned into his body like a cat begging to be stroked. "And I'll not complain if you continue what you're doing."

He led her to a chair and pushed gently until she was seated. Ian traced his hands over the smooth column of her neck, stroking her warm skin, then feathering his fingertips along the creamy flesh. Taking up her braid, he ran his hands caressingly down its length before he unplaited it.

"What are you doing?" Lily asked, the drowsy purr of her voice streaking along Ian's spine. His mouth suddenly dry, he swallowed and took a deep breath. Spying her brush on the table next to the bed, he reached over and snatched it up, then stood staring down at the top of her head.

A fine tremor ran through his fingers. How he wanted her! He felt like a youth with his first woman—his reaction unchanged, it seemed, no matter how often they made love.

"Ian?" Lily spun in the chair and gazed at him quizzically. "Is something wrong?"

"Nay," he said, shaking his head to rid it of the enticing thoughts racing through his mind. "I was getting this." He held up the brush.

Lily's face brightened with anticipation, and she turned so that he could reach her hair. "It felt wonderful when you combed it before."

Capturing the soft copper strands in his hand, he drew the brush slowly through her hair. Sighing, Lily closed her eyes. She looked as if she might drift off where she sat.

"Don't go to sleep," he whispered in her ear. "We cannot let this bath go to waste. Stay awake, and I'll help you wash," he promised.

Lily turned her head just far enough to see him. "Are you trying to lure me there, Dragon? If you wish to join me, all you need do is ask."

She looked intrigued by the idea. And the eagerness he saw in her eyes matched that in her voice.

He came around to the front of the chair and dropped to his knees. "I'll do anything you wish, Lily." He framed her face with his hands and stared into her eyes, trying to express the things his lips feared to say. "I will give you whatever you desire, if I can."

Ian went to the tub and trailed his fingers through the water, inhaling deeply of the herb-scented steam rising from its surface. Anticipation singing through his veins, he knelt on the hearth and stirred up the fire; this bath might take a while, if he had his way.

He rose and went to stand before her. "There is nowhere I'd rather be than here with you." He held out his hand.

"Stay with me, Ian." Placing her hand in his, Lily stood and let him lead her to the tub. She raised her hand to the lacings of her gown, but hesitated there. "Will you help me, milord?" she asked. "You're much better at this than I am." Her eyes promised him a world of delights—a world he intended to explore completely before this night was through.

Ian gently moved her hand aside and tugged the laces free. "You must be tired," he teased, lifting her bliaut over her head and tossing it aside. "You don't even have the energy to undress."

Lily's face flushed, her tongue darting out to moisten her lips. "You must be weary, too, Dragon. Here, let me help you," she whispered. She raised her hand to the neck of his shirt and slowly untied it. "I'm not used to this. It could take me a while." Her gaze holding his, she sent him a sultry look. "But I'm sure I'll learn."

Lily pushed open the neckline of Ian's shirt, leaned toward him and brushed her lips along the exposed flesh, then lightly nipped at the base of his throat. He tasted of sweat and the unique scent of Dragon. "You've been hard at work, I can tell," she murmured, soothing the spot with her tongue.

Ian groaned. The sound sent a surge of heat through her. She laughed, deep in her throat, as he redoubled his efforts to undress her. His eagerness made her feel powerful—all woman.

Was she powerful enough to control the Dragon?

"Slowly." She placed her hands over his as he sought to tug her undertunic up and over her head. "We've no need to hurry."

But she *did* want to see him—all of him—with the flickering firelight shimmering on his wet skin.

Ian stood and permitted her to undress him, his gaze following her every movement as she bared him to her eager scrutiny. She ran her hands over him from shoulders to hips, taking her time and making him shudder.

Ian's breath hissed between his teeth. "Temptress," he growled.

Lily toyed with the curls covering his chest, then drew her fingernail slowly along the cloud of hair covering his stomach. But she refused to touch that part of him that was standing to greet her.

Although her attention remained focused upon the fascinating musculature of Ian's chest, she could feel his gaze burning through her garments. She felt stripped bare, despite the fact that she still wore her clothes.

But she could hardly wear them into the bath. Stepping past Ian, Lily tested the herb-scented water with her finger. Perfect.

Smiling, she dragged her fingertip over Ian's lips, wondering why she didn't burst into flames from the heat of the passion burning in his eyes. "Are you ready to bathe, milord?" she asked.

"Aye, wife," he said. The rough timbre of his voice made her heart beat faster, if that was possible.

Slowly, Lily drew off her undertunic. She took even longer to wriggle free of her shift. Finally she stood naked before him, her only covering the shifting veil of hair hanging to below her hips.

Ian made a leisurely survey of the treasures before him, his gaze finally centering on her face.

A delicate bloom of color rode high along her cheeks—a tinge of embarrassment because of her boldness? He had enjoyed every moment of her teasing.

She resumed her stroking caress of his chest and stomach, her touch sending a fine tremor through his body. Ian knew the instant she felt it, her eyes darkening to a smoky green. Gliding her hands slowly over his neck and shoulders, she moved closer, until her breasts brushed against the curls matting his chest.

Closing his eyes for a moment, Ian searched within himself for the patience to make this feeling last. His body urged him to grab Lily, carry her to the bed and drive his aching flesh into her welcoming warmth.

But he wanted to linger over the pleasure, to share with Lily all the facets of passion, not just the urge for completion. Ian wanted to imprint himself upon Lily, to lose himself in her, to give himself to her—and receive the gift of Lily in return.

He could see her growing sense of power in her eyes, feel it in the sure touch of her hands on his body. It was her turn to lead the way, after their loving of the night before. He intended to savor every moment of Lily's boldness; he'd never felt so appreciated by a woman.

"Come, Dragon. Let me help you bathe," she murmured, taking his hand and stepping into the steaming tub. "'Tis wonderful."

Ian climbed in after her and tried to decide how they'd both fit. Laughing, she scooped water into her hand and splashed him.

"Careful," he warned. "We don't want to start a flood."

He grabbed her about the waist and pulled her into

his lap, sending a surge of water over the sides of the tub.

Lily shrieked, the sound swiftly cut off when Ian covered her mouth with his own. She offered no resistance, her tongue slipping through his lips to mate with his as he settled her more comfortably atop his lap.

Lily sank into the warm water and Ian's embrace, until she lay draped over him, her legs about his lean waist. His kiss alone was pure seduction, his tongue thrusting and taunting, drawing her deeper into the dark, whirling pool of his desire. He drew his hand slowly up her stomach and captured her breast, toying with the nipple and sending a bolt of fire to her very core.

She was content, now, to share the power in this battle.

A low moan rising from her throat, Lily sank deeper into the water, tightening her legs around Ian until the welcome heat of his manhood pressed against her aching flesh. He tore his mouth from hers, soothing her loss by nipping at her lower lip.

"You make me burn, sweeting," he murmured. Easing back slightly, he took her hand in his and dragged it down his chest until she encountered his arousal. "Feel how I want you." He closed her fingers about his flesh, hissing through his teeth when she slowly caressed him.

He was like silk beneath her touch, smooth and warm, pulsating with life. The water embraced her, intensifying her awareness of Ian's touch. It suddenly struck her that he intended to make love to her in the tub.

She found the idea appealing, although she wasn't certain it was possible. But as Ian continued to lavish attention on her aching breasts, stoking the flames smoldering within her, Lily became impatient. "Shouldn't we get out of here?" she asked, moaning against his neck as he slipped his hand over her stomach to the pool of heat between her legs. "Are you trying to drive me mad?"

"Aye." He took her mouth at the same moment he slid his fingers into her, her body arching into his at the sudden onslaught of pleasure. "I want to make you forget that anything exists but me. I want to hear the sounds you make when I give you joy, see it reflected in your eyes—" he nipped at her earlobe "—feel you melt around me when we become one."

Shifting beneath her, Ian grasped her about the waist and impaled her with his shaft. "Still want to leave?" he asked, his breath coming in short gasps.

Lily's aching body accepted him eagerly, rippling around his flesh in a spasm of pleasure. Her eyes opened wide, and she stared into his. "Never," she moaned. The possession in his eyes sent another bolt of fire searing through her to pool where they were joined. "Never leave me, Ian."

His hands still firm about her, he helped her move in a languid rhythm, while continuing to stare into her eyes. The water lapped about her breasts, its delicate caress intensifying everything she felt until her entire body became a pleasure point, every brush of sensation adding to her desire.

Ian slowed the rhythm of his thrusts, moving within her with a maddening languor. "Take me, Lily," he whispered, his breath against her ear weakening her grasp on reality.

"I am."

"Nay. Not just my body. Take me. Everything I want to give you." He maintained his leisurely movements.

"I'll give you happiness, if you let me. A child of our bodies—" he thrust harder "—if 'tis what you desire."

His words pushed Lily closer to the edge of the peak. Fire searing her veins, she gazed into his face, still reluctant to believe.

"But you must give me yourself. All of you." He leaned closer and brushed his lips against hers. "Please," he whispered, "give me my heart's desire."

Lily had no strength to resist the sincerity in his eyes. He lured her into the unknown depths with the promise of trust, of excitement—of love. How could she defy such a challenge? Throwing caution to the winds, she let her body welcome everything Ian offered.

"Yes." Her lips curled into a shaky smile. "Yes," she moaned as her body soared free.

The awareness that Ian watched her face as the spasms shook her sent Lily into a deeper realm of pleasure. And he waited until her eyes were fixed upon him before giving in to his own.

The intimacy of the gesture sent renewed heat shimmering through her. Gasping, they slumped together in the water.

As the blinding pleasure faded, Ian became aware of Lily draped limply over him, her hair floating in the now cool water.

"I cannot move," Lily mumbled against his cheek.

"What?" Had she come to harm from their lovemaking? Gathering himself, Ian pushed up against the side of the tub and lifted her so that he could see her face. "Is something wrong?"

Her eyes opened slowly. "Not a thing," she said, her voice a raspy purr. Her lips curled into a smile that was pure seduction. "'Tis just that you turned all my bones to mush."

She had the look of a thoroughly satisfied woman. Ian had never realized how arousing it could be, to know he'd put that look on her face, that hum of pleasure in her voice. His manhood began to stir. Impossible! he thought. But he couldn't deny that he wanted her again.

However, she'd been exhausted when she came into the room. He was greedy for her, 'twas true, but surely he could restrain himself long enough to allow her some well-earned rest.

And they needed to talk. Ian would never have believed he'd think such a thing. Discussing feelings and emotions was a woman's province. But they had gone deeply into something important, though they'd said barely a word about where they were headed.

He wanted to know what his wife felt for him.

The best thing would be to get out of the tub and dressed. Perhaps that would lessen the temptation to drag Lily beneath him and have his way with her. He looked at her again, keeping his gaze above her neck, but it didn't matter. He still wanted her.

Seeing the circles of weariness beneath her eyes, he knew he wouldn't try to take her.

Ian picked Lily up and climbed from the tub, then set her back in the water.

"What are you doing?" Her hand trailed lingeringly along his arm.

"You should finish your bath and rest now," he said. Picking up a clump of sweet-scented soap and a washrag, Ian knelt beside the tub.

"Ian...I thought you wished to bathe, too." Lily looked at him in confusion.

"If I get into that tub, there will be precious little bathing going on," he said shortly. Reaching into the water for her hand, he lifted her arm and began to rub the soapy cloth vigorously over her arm, then moved up to scrub at her upper chest and the column of her neck.

"But—"

Letting the rag fall into the water, Ian took her by the shoulders. "I want you again—now—but you need to rest. See what you do to me?" He glanced down at his manhood, jutting out from his thighs. "I'm becoming a rutting beast, wife," he said with disgust.

Lily's face colored slightly, but she continued to gaze at him. His body reacted accordingly, swelling his arousal even more. She reached out and cupped him in her palm. "I'm not that tired," she said, meeting his eyes with a searing look.

"By Christ, Lily. You'll drive me mad." Closing his eyes, he savored her touch. Her fingers cherished him, smoothing over his heated flesh until he was aware of little save the driving need to join with her again.

"Are you sure?" he asked, bending to rinse the soap from her glistening skin, then scooping her into his arms. She nodded, looping her arms about his neck and nuzzling at his throat.

There would be time for bathing—and talking—later. Three strides took him to the bed. Capturing her lips, he fell across the mattress and made her his once again.

They dozed for a while, but eventually neither could pretend to be asleep any longer. Ian rolled onto his side and looked down at Lily's beautiful face.

Their lovemaking had been amazing, each time more incredible than before. He had never imagined himself capable of the depth of feeling Lily could evoke with the simplest of caresses.

But life, once again, had intruded upon them. Although Steffan could not harm anyone now, Ian knew 'twas a matter of time before he—or they—were attacked again.

He could not bear it if Lily was harmed, but to have it happen when they were after him...

He would rather die than allow that to occur.

He kissed her lips gently, the only way he dared show Lily how he felt. The words to express his feelings were foreign to him, although perhaps he'd be able to say them, in time.

But time was something they might not have.

"I've been thinking," he whispered. "Trying to decide what to do." Lily stroked her fingers over his lips, making his blood begin to simmer once more. He captured her hand and laid it on his chest, over his heart.

"And what have you decided?"

"You realize we cannot go on like this, sweeting?"

"Like what?" she asked, looking confused. Perhaps he needed to go back to the beginning; he'd been turning ideas over in his mind for so long, he'd forgotten that she might not know what he was talking about.

"I have a home, a modest estate not so very far from here. Now that Llywelyn has branded me outlaw, my lands are likely forfeit. I need to find a way out of this coil, Lily, so that I can give you a home, and a life. We cannot run forever."

"Is there no place else we can go?"

Her shook his head. "Nay. Most of my power, such as it was, came from my position as Llywelyn's enforcer, not from lands or hereditary rights. So now I have nothing to offer you. Not even a roof over your head.''

"That doesn't matter to me, Ian. So long as I have you, I need nothing more.''

"But you will." He placed his hand over her stomach. "Even now, a tiny dragon may slumber here. You would not wish a wandering life on a babe. I know that, and so do you. The only way I can provide for you now is to hire out my sword. While I don't doubt I could do well at it, I don't believe you'd enjoy the mercenary's life."

Her eyes were soft when they gazed into his. "Such trifles do not matter, Ian," she said.

"I'm afraid you would find that they did, love. After living your life in an abbey, a mercenary's lot would seem to you as hell on earth. Ask Nicholas, if you don't believe me."

"How could he know?"

"His father was a mercenary, and so was he, briefly, before he inherited the honors of Ashby. His king never allows him to forget where he came from, and I'm certain he's not the only one. 'Tis a harsh life, with no hope of salvation. I refuse to subject you to it, if I can avoid it."

"But what can we do?"

"There's only one thing I can do. Go to Llywelyn and see what I can salvage of my life."

He hated the way her face turned pale and shadows clouded her eyes. "I don't know if he even knows the truth of anything that has happened."

"If you go to him, he'll kill you, or lock you away in those vaults!" she cried, burying her face against his chest. He could feel the warmth of her tears as they seeped from her eyes and ran over his flesh. They burned him, seared him with a sense of hopefulness, despite their situation.

Lily wouldn't cry unless she cared for him. Knowing that she cared, he was willing to try anything to give her all that she deserved—a life, a home, children, whatever she wanted.

"I think I know a way, a bargain I can strike with Llywelyn to get back what I have lost. I want to take you back to Gwal Draig with me, show you the Dragon's lair. If my idea works, I can give you the life you deserve, Lily."

And if it doesn't, I pray our family can protect you.

No doubt Llywelyn's vengeance would know no bounds.

Chapter Nineteen

"Please, Rannulf, tell him he's mad to even consider returning to Dolwyddelan. Why can't he see how dangerous it is?" Lily pleaded with her brother-by-marriage, although she feared it would serve no purpose.

He seemed as enamored of the idea as Ian. Perhaps they saw the situation differently, being men. She did not know. But she had to do *something*.

She looked across the solar to her sister, who was sitting by the fire, sewing, as usual. "Gillian—can you not reason with him?"

Gillian shook her head. "I agree with you that it's probably foolish to put himself into Llywelyn's hands. We've all seen he cannot be trusted," she added bitterly. "But I know Ian, and he will not rest until this situation is resolved." Her expression sympathetic, Gillian shook her head. "I'm sorry, Lily, but there is nothing we can do to stop him."

"Thank you for your faith in my abilities, cousin," Ian said dryly. He leaned back against the mantel and watched Lily. She refused to look at him, but she could feel the power of his gaze. "It's a pity my wife doesn't feel the same."

Lily fought back tears. They had been through this argument over and over. Ian refused to listen to anything she said. It felt as though he were mocking her concerns, and that hurt her, deeply.

They had just begun their life together, and what he wanted to do could bring it all—including Ian's very existence—crashing to an end.

"Don't you understand? I want us to have a future together." She jumped to her feet and took a turn about the room. She wanted to scream, he infuriated her so! "I don't care where we live, or how, so long as we're together."

"And don't you understand me?" Ian asked, low-voiced. "I have devoted myself to Llywelyn's cause for many years. It's as much a part of me as my hands, my eyes. He has to realize that will not change. He can trust me in this, at least. And if he needs me badly enough, perhaps he'll be willing to bargain."

She glanced at him, making no effort to stem the tears streaming down her cheeks. "And if he's not? What do you think will happen to you then? Or to me, not that that matters?"

Ian crossed the room and knelt by her side. "Nothing will happen to you. Rannulf won't allow it, will you?" he asked, glancing Rannulf's way.

"Of course not," Rannulf said. "You mustn't worry, Lily. You are family. I protect what is mine."

Were all men so dense? Lily reached out and framed Ian's face in her hands. "But how will I survive if something happens to you? Please, Ian."

He pressed a kiss in her palm, then gently pushed her hands away. "No. I'm sorry, sweeting." He stood. "I cannot do as you wish. Rannulf, may I speak with you outside?''

Lily watched them go, then buried her face in her hands as soon as the door closed behind the men. Gillian came to her and held her, smoothing away her tears.

"You cannot push him to it, Lily," she chided. "It will simply make him more stubborn."

"I truly don't understand him. Isn't it better to be alive somewhere else, even if it means changing your dreams, than to have done the honorable thing and be dead because of it? Perhaps it would make more sense to me if I'd grown up around men. I really haven't had much contact with them."

Gillian laughed, startling her. "It wouldn't make a whit of difference, believe me. I spent the first twelve years of my life almost exclusively with men, and while I might know how they think, I don't understand it, either. And I never learned to think like them. Thank goodness," she added with a rueful chuckle.

Lily scrubbed the trailing end of her sleeve over her eyes and stood. "What should I do, Gillian?"

Her sister put her arm about Lily's shoulders. "Kiss him goodbye with all the love in your heart, and smile as he rides off, in case he looks back. You're not going to change his mind, Lily, whether you rage and plead or weep and moan. At least let him remember you smiling, so that he's not distracted with worry while he's away." She kissed her cheek and stepped away. "Savor my pearls of wisdom, sister, for you won't hear many from me. But this I know to be true. If you love him, let him go with your smile in his heart, and pray for his safe return."

Lily thought about Gillian's words as she went about the tasks her sister had set for her. There was nothing she could do to help Ian prepare for his journey—except pray, as Gillian had suggested.

But as the time approached for Ian's departure, her heart grew so heavy, she didn't know if she could bear to watch him ride away. She feared what Llywelyn would do to him, even if he did not.

She took refuge in their chamber when she felt as though she could no longer hold back her tears. She sprawled across the bed, her hair lying about her in complete disarray.

Lily was so engrossed in her own thoughts that she didn't realize Ian had entered the room until she felt his fingers brush aside her hair, exposing the back of her neck. His touch sent shivers down her spine.

She tried to roll over to face him, but he prevented her. "Nay, just lie here, sweeting, and let me hold you."

He wrapped his arms about her and cuddled her into his body spoon-fashion, nuzzling her nape with his lips. She smiled to herself when she realized she was not the only one affected by this play; she could feel his manhood pressing firmly against her buttocks.

But still he refused to permit her to turn and face him. Instead, he slipped his hand inside the bodice of her gown, his fingers skimming over her sensitive flesh until she felt a rush of warmth at her core.

"Ian," she moaned, trying to squirm around. She managed to move her hand behind her and reach him.

She teased his shaft through his clothes, and his sighs of pleasure were soon rising to join hers. Finally, his hands frantic, he pushed at the hem of her bliaut and shoved it up high enough to reach beneath it to her woman's flesh.

She ached for him, but he tempted her even as she

did the same to him. She didn't understand his intentions when he raised one of her legs and slipped between her thighs, but when he slipped his shaft into her waiting flesh, all thought fled.

Afterward, they lay nestled together in the center of the bed. Content, Lily drifted off to sleep in Ian's arms.

When she awoke, she was alone. She could tell from the fading light that the day was nearly done.

It felt as though her heart leaped into her throat as she crawled off the bed and straightened her twisted garments. He couldn't have left her without saying goodbye.

Could he?

She tugged the door open and ran out into the corridor. "Ian? Gillian? Is anyone here?"

The sound of boot-clad feet mounting the stairs caught her attention, and she raced to the stairwell. "Ian?"

Swen caught her about the waist before she could run down the stairs. "He's already gone, Lily," he said, swinging her around and settling her gently on a stool. "There's no need to hurry."

"He left without saying goodbye?"

"Aye."

She fought back tears, unsuccessfully.

"He didn't want you to cry," he said, his voice kind. He had no mocking grin for her now. "And I think he didn't want to let you go. 'Twas easier for him this way. Don't blame him."

He stood patiently, waiting while she tried to collect herself. When the tears had finally ceased, he said, "I have just the thing to make you smile. Come with me. Lady Gillian has brought Katherine outside to see a new litter of pups. I promise she'll make you laugh."

She took the hand he held out to her, and allowed him to lead her outside. But as kind as Swen was, she knew she could not forget Ian, not for a moment.

And though her tears had dried for now, she knew that even if Ian survived, he would make her weep again.

The road to Dolwyddelan seemed far longer upon Ian's return than it had when he left. Despite taking a much more direct route, he found the journey dull and slow without Lily by his side to brighten his way.

Rannulf and a full troop of his men accompanied him, well-trained soldiers he trusted with his life. This journey back might very well be a matter of life or death, for unless he could somehow make his peace with Llywelyn, he had no life to offer Lily. His pride would allow nothing else.

They carried Steffan's body with them, preserved for the trip in a barrel of brine. Lily had been horrified at the thought, but Ian wanted Llywelyn to see just what Steffan had become. Perhaps he'd find some lesson in that.

He and Swen had argued mightily over whether Swen ought to come with him. But Ian had won the day in that battle of wits. Considering that he didn't know what his reception would be when he arrived at Dolwyddelan, Ian didn't want Swen to be tarred with the same brush as he. Chances were strong that Llywelyn didn't know Swen had joined forces with the Dragon. It would be best if it stayed that way.

Rannulf had come to lend his support when Ian presented his bargain to the prince. The Norman had always gotten along well with Llywelyn; perhaps his presence would serve to keep the prince's temper under control.

When Ian arrived at Dolwyddelan, it was sheer luck that the guard at the gates was a man whose loyalty was more to the Dragon than to Llywelyn. Thus, Ian was able to bring Rannulf's troops in with him, though whether that would prove beneficial or not, he could not have said.

However, he was glad of their company.

The guards permitted him to make use of his chamber before they took him to see Llywelyn. He used the opportunity to wash and shave, and to garb himself in his finest clothes. Most of the time, what he wore made no difference to him, so long as the clothing was adequate for his needs. However, today he wanted every advantage he could find.

He was Lord Ian ap Dafydd of Gwal Draig, the Dragon, cousin to Welsh royalty. He refused to be cowed by anyone.

Not even Llywelyn himself.

Lily bounced along in the saddle, trying not to moan, despite the cramps in her legs. It had taken her so long to convince Swen he must bring her to Dolwyddelan, they'd had to travel at a headlong pace to make up for lost time.

She only hoped that once they arrived, she'd be capable of movement. Although, if she was desperate enough, Swen could always carry her in.

What an entrance that would be!

Lily found a certain irony in the fact that today she was permitted to ride straight through the gates. But, like the last time she'd come to Dolwyddelan, she was taken into custody immediately.

She hoped her guard would be stupid enough to put her in the same room she'd occupied so briefly. Not that she wished to leave the keep at the moment, having come here of her own free will, but who could say when she might need an escape route? Unfortunately, they brought her to a chamber near the prince's. There was a constant parade of people in and out of Llywelyn's meeting room, as well as a bevy of others lounging about in the corridor outside.

She scarcely had a chance to change into the garments Gillian had sent with her—clothing much finer than anything she'd ever worn—before a servant came to take her to meet with Llywelyn.

Her reception—and accommodations—certainly were very different from her previous stay here. But those things didn't matter.

Saving Ian did.

Swen stood outside her door with a guard of his own. For once, his smile was nowhere in sight. "The Dragon will skin me alive when he sees you here," he said, low-voiced, glaring at a pair of men trying to listen to their conversation. "He didn't even want me to come here, or be associated with him in any way. What will he think when he discovers you're here?"

"He'll think that you're a fool where women are concerned," she whispered. "There are worse things."

"Do you think I should have stayed outside the castle walls?" he asked.

She poked him in the arm. "Aye. But I told you that before you so stupidly rode in here anyway, if you recall. Don't blame me if you're sorry now."

Despite her harsh words, Lily was concerned about Swen. She'd grown fond of the brawny Viking, and she wished him no harm. However, she very much feared that his fate would not be any better than Ian's, simply because of his involvement with her.

A servant motioned them forward and held the door for them. Swen went in first, with Lily right behind him. Then, side by side, they stood before Llywelyn.

The prince sat in state in a huge chair at one end of the room, surrounded by people—men, mostly. The babble of voices died down to a whisper as all eyes focused on them.

Llywelyn motioned them forward. Lily took a deep breath and forced steel into her backbone. She'd gain nothing if she behaved like a puling weakling.

She was the Dragon's mate. She'd prove to these men that she was worthy of that honor.

Head held high, taking her time, as though she, and not Llywelyn, controlled this meeting, Lily glided across the room. Upon reaching the prince, she sank into a deep curtsy.

"Cousin," she said clearly, inclining her head in a regal gesture she'd copied from the abbess. "I thank you for allowing me to join you."

"Milady," Llywelyn murmured, with a nod of his own. "Please, be seated here, near me." He gestured toward a bench along the wall.

She took the place he indicated and settled to watch and wait.

Swen made a bow to Llywelyn, as well, receiving only an absentminded nod in acknowledgment. His wide shoulders dipping into a shrug, he came to stand near her.

Another murmur of voices forced her attention to the door. Ian and Rannulf stood there, scanning the room.

Lily knew the instant her husband saw her. His face,

already set in harsh lines, seemed to tighten into an expressionless mask.

And the look in his eyes would have frightened her, had she not been so frightened *for* him.

"FitzClifford," Llywelyn called. "Welcome to Dolwyddelan. Come and tell me why you're here."

Rannulf and Ian went to stand directly before the prince. Llywelyn did not acknowledge Ian in any way.

Rannulf bowed. "I have come to you, Llywelyn, on behalf of my brother-by-marriage, Lord Ian ap Dafydd of Gwal Draig."

"That honor is his no longer," Llywelyn snarled. He rose from his chair. "And what do you mean, brother-by-marriage? You wed his cousin, not his sister."

"Aye, sir, that is true." Rannulf came to Lily and, taking her hand, helped her to rise from her seat. "But he is wed to my wife's sister." He presented her to Llywelyn with a flourish. "Lady Lily de l'Eau Clair."

A loud hum of conversation rose from the crowd around them, and Lily felt herself to be under scrutiny from a hundred pairs of eyes. Although she knew that was an exaggeration, she didn't like the sensation.

And evidently Llywelyn didn't care to have all these people know his business. "Clear this hall!" he cried, then remained silent until all the hangers-on had left.

"You have wed the Dragon, madame?"

"Aye, milord." She turned to the side, just far enough to see Ian's face. "We are most assuredly husband and wife."

Llywelyn's eyes narrowed. "Is it not true, Dragon, that you married this woman simply to spite me, to destroy my plans for her?"

"No, milord, that is not true. I wed her because she is courageous and beautiful, with a kind heart." Ian met her gaze, and she smiled at the emotion darkening his eyes. "I married her because I love her. If that upsets your plans, milord, then be damned to you."

"Your tone is not what I would expect from a man who has been branded outlaw and traitor."

"Outlaw I may be, but I am no traitor!" A flush suffused Ian's face, and his voice shook. "I will kill any man who calls me thus."

Llywelyn could have chosen no worse term to label Ian; despite all that had happened of late, his loyalty to Wales was above reproach.

Llywelyn laughed, startling them all. "I have no doubt but that you've killed him already, the jealous bastard. Sion was the first to go after you once I declared you outlaw."

"Aye, he's dead, and many others with him," Ian said. "Do you have so many men to spare, that you send them to their deaths to punish one man? It makes no sense, milord. You need them for Wales, not for vengeance."

Rannulf stepped into the conversation. "We have come here, sir, to make you a proposition. In return for Ian's help in the negotiations currently under way in London, he will regain everything you have declared forfeit. In addition, you will swear you have no further plans for Lily."

Llywelyn stared at Lily for a long while. "Do you realize what you set in motion, girl, because you refused to stay where you belonged? You have been nothing but trouble from the moment you arrived here."

"Then you should have no objections to transferring possession of me to Ian, if he still wants me. And I am willing to stay here, or at another keep of your choosing, as surety for Ian's return."

"Lily," Ian growled. His gaze promised retribution. She could hardly wait.

But she returned her attention to Llywelyn.

"If I agree to this, what benefit do I gain?" he asked—needlessly, Lily thought. If the prince didn't know that, he didn't deserve to rule.

Ian stared him straight in the eyes. "You gain my goodwill and loyalty, milord, despite my opinion of your actions with regard to my wife. And you retain my ability as the enforcer of your justice." His grin would have done Swen proud. "Instead of as your enemy."

"And you're willing to travel to London to represent our interests in the matter of this charter?" Llywelyn asked.

Ian nodded.

"Then sit yourself down, Dragon. I've important work for you."

Chapter Twenty

The door to her chamber slammed shut behind them. Ian looked as stone-faced as he had when facing down Llywelyn, which did not bode well for the brief time they had left together.

Once Llywelyn decided something, he wasted no time in implementing his plans. The man was a born schemer—and meddler. Lily could only be glad she shouldn't need to deal with him often.

But now she should start behaving as a wife ought to. It wasn't too late to begin. She rose and poured a mug of mead from the pitcher on the table. "Please sit." She indicated a bench. "When did you last eat?" she asked, handing him the cup.

"This morning sometime—I don't recall exactly when." He drank the mead in one long swallow, then held out the mug for more. "'Twas a long and dusty ride."

Lily refilled his mug, then opened the door and asked that food be brought. She was surprised when the servant left to fulfill her request. She returned to Ian, not wanting to waste a moment of their time together.

She felt nervous, unwilling to meet his eyes.

"I never planned on telling you as I did. I thought we'd be abed, or perhaps taking a bath," Ian said lightly.

Lily looked up swiftly at his teasing tone. The veil of weariness had lifted from his eyes, leaving them a beautiful dark green. A wry smile lifting one corner of his mouth, his expression taunted her, challenged her, dared her to come closer.

When he held out his hand, she couldn't resist.

No sooner had Lily stepped nearer than Ian stood and swept her into his arms. Lifting her until her feet left the floor and her eyes were level with his, he took her mouth in a demanding kiss.

By the time his lips abandoned hers, both of them were short of breath. "I've hungered for you since I left you," Ian whispered. "'Twas torture to leave you as I did, but it was the only way I could leave you at all." He slowly slid her down his body, nudging her gently with the proof of his desire before her feet touched the floor. "But it seems I'll be satisfying a different hunger for the moment," he said as a knock sounded at the door.

He nodded to the manservant who placed a tray of food on the table.

His attention on them instead of his task, the man bumped the pitcher of mead and set it wobbling. Lily didn't care for the smirk on his face.

Evidently Ian didn't, either. "You'd do well to attend to your duties," he snarled. He grabbed the pitcher before it could topple over. "And you'll show respect to the lady, else you'll be dredging out the garderobe pits."

The color draining from his face, the servant bowed

low. "Aye, milord. Beg pardon, milady." Snatching up the tray, he hurried back to the kitchen.

"Insolent knave," Ian growled, pulling the bench up to the table. He met her gaze before he sat down. "I apologize for his discourtesy. God knows, they know little of manners here, but it will not happen again, I promise you."

She knew she could count on that. It surprised her to think that any servant would risk angering the Dragon. She sliced cheese and meat, placing them on a trencher of dark brown bread. "This fare is better than what I ate the last time I was here," she said, placing the food before Ian and pouring more mead.

She saved her questions for later.

He continued to tease her throughout the meal, until she was ready to strangle him. This was an Ian she did not know, although she found this side of him appealing.

"Calm yourself," he said, smiling. "I vow I've never met a woman as easy to provoke as you." The look Lily sent him would have brought most men to their knees to beg for mercy.

But not Ian. "Messengers will go out to Ashby, Gwal Draig and l'Eau Clair at first light." He picked up her hand from her lap and began toying with her fingers. "I wish you hadn't come here, love. I'd have felt much better about this if I knew you were with Gillian or Catrin."

"I'll be safe here," she assured him. She felt that was true. "But I worry about you, journeying so far from home."

"We'll go well guarded. And now that I'm no longer an outlaw, I should be safe enough. 'Tis not like the last time."

What she'd intended to say flew out of her brain when Ian stroked his fingertip along the sensitive flesh of her wrist, sending a shiver of reaction down her spine. An intimate, knowing smile and the warm glow in his eyes were his only response.

He raised her hand to his lips and kissed her fingertips one by one.

Lily hadn't objected to Ian's affectionate display; truthfully, she had no wish to stop him. He made her feel as if she were the focus of his attention, her opinions and her person valued and desired. It was easy to forget the realities of life, away from the rest of the world.

Her attention focused on Ian, Lily wasn't aware anyone had entered the room until Ian spoke. "What is it?" he asked, his voice hoarse. He clasped Lily's hand when she would have pulled it away.

Lily lowered her gaze, refusing to look at the man. Doubtless her desire for Ian was written on her face. And right now, her face felt as hot as her blood.

"Beg pardon, milord, but the master says 'tis time to leave," the servant mumbled, bowing slightly.

"I'll be along directly," he said, dismissing him. Not until the servant was nearly to the door did Ian stand. "You have a powerful effect on me, love," he said softly, casting a rueful glance at his body.

Lily's flush deepened when she noted his swollen manhood. "I'm sorry."

"Don't be. I'm not." Catching her chin in his hand, he bent and brushed his lips across hers. "I'm only sorry we weren't alone." Reaching down, he grasped her about the waist and lifted her from the bench. "This will have to last us." Clasping her tightly to his still-aroused body, Ian ravished her mouth with his. When he'd reduced her to mindless confusion, he set her back on the bench.

"I love you, Lily. Don't ever forget that." He trailed his fingers over her cheek, then was gone.

Ian and Rannulf left Dolwyddelan the same day they arrived, heading for Ashby to meet Nicholas. They took Rannulf's troop with them; all three of them were exceptional fighters, but there were bandits and criminals everywhere.

It galled Ian to leave Lily with Llywelyn, but he tried to console himself with the fact that at least she should be safe there. As long as he believed she would be safe, he could concentrate all his attention on trying to gain what concessions he could for Wales.

He found the thought of traveling all the way to London terrible. 'Twas a long journey, and bound to be hellish with mud and bad roads this time of year.

And who knew what they would discover once they arrived?

The situation between King John and the rebels had dragged back and forth since before Christmastide. The king had until Easter to come to some sort of decision about what to do. It didn't appear that he intended to do much of anything, except stalling.

Ian knew Nicholas and Rannulf were torn between their duty and the fact that many of the claims and complaints made by the rebels had merit.

And both men had no desire to leave their wives and homes to rejoin the back-stabbing and petty squabbles of their fellow noblemen.

But despite that, they felt a duty to go and add their support to the king. Though he knew that both despised the man, for numerous reasons.

King John was Nicholas's overlord, and Rannulf's, through Gillian; her father, like so many marcher lords, had held l'Eau Clair directly of the king.

Ian had been surprised at their willingness to make the long journey to London. But as they eased the weariness and boredom of the trip with talk and discussion, he came to understand his two brothers-by-marriage better, to know them as men.

Rannulf, in particular, had decided to go because of his loyalty to his foster father, William Marshall, the earl of Pembroke—who also happened to be Gillian's godfather. When Rannulf and Gillian wished to wed, only Marshall's intervention with the king had made their marriage possible. Otherwise, she'd be unmarried still, or wed to Nicholas, whom the king had appointed her guardian.

Ian found he missed Lily more and more each day they were apart. He felt as though a huge hole had been ripped in his soul. The thought that it might possibly be months before they were together again made him resent the necessity for this journey all the more.

His companions seemed no more eager to be away from home than he. It was a miserable and morose group of men who finally arrived in Pembroke's camp.

Ian dreaded the thought of trying to make the Norman—no, English, he reminded himself—king see the merit of Llywelyn's requests. The fact that John also happened to be Llywelyn's father-by-marriage would matter not at all. John and Llywelyn had a battle-strewn relationship, and since neither man was willing to give an inch, no charter was likely to change that.

But Ian would do what he could, for Wales, if not for her prince.

He understood his duty, all too well.

And he would have done his duty whether Llywelyn held Lily as surety or not.

Once they arrived, Ian swiftly realized that he would find it next to impossible to stay at the loyal barons' camp. Nicholas and Rannulf remained fixed there with their compatriots, but he didn't belong there.

Unfortunately, he didn't belong with that lot of idiots in the rebel camp, either.

He found himself an inn near where Nicholas and Rannulf were located, and settled in to wait.

Even the English had heard of the Dragon, so he had little difficulty in obtaining an interview with King John himself.

He found that Nicholas's description of the English king had been very accurate. It helped him keep his temper, though he wanted to snarl when the frustration of dealing with these fools became too much. He was surprised to discover that Llywelyn seemed a very reasonable leader in comparison.

Nicholas and Rannulf sought him out late one evening, nearly a month after they arrived. They were waiting for him when he returned—hot, tired and angry—from another foray at court.

He invited them into his room and offered them mead. "Though I must apologize for the poor quality. I cannot find much of anything, food nor drink, worth the money they charge for it here."

Nicholas nodded. "Aye. Everyone's been here too long. Tempers are short, the weather is too hot—everywhere there's the stink of too many people. Our encampment smells like a midden. If something isn't resolved soon, we'll have a battle on our hands right here."

"Have you heard anything from Lily?" Rannulf asked.

Ian shook his head and frowned. "Nay. I'm not sure if it's because Llywelyn won't allow it, or if she simply didn't think to send me word of her."

"A messenger arrived from l'Eau Clair this morning, the first since we got here. Gillian sent Swen to Dolwyddelan to see her, thinking we'd want news of her. The prince left the keep long ago—shortly after we did, as a matter of fact—but he's keeping Lily there, as a guest of sorts. Swen said she's hopeful she might be permitted to go to Gwal Draig soon. I guess she doesn't like being mewed up under someone else's thumb," he added with a chuckle. "I wonder how she'll like being married to you, once the newness wears thin." He raised an eyebrow.

Nicholas punched Rannulf in the arm. "Don't you start. Do you want to have to battle your own brother-by-marriage?"

Ian waved them to silence. "Nay, I'll fight neither of you. I, too, wonder how Lily will find married life, once we have the chance to spend much time in each other's company."

"Aye," Nicholas said with a wink, "and you have to leave your bedchamber eventually, more's the pity."

"I wouldn't worry about that, if I were you," Rannulf said. "'Tis clear as a summer morn that Lily loves you. I just hope, for your sake, that she has a temper like her sister's," he added with a laugh. "I love to argue with Gillian, I must admit."

"That's because you enjoy making up with her," Nicholas said wryly.

"We came here to bring you with us to Pembroke's camp," Rannulf said. "I think you'll find more opportunity to discuss Llywelyn's aims with the men there than with the ones you've dealt with at court.''

What harm could there be in it? Ian buckled on his sword belt and left the stifling confines of the inn. Anything to hurry along these ceaseless arguments disguised as negotiations, he thought with a frown.

At this point, he'd do just about anything, if it meant he could rejoin Lily soon.

Lily swiftly grew to dislike Dolwyddelan just as much as she had Saint Winifred's, and for similar reasons. Once again she was a prisoner.

But it was far worse this time. She'd tasted freedom, adventure, love. Now that she'd experienced those things, the walls of her prison felt that much higher.

Sometimes she wondered if she would ever be free again.

At least Llywelyn was no longer here. She'd found that simply being in his presence was a trial. She couldn't look at him without remembering all she had lost due to his machinations. She didn't know if she'd ever be able to forgive him.

Lily tried to remind herself that she'd come here of her own free will, to help save the life of the man she loved. But as the weeks went by with no word of Ian, she began to wonder whether it had all been for naught.

What if something had happened to him, either on the journey or in England, a foreign land? Despite reminding herself that Rannulf or Nicholas would surely tell her if something had happened, she couldn't bury her fears completely.

Swen had been to see her, at Gillian's behest, several times since Ian had left for England. The Viking was always good company, but it came to the point where even he could no longer lift her spirits.

Finally, on another warm, sunny day—a day when she longed for the freedom to simply leave the castle walls and run wherever she willed—a visitor arrived.

She returned Gillian's embrace, tears streaming down her cheeks. "I'm so glad to see you," she said, unwilling to release her sister.

"And I you."

Lily finally stepped back and gave Gillian a watery smile. "It's been so long since I came here." She motioned for the other woman to take a seat in the room's only chair. "All too often of late it seems like everything that came before—marrying Ian, finding you—is naught but a wonderful dream."

Gillian smiled. "'Tis no dream," she assured her. "And neither is the news I bring you. I petitioned Llywelyn on your behalf. He's willing to allow you to go home, to Gwal Draig."

"I'm free to leave this place?"

"Aye, but only to go to Gwal Draig. The prince wants to know where you are. I think he finally overcame his anger with Ian, and has come to realize that this gesture of goodwill and trust could make up for a great deal. He realizes how valuable Ian is to him. No good can come from keeping him on too short a lead, else he'll simply decide to leave after all."

Lily shook her head. "Nay, Gillian. Believe me when I tell you that will never happen," she said bitterly. "I tried to get Ian to leave, to start our lives over someplace else, but he'd have none of it. Wales is his home. He will not leave it."

"As I said, I don't think he needs to worry about

Llywelyn's wrath falling upon him again.'' She settled back in the chair and ran her gaze critically over Lily.

Lily flushed beneath her sister's scrutiny and turned away to begin gathering together her few belongings.

"Have you been ill in the mornings?'' Gillian asked.

Lily swung around and stared.

"Have you?''

Lily sank down on the edge of the bed. "Aye, and other times, as well.''

"You *do* know what that means?''

"I'm not so ignorant as that!'' she said hotly.

Gillian laughed. "Peace, sister. Since you were raised by a bevy of nuns, I doubt you had much exposure to the realities of life.''

"In the company of women, childbearing is a universal topic. Several of the other boarders had been wed and had children. I do know where babies come from,'' she said, grinning. "At least, I do now.''

"Obviously.''

"Do you think Ian will mind?'' she asked, giving voice to one of the many questions that had haunted her of late.

"How can he mind? He had something to do with the condition you're in. Despite your holy upbringing, I refuse to believe God had anything to do with this,'' Gillian said dryly.

"I doubt it.''

Gillian stood and began helping Lily fold her clothing. "Are you well enough to travel? Gwal Draig is not far from here, but if you think riding would—''

"I'll be fine,'' Lily assured her. "Most likely much of my malaise is due to the fact that I feel imprisoned here. I should be better away from Dolwyddelan.''

"Good. I'll stay with you for a while, if you wish,

until you are settled. Soon, pray God, our husbands will return.''

It couldn't happen too soon for Lily.

Chapter Twenty-One

Finally the day arrived for which Ian had waited— forever, it seemed. After continuing to argue up to the last moment, King John agreed to meet his barons at the water meadow of Runnymede.

Ian wouldn't have bothered to stay for the event if he hadn't feared that Llywelyn might claim—and rightly so—that he hadn't seen his task to completion. Given the king's wavering nature, Ian wouldn't believe the charter had been accepted until he saw it for himself.

Nicholas and Rannulf were likewise eager to be quit of the place. By now, summer had arrived, and all three men had too much to do at home.

So few barons had stayed at John's side throughout the negotiations that the king's train was meager indeed. So much for loyalty, Ian thought. 'Twas the same everywhere, unfortunately. Few men valued honor anymore.

The actual meeting with the king proved anticlimactic. Considering what the charter stood to do for the barons, it should have been a far more momentous occasion. But perhaps everyone else was as tired of the entire situation as Ian, Nicholas and Rannulf were.

As soon as they could get away, the three gathered

up their gear and their men and set off for home, eagerness lending speed to their journey.

Lily settled in at Gwal Draig with surprising ease. She couldn't decide if that was due to Gillian's presence or to the fact that Ian's people were happy to have a woman about to keep the household running smoothly. They'd had no mistress since Catrin's marriage to Nicholas, and it showed.

Lily had a great deal to learn about housewifery, and was especially thankful for her sister's help. She was skilled at managing a manor, and good at dealing with people, and Lily found it amazing, the amount of work Gillian could get out of people by the simple expedient of praising their efforts.

This method was completely foreign to Lily, since the abbess of Saint Winifred's had done little except carp and complain. Lily had noticed how Gillian went about it in her own home, however, so she quickly set about implementing the same technique at Gwal Draig. She could see the merit in Gillian's skillful handling of servants, for they worked harder, and seemed to like her, as well.

Thinking of the child she carried, Ian's child, helped her when she found herself floundering for want of him. She'd come to depend upon him so quickly, it surprised her, and she felt his loss keenly. As the weeks passed without word of him, so did her worry increase.

She was disgusted that she cried so easily because of the babe, but Gillian simply laughed and told her 'twas normal. Thankfully, it shouldn't last.

She hoped not. She despised herself each time she dissolved into tears. And she doubted Ian would find it attractive.

In June, one of Gillian's messengers arrived at Gwal Draig with welcome news.

"They should be home soon," Gillian said, her voice filled with excitement.

"Are they all well?"

"Aye, just bored and tired of waiting. Rannulf says to tell you that Ian has grown thin and wan for want of you," she read with a giggle. "He hopes you're prepared to nurse him back to health."

"You don't think Ian is truly ill, do you?" Lily asked, all her concerns rushing to the fore.

"Of course not," Gillian said, waving the parchment about. "'Tis just Rannulf's way of telling you that Ian misses you dreadfully—no surprise there."

"I'd better set to work to prepare everything for their arrival. They are all coming here, aren't they?"

"I'm not sure about Nicholas. He may go directly to Ashby. Perhaps it will just be Ian and Rannulf and their men."

Lily smiled at Gillian and returned her embrace. "I hope they arrive soon. I'm eager for our life together to finally begin."

Ian's blood thrummed with anticipation as they drew closer to Gwal Draig. Since Rannulf had told him that Lily was there, he had not been able to stop picturing her in the hall, the gardens—his bed.

But there was so much they needed to set straight before they started their life together. Everything had happened so quickly. They'd met and married within just over a sennight. No wonder he felt such uncertainty about whether Lily would still want him, once she learned to know him.

Yet he was a better man for having met her. She

brought out a side of himself he'd thought lost forever, a trace of the idealistic youth he'd once been. And he no longer saw himself as the sole savior of Llywelyn's plans. Let the prince scheme and plot as he would; he did not always need the Dragon to enforce his law.

Let some other poor fool take up that thankless chore. Ian had other tasks, more dear to his heart than even his beloved Wales.

The weather turned nasty as they got closer to home. Gwal Draig stood surrounded by forest and rugged terrain, and the rain and fog that had descended upon them from the mountains made the going slow.

Impatient now that he was nearly there, he could have snarled in frustration.

They were almost to the village when the attack came out of nowhere, startling their mounts and catching them foolishly unprepared. Their attackers were on foot, and outnumbered them, from the sound of it—'twas difficult to see—so the men split up and joined the battle.

"Hurry!" Ian shouted to the others. "They're attacking the town!" He spurred his horse along the track. "Follow me!"

A muted cry echoed through the trees, followed by the unmistakable clash of steel against steel. Some of their men had gone on ahead; clearly, they'd already met with trouble.

Hoofbeats pounded as the two rear guards rushed past them. Rain flung from the sodden branches whipped at their faces as they raced through the trees toward the sounds of battle.

A woman ran past, her gown torn and scarcely covering her nakedness. 'Twas all Ian needed to see. Leaping from the saddle, he shoved past Rannulf, racing over the uneven ground to the pair writhing on the grass.

Leaping the last few yards, he hit the man square in the back, sending him flying.

Roaring his rage, Ian grabbed the churl by the tunic and jerked him to his feet. The man didn't even have a chance to straighten before Ian planted a fist in his face, forcing him to his knees. Ian grinned at the satisfying crunch of bone beneath his knuckles. "Get up, you coward," he snarled, motioning with his hands for the man to stand. "I've not even started with you."

Breathing noisily through his crushed nose, he lurched to his feet and, clasping his hands together, swung them at Ian's head. Ian evaded the blow easily, taking advantage of the other man's momentum to knock him to the ground again.

There was no challenge to this, Ian thought, disgusted by the whimpering sounds stealing through his opponent's lips. He waited impatiently for him to regain his feet, then stalked him around the clearing. "Fight back, damn you," he growled. "Or do you only hit women?"

His body swaying, he simply stood and stared at Ian, his only response to the insult the fire flaring in his eyes.

"Do you know what I'm going to do to you, you miserable son of a bitch? Once I've beaten you bloody, I'm going to rip off your—"

Snarling, teeth bared in a terrible grimace, the other man dived at Ian.

Finally, Ian thought, the exultation of battle rushing through him. There was no challenge—or honor—in pounding on a puling craven who wouldn't fight back. But now he felt the honest satisfaction of defending the innocent. This churl would die today, one way or another, for the things he'd done.

Hands at each other's throats, they rolled across the

rocky ground, their struggle punctuated by grunts and moans.

Finally, Ian felt the man go limp beneath him. Leaving him lying there, Ian grabbed the reins and swung back into the saddle, heading for the village.

He discovered a group of men on the road leading away from the village, loaded down with their ill-gotten gains. A ragged band of fighters ran from the trees and joined their fellows, their crude weapons at the ready.

They attacked immediately, reaching to pull him from the saddle. He looked about for any help, but none of his men were near. No matter. He could manage on his own.

Slashing about him with his sword and kicking out at the cudgels raised against him, Ian sent several men to their knees, blood streaming from their wounds. He swung his sword in a wide arc and sent a subtle command to his mount. The stallion reared up, hooves flailing out to strike at the men before him.

A bolt of fire shot through his shoulder. Sucking in a deep breath against the pain, he stared at the arrow piercing his flesh. Damnation, but it hurt!

His attention faltered, and the stallion lowered his hooves to the ground.

Before he could urge the horse to a gallop, the group moved in to attack again. He could not beat back this assault. Ian cursed as they pulled him from the saddle and continued to rain blows upon him, despite his struggles.

They finally pinned him to the ground. He felt a sharp blow to the head, making his body jerk and his vision dim.

His last thought before the darkness claimed him was of Lily.

When Ian regained his senses, he lay flat on his back, soaking-wet and shivering with a bone-deep chill. The icy moisture soothed his aching body, bringing him back from the darkness still muddling his mind. He rolled onto his side, groaning when he hit the arrow in his shoulder. He had to get up. His attackers seemed to have left him alone for the moment, but they might return to resume their assault.

He shifted and lifted his uninjured arm, surprised at how unsteady he felt.

Where were Nicholas and Rannulf? he wondered. Had they managed to survive this, or were they, like him, lying wounded somewhere?

He struggled to sit up, a sharp pain in his right leg telling him he'd been hit by another arrow. He reached down and felt the shaft, just below his knee. He didn't think the wound was bleeding, but it certainly would make it difficult to walk.

Head pounding, he struggled to his feet, ignoring the way his stomach churned. His sight wavered and blurred.

Ian lurched across the uneven ground, managing only a few stumbling steps before his knee gave out.

He landed hard on his side, his head swimming giddily for a moment. Sweat ran down his face and neck as he rolled onto his good knee and tried to rise again.

Ian pushed himself upright, shoving wet hair out of his face with a shaking hand. He scanned the area. The fog, combined with his headache, lent an eerie glow to the landscape. Though he knew he could only be a few leagues from Gwal Draig, nothing looked familiar.

Nothing moved. All was silent save for the steady drip of rain off the trees.

He should move, look at the bodies laying along the

trail. He knew he'd recognize the victims—they were his people, after all—but he doubted Rannulf or Nicholas would be among them. He hoped not. He already dreaded the tally of carnage from this day's work.

He staggered along the road, clutching his shoulder and dragging his right leg. Before he'd gone twenty yards, his leg collapsed under him and he fell to the ground.

Though he struggled against it, darkness claimed him once more.

Rannulf spurred his horse back along the trail, Nicholas riding hard beside him. It had taken a while, but they and their men had managed to help the villagers beat off the attack. Casualties among the villagers appeared high, but nowhere among the bodies strewn throughout the area around the town had they found Ian.

No one had seen him since he'd leaped back onto his horse after beating the rapist into the ground. It had been too hectic for them to keep track of each other in the fray.

They'd search every inch of the forest if they had to, but find him they would. Rannulf had no intention of going to Gwal Draig without him, or of telling Lily her husband was dead. Ian was alive, and they would find him.

They nearly rode right over Ian's prone body where he lay sprawled in the middle of the road. Even the thundering hoofbeats of the horses hadn't seemed to rouse him.

Nicholas jumped from the saddle and ran to Ian, carefully easing him over onto his back. "An arrow in the arm, another in the leg, and bruises about the head," he said as he examined him.

"Look at his leg." Rannulf pointed toward Ian's knee, twisted at an odd angle below the arrow.

"At least he still lives," Nicholas said. "Come on, we've got to get him home." Together they picked him up and moved him to the side of the road.

"It's not far to Gwal Draig from here." Rannulf sat back on his heels and pondered the situation. "'Twould be best to get a hurdle. Some of the townspeople—or we—can carry him there."

"Aye. With the lumps on his head and the fact that he hasn't awakened, we'd better not try to move him with a cart or horse. He shouldn't be jostled about. There's no telling what shape his head is in."

It took a while, but eventually they found two able-bodied young men who were very willing to do what they could to help their lord. Rannulf sent a boy running ahead to Gwal Draig with a message for Lily, warning of what had happened. She would surely need to prepare medicines, or some such.

Lily and Gillian waited impatiently in the courtyard for the men to arrive with Ian. The guards stood ready to throw open the gates as soon as they got there.

From the moment the messenger arrived, Lily's stomach had been trying to rebel. How could he get so close to home, after being gone for so long, and be attacked in his own village?

It made no sense.

But she refused to consider that they might not save him. She would not let him die. She loved him too much, and she wanted the chance to show him.

She met them as soon as they entered the bailey, directing the men where to take him. She was vaguely aware of Rannulf and Gillian exchanging a hurried embrace before they joined Nicholas to follow the procession up the stairs.

"What happened?" she asked.

"When we got to the outskirts of the village, we saw that it was under attack," Nicholas told her. "Outlaws, apparently."

"I'm surprised they didn't come here, as well," Rannulf added. "Although they weren't well armed. But there were a number of them—a large band, from the look of it. As soon as you get Ian settled here, Nick and I will take some of your men out to find the bastards."

"There's nothing you can do here," Gillian said, her attention on Ian as they transferred him from the hurdle to the bed. "Go find the men who did this."

Rannulf dropped a kiss on his wife's lips, then placed a comforting hand on Lily's shoulder before he and Nicholas headed out the door.

Lily wasn't certain where to start. Ian looked terrible, streaked with blood and dirt, the arrows still sticking out of his shoulder and leg. His leg was badly swollen.

"Sit down," Gillian told her, moving her to a stool beside the bed. "I'm used to this kind of thing, and I can see you're not. When I need you to help me with anything, I'll tell you." She began cutting off his leggings. "You sit there and talk to him, let him know he's home with you."

Lily maintained a steady stream of conversation as Gillian ministered to Ian's injuries. It terrified her to see him lying there so still, pale but for the bruises discoloring his face.

Gillian paused beside her. "Will you be all right here, alone? I'm going to get you something to eat and see if I can discover what Rannulf's found out."

"I'll be fine," Lily whispered. "Is there anything I should look out for?"

"Just don't let him move about too much if he should awaken." Gillian placed a comforting hand on her shoulder. "I'll be back soon."

Lily moved closer to Ian, leaning over the bed to softly kiss his lips. She nearly jumped when she felt him respond with a weak kiss of his own.

"Lily?" he asked, his voice barely audible.

"Aye, sweeting, 'tis Lily." She carefully sat on the edge of the bed. "How do you feel?"

"Like I tried to dance with Mouse," he said with a shaky laugh. "And he tripped."

"I'm so glad you're home," she said, resting her cheek on his uninjured shoulder as, against her will, the tears began to flow. "I've missed you so much."

He squeezed her hand. "Hush, love. Don't cry. It would take more than this to kill me. I won't leave you, I swear. I've waited too long for us to be together."

Lily stretched out beside him, taking comfort from the heat of his body next to hers. "I'll hold you to your promise," she said, reassured that he meant what he said.

It took more than this to kill a dragon.

Epilogue

Ian sat in state in his bedchamber at Gwal Draig, his leg propped on a footstool. Lily had ensconced him there, refusing to allow him to do much of anything until he recovered completely from his injuries. This was the first day in over a week he'd even been allowed out of bed. He wouldn't have minded so much, especially after his long absence, if his wife had joined him there. But she'd not yet felt he was up to it.

Ha! She couldn't possibly have missed noticing just how ready for her company he was.

But how could he complain? If his lovely wife wished to treat him like a king, he'd not say her nay. Wasn't that a husband's duty, after all, to be treated like a king?

He was an obedient creature, he thought with a snort. Obeying his liege, however reluctant he'd been to leave Lily to do it, had given him his heart's desire, without fear that she'd be taken from him. He knew Llywelyn would not go back on his word in this. Especially since Ian had the backing of two powerful marcher lords, he thought with a chuckle. If he hadn't gone to London about Llywelyn's business, he and Lily would likely be living in the forest somewhere, part of an outlaw band struggling to stay alive.

Like the men who had attacked the village. Rannulf and Nicholas had run them to ground without much difficulty, loaded down as the miscreants had been with loot from his village.

There was certain irony to the situation, he thought. First, that such a large group of renegades should have chosen his forest for their lair. They'd known he was seldom home, being as busy as he was on Llywelyn's business.

And he found it particularly ironic that, in the times he'd been attacked when he was outlawed, no one had come as close to killing him as these ill-equipped men.

But still he couldn't regret going to London. Without making his bargain with Llywelyn, he'd probably have wound up dead eventually, and Lily married to some idiot of Llywelyn's choosing.

And if he hadn't met Lily, he would still be a blind, emotionless fool.

How could he have known he needed a woman like Lily, to awaken the heart of the Dragon? Courageous and loving, fearless enough to match him word for word, passion for passion. Powerful enough to hold the Dragon's heart in her hand.

For though far from tame, he was not the man he'd been when he met her. And he thanked God he was not. That poor fool had been so blinded by his goals, his duty, that he'd forgotten how to be a man with compassion, as well as fire.

In Lily he'd found the perfect mate. Now all he needed to do was convince her of the fact.

He smoothed his hand through his hair, then twitched at the cuffs of his shirt. Why hadn't Lily gotten here yet? Today, of all days, she'd kept away from their chamber. He'd sent a servant to bring her to him, for his injured leg made it difficult for him to walk yet. He hadn't been out of this room since Rannulf and Nicholas carried him up here more than a week ago.

His leg throbbed in remembered agony. The journey back to Gwal Draig was a long, pain-filled blur in his mind. But he'd recovered quickly. Though his head still pained him on occasion, his shoulder was healing nicely. He felt much better now, ready for any confrontation.

Hopefully it wouldn't come to that, he thought, sitting up straight as the door opened.

Lily's face brightened when she saw him, those delectable lips curving in a smile. "You must be feeling better," she said, crossing the room and sitting beside his foot on the stool. She felt his forehead for fever, then poked gently at his knee, eliciting a mock grimace of pain.

"There's not enough room for you there," he said, nudging her off the seat with his foot. "Come sit up here with me." He patted his good leg. "'Tis a far more comfortable chair."

She had no choice but to stand; otherwise, she would have landed on the floor. "Do you think that's wise?" she asked primly.

"Come here," he growled, tugging her onto his lap. She landed sprawled over him. She squirmed into a more settled position, the movement sending shards of pleasure through him.

He wrapped his arms about her tightly and held her for a moment, savoring her warmth and sweet scent. Lily's arms slipped about his waist and, sighing, she nuzzled the base of his throat. His arms tightened about her. "I've missed you. I hope I am never away from you for so long again."

"Aye. This is wonderful, don't you think? We've had so little peace since we wed," she murmured. "I never realized I wanted it, but sitting here like this makes me complete. I have you, and a family. And there's more," she added, sitting up to gaze into his eyes. He couldn't understand what she was trying to tell him, but it seemed to be something good.

"And what might that be?" He pressed a kiss to her throat. "I find I'm feeling quite content, myself. And I like it," he said, surprised to find it true.

"You've been too ill to notice the change, perhaps. But I've grown in the time you were gone."

Grown?

If by that she meant that her body had become more rounded, he had noticed. A certain lushness about her breasts—making his mouth water for a taste—and a sweeter curve to her hips. Tonight, perhaps, he'd finally be up to the challenge of reintroducing his wife to passion.

If she'd allow it. Perhaps he'd better start trying to convince her now.

A glimmer of hope warmed Ian. "Aye. I might go an entire hour without noticing you—and wanting you—if I really try." He laughed, then looked down at her face. "But only if you truly feel that way. I love to make love with you. Do you feel the same?"

"How could you doubt it, Ian?" she asked, her voice a purr as she nipped lightly at his neck. "But do you like the changes in me?"

He ran his hands lightly over her from shoulders to thighs, savoring the way her eyes darkened and her breath caught in the back of her throat. His body liked the changes, very much, indeed.

She took his hand and held it over her stomach, gently rounded beneath his palm.

Could it mean—?

"A babe?"

She nodded in response to his question, her mouth curving into a loving smile.

He felt a tiny fluttering under his fingers, the movement almost imperceptible. He felt a corresponding movement in the vicinity of his heart.

"The baby dragon is fluttering his wings," she murmured. "'Tis early yet, but he's strong. I think he has your fierceness, Dragon."

"Not all the time, I hope," he said wryly. "Else you'll never have a moment's peace."

"I love your fierce nature, your determination. That determination saved my life, found my family, made you mine. A child could inherit worse qualities," she said, kissing him lightly on the cheek. "I hope our son is just like you."

"It could be a daughter, sweet and kind and beautiful like her mother." She smiled at his description. "Are you sure you like those things about me, Lily? I don't know if I can be any other way."

"I have no desire for a milksop, meek and compliant. I'd die of boredom. But you fire my blood, Dragon," she said.

"You make me see life differently, Lily. I've come to see that I love a challenge."

He lifted her chin and gazed into her eyes, losing himself in their cool green depths. "Challenge me, Lily. Every day of my life. I need your fire, your passion. I need you, wife." He brushed his lips over hers. "I love you."

Lily snuggled deeper into his embrace, wanting to believe, but not quite trusting that fate would be so kind. Could she really have everything she wanted?

"The past is done with. I doubt Llywelyn will bother you again. But even if he tried, I would do whatever I had to to protect you. You are mine," he vowed. "I love who you are, Lily. I don't want to change you." He smoothed her hair back. "Never leave me. Help me learn to live a more peaceful life. I can no longer be Llywelyn's Dragon, Lily. But I can be yours."

"Yes," she whispered against his cheek. Reaching up, Lily drew his mouth to hers. "I love you." He took her lips in a kiss of complete possession.

Her heart light as a feather, Lily gave herself up to his caress. The darkness of the past faded away, leaving only the bright glow of the future.

She'd found a home, a life, with the Dragon. She would never be alone again.

*   *   *   *   *

Bestselling Medieval author of
KNIGHT'S RANSOM

Suzanne Barclay

Continues her exciting
Sommerville Brothers series with

Knights Divided

Watch for the spectacular tale of a valiant knight accused
of murder and a beautiful woman who takes him captive!

Don't miss this searing story, available in March,
wherever Harlequin Historicals are sold.

From the bestselling author of *Scandalous*

CANDACE CAMP

Cam Monroe vowed revenge when
Angela Stanhope's family accused him
of a crime he didn't commit.

Fifteen years later he returns from exile, wealthy
and powerful, to demand Angela's hand in marriage.
It is then that the strange "accidents" begin. Are the
Stanhopes trying to remove him from their lives
one last time, or is there a more insidious,
mysterious explanation?

Impulse

Available this March at your favorite retail outlet.

Heartbreak RANCH

Four generations of independent women...
Four heartwarming, romantic stories of the West...
Four incredible authors...

Fern Michaels
Jill Marie Landis
Dorsey Kelley
Chelley Kitzmiller

Saddle up with Heartbreak Ranch, an outstanding
Western collection that will take you on a whirlwind
trip through four generations and the exciting,
romantic adventures of four strong women who
have inherited the ranch from Bella Duprey,
famed Barbary Coast madam.

Available in March,
wherever Harlequin books are sold.

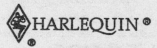

HARLEQUIN ®

LOVE *or* MONEY?
Why not Love *and* Money!
After all, millionaires
need love, too!

How to Marry a
MILLIONAIRE

Suzanne Forster,
Muriel Jensen
and
Judith Arnold

bring you three original stories
about finding that one-in-a million man!

Harlequin also brings you
a million-dollar sweepstakes—enter
for your chance to win a fortune!

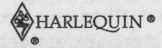 HARLEQUIN ®

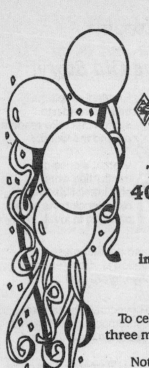

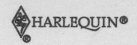 **◈ HARLEQUIN®**

Not The Same Old Story!

Exciting, emotionally intense romance stories that take readers around the world.

 *Harlequin Romance®*
Vibrant stories of captivating women and irresistible men experiencing the magic of falling in love!

 **HARLEQUIN® Temptation**
Bold and adventurous— Temptation is strong women, bad boys, great sex!

 **HARLEQUIN SUPERROMANCE®**
Provocative, passionate, contemporary stories that celebrate life and love.

 **AMERICAN ◈ ROMANCE®**
Romantic adventure where anything is possible and where dreams come true.

HARLEQUIN® INTRIGUE®
Heart-stopping, suspenseful adventures that combine the best of romance and mystery.

 **LOVE & LAUGHTER™**
Entertaining and fun, humorous and romantic—stories that capture the lighter side of love.

Look us up on-line at: http://www.romance.net   HGENERIC